# He Sees You When He's Creepin'

## Tales of Krampus

Edited by

KATE WOLFORD

WORLD WEAVER PRESS

HE SEES YOU WHEN HE'S CREEPIN': TALES OF KRAMPUS



Published by World Weaver Press, LLC
Albuquerque, New Mexico
www.WorldWeaverPress.com

Cover Illustration by Samuel Connor Anderson
SearingLimb.com
Cover layout and design by Sarena Ulibarri
Additional cover images used under license from
DepositPhotos.com

First edition: November 2016
ISBN-10: 0-997788844
ISBN-13: 978-0997788846



Also available in ebook

# HE SEES YOU WHEN HE'S CREEPIN':
# TALES OF KRAMPUS

# INTRODUCTION
## KATE WOLFORD

When you think Krampus, what do you see in your mind's eye? Horns? A ghastly tongue? Sly eyes? Hooves and a whole lotta fur? Add a few chains, a basket, and a switch, and there's your man-demon, all dressed up and ready to serve up his own brand of justice.

Think about that last word. Let it settle. "Justice."

Krampus traditions suggest that his duty is to provide a balance for the gentleness and generosity of Saint Nicholas. After all, most children are naughty sometimes, and some kids are just plain rotten. The presence of Krampus suggests that for hundreds of years, long before the Christmas season began to be a materialistic bacchanalia, adults began to want to see the darker side of Santa. After all, it's parents who allow children to partake in traditions, and what parent doesn't want an antidote for impudence?

In the countries where Krampus has long been popular—Germany, Austria, and northern Italy—Christmas festivities kick off in early December, the sixth, to be exact: Saint Nicholas Day. The American style of Santa Claus, while influential worldwide, is not the classic Saint Nicholas. The latter is tall, rather slim, and is decked in regalia more associated with bishops than with the big fat man we call Santa. He's a kindly, but more serious figure. The gifts associated with his feast day tend to be simpler, perhaps some candy or small toys.

Krampus fits into the celebration as discipline embodied. With his basket, just the thing for dragging brats to hell; his chains, gotta corral the kids to get them into the basket or drag them behind if it's too full; and his *ruten* or switch, when a brisk beating is all that's needed to get the message across, Krampus exists to remind children they'll get a hell of a lot worse than coal in their stockings if their behavior is rotten enough.

As for hell, Krampus may be the son of Hel, a Norse goddess who rules over the dead. His name, Krampus, is connected to *krampen*, which means claw in German. Hell and claws suggest that Krampus was meant to be a fierce creature from his earliest origins. And, although you should be very suspicious of any attempts to definitively explain Krampus' origins, it seems that he springs from old, pre-Christian traditions that weren't too far away from Pan, a horned Greek god.

But does he deserve the name "Christmas Devil"? After all, he is often shown as a companion to St. Nicholas, not as his sworn enemy. (Certainly a saint would not allow a devil to have his vicious way with children without the good companion's blessing.) Heck, even the extravagant, indulgent US Santa tradition threatens bad kids with coal, sans Krampus. Yet even our anemic coal tradition winks at the idea that Santa and parents believe children need both the carrot and the *ruten*. So, in his own creepy, horned way, Krampus may be necessary, if entirely over the top.

He even has his own special night in European countries that celebrate Krampus, and, increasingly, in Canada, the U.K., and the US. Traditionally, the night of Krampus, *Krampusnacht*, December 5th, features the *Krampuslauf*, or run of costumed revelers. It should come as no surprise that the Krampus runners are usually drunk and determined to scare the townspeople, young and old, with their wild ways, and, increasingly, very elaborate costumes.

Just how Krampusnacht got started is unclear, but it could spring from the ancient European custom of mummery, which features costumed players frolicking about and calling back to even more ancient religious traditions and stories. But mostly, Krampusnacht probably has always been about having scary fun. And giving bad kids what for.

Why is Krampusnacht an increasingly popular tradition in the US? Who knows? But it's probably because people, especially college age ones, like to get drunk and wear costumes and behave badly. Think of Krampusnacht as second Halloween, and you've got the idea.

In this volume, Krampus is thrown into some very odd, terrifying, funny, and thought-provoking situations. The twelve stories demonstrate that Krampus provides rich material for writers.

In Steven Grimm's "Villainess Ascending," Krampus and Cinderella meet, and there is no way you'll be able to predict what happens.

In Lissa Marie Redmond's "He Sees You When You're Sleeping," a hipster coffee shop owner named James, with a history of dealing with the supernatural, helps a good friend in a terrible situation. (This is the second outing for James. His first appearance is in the anthology *Frozen Fairy Tales.*)

In Beth Mann's "Santa's Little Helper," Krampus has a life-changing encounter with an attractive and devilish woman who gives him a big assist.

In Anya J. Davis's "The Business of Christmas," a talented artist becomes an employee of "Petra Krampus," who has an essential business plan to save Santa from his worst impulses.

E.J. Hagadorn lets Krampus have his way with a genuinely horrible monster kid named Rolf. Things get enjoyably rotten for Rolf in "Schadenfreude."

In "Family Tradition," by S.E. Foley, a bold, creative, guitar-playing big sister named Laney fights the good fight against the horned one to save her family.

In Brad P. Christy's "Krampus: The Summoning," we go back a thousand years to the vengeful beginnings of a Christmas tradition.

In "The Outfit," by Ross Baxter, two boys are out to enjoy Krampusnacht, but one of them is in a truly transformative costume. His pal doesn't fare too well.

In "Family Night," by Nancy Brewka-Clark, Krampus is a family man who faces the frustrations of being a parent, but his troubles are far from ordinary.

"A Winter Scourge," by Tamsin Showbrook, places a British detective in Florida at Christmas time. She encounters both Santa and Krampus in surprising ways. Mayhem ensues.

"Bad Parents," by E.M. Eastick, has Saint Nick begging Krampus to come out of retirement to save a village that is going to hell thanks to idiot parents.

Rounding out this collection is Jude Tulli's "Memo From Santa," in which Krampus lays out the way Christmas will be for kids in the future—and it's not all sugar plums and toys anymore.

I hope you'll like this book. It's a companion to *Krampusnacht: Twelve Nights of Krampus*. So if you need another Krampus fix, go to WorldWeaverPress.com to find out more.

Kate Wolford
Editor

# VILLAINESS ASCENDING

## Steven Grimm

It was not that Cinderella. It was this Cinderella. There have been hundreds of Cinderellas, and we find tonight's in Vienna in 1792 or 1803 or 1814. What matter the year, when the men keep the hours? In any case, this Cinderella is akin to others you may know.

A devoted mother, dead. A father, remarried. A stepmother who was kindness personified until, after her husband's death, she became cruelty incarnate, casting the man's daughter low while raising her own daughters from a previous marriage high. Having found this Cinderella, we leap ahead to the end of her story. The third night of the ball.

"Where is she?" Cinderella paced the cellar in her rags.

It was twilight. She knew that the first of the ball guests were now pulling up to one of Vienna's grandest palaces. Not the old imperial one in the heart of the city, which Cinderella thought looked like a pile of rocks, but the imperial family's country palace, Schönbrunn, which she always thought must be at least as pretty as Versailles.

Her stepmother and stepsisters had already departed for this final night of the balls, spending the last of their inheritance—which should have been hers—to hire a carriage to convey them to the palace. Her stepmother, who had the instincts of a viper, ever ready to sink her fangs into easy meat—as the damned snake had done to her father—surely had her brood of two slitherettes there already, waiting in the line of carriages at the front steps of Schönbrunn.

They lived only an hour's stroll away, just inside the old city walls, but while Cinderella could fault them for many things—and daily, did—she couldn't criticize the decision to hire a carriage tonight. A snowstorm, the likes of which no one had ever seen, had come out of nowhere, only hours ago, blowing in from no cardinal point. It had come from above, dropping the downiest and heaviest of flakes, blanketing Vienna.

Cinderella would have done the same in her stepmother's position. Hobbling the cobbled lanes in heels, trailing satin and silks, clutching feathery accoutrements, trudging through snowdrifts that seem pristine but veiled the sludge of crowded Vienna life…?

Slippery corruption!

"If she's late, I'll be late." Cinderella pressed her hand against the cellar window, melting the frost that had caked the inside of the pane. She pulled her chilled hand back, rubbed it in the other, huffing hot breath that came out in plumes. She wondered how cold it had to get before the imperial family would cancel a ball, how dangerous before people would stay home? Cinderella knew what every living soul in Vienna knew, of course: invitations to balls were rare, and the happy endings found there, even rarer. But if there was a chance of securing a prince? If not that, a duke? And if not that, an ongoing liaison as a secret paramour?

Even a priest, if it came to that?

She'd do anything.

Be anyone.

And for two nights, with the Godmother's help, she had—though anything was merely dancing with every man, and anyone meant whomever each man wanted her to be. Pretty and vapid? Easily done.

She needed only keep her opinions to herself. Pretty and coquettish? Tricky, for one wanted to appear selective, but quite doable. Pretty and witty? A stretch, for she disliked wit because it seemed the gussied-up cousin of sarcasm. That she despised, being on the lash end of sarcasm so often in this house—her cooking, her cleaning, her devotion, ridiculed at every turn. Still, she found she could ape wit simply by smirking at a man's jest.

After two nights though, Cinderella had failed to secure her happy ending. It had to be tonight, the third and final night.

Cinderella peered through the slush dripping down the glass. Her heart quickened as she saw a dark shape pass by. The Godmother? Not at all. A figure bulky as a yak. Lumbering. She watched him go by the other cellar windows, where he stopped at the door above.

He knocked once, loudly.

She had no time for visitors, not tonight, especially since visitors only came for her stepmother or stepsisters. But no matter who it was—bill collectors, old widowers, penniless suitors, pastors collecting alms for the poor, paupers rattling their tin cups—she didn't have time for it. Vienna was stuffed with a hundred-thousand people at each other's throats over a handful of coins. There was nothing left in their house to give to anyone. No love, money, or charity. Theirs was a house of misery, a theater where her stepmother acted like they weren't in poverty, an opium dream where her stepsisters lounged all day long. Only Cinderella was in touch with their fell and famished state; of course, she'd learned, only servants knew the truth about anything. And yet, what she wouldn't do to get to that ball—no longer anyone's servant.

The figure knocked again.

"They're not here!" shouted Cinderella. "Come back tomorrow!" Feeling the pain of the chill in her palm, she whirled from the window, turning her back on the visitor, and then crossed her arms, the better to slide her hands under her armpits, but also to register her displeasure.

How could the Godmother do this to her? Two nights of hope, only to snatch it away on the third? But tonight she had to lay claim to her groom, her future. All the finest diplomats of Europe, as well as a few princes, had been in Vienna for weeks to negotiate some sort of nonsense. The men wanted to forget their quarrels, which had grown hostile in recent days. The imperial family had arranged a ball, inviting the loveliest ladies around to ease their eyes and minds. Cinderella couldn't fathom how her stepmother had gotten an invitation.

The figure knocked a third time.

The force of it jarred Cinderella as she heard a splintering sound—a crack in the thick frost of a window, a crack in the glass itself. She realized that he hadn't knocked, but stomped a foot, heavy as a sledgehammer. "If you've come for—!" And then she said the viper's name, and those of the two in her brood. "—then you'd better make for Schönbrunn!"

Cinderella spat.

The Godmother had to show up soon. Getting there on time was the least of her problems on this third night of the ball. She'd awoken this morning to find that there was nothing left to turn into a carriage, the coachmen, or horses. Not that there had been much in their house on the first two nights, as her stepmother had sold everything off to buy dresses for the balls, but the Godmother had said to never fear, that she could bring out the best in anything with her magic.

And she had—from rats, a gourd, and spiders.

But in the severe cold that had just descended on Vienna, all the rats had all run away in search of warmer crevices. So much for coachmen. Still, good riddance. They'd stolen all the cheese from the ball during the first two nights, and both rides home had been a flatulent nightmare. Also, their one gourd had split open in the deepening chill. And so, no carriage. She'd had no complaints there—a very pretty carriage it made—though her derrière was pricked by the seeds in the cushions, and if pressed to confess, the gourd gave the vehicle a green-yellow hue, somewhere between absinthe and jaundice. Unseemly.

Oh, and the spiders were all gone but one. They'd made for ghastly horses anyway. The stallions kept fighting each other for the right to mount the one mare in their midst—as male spiders did a female—which made for a bumpy ride, while the mare whinnied in delight. This morning, Cinderella had found the webs in her rafters devoid of spiders, save for just the one female. She was sitting in the center of her web, all the other challengers wrapped in silky bundles, and she, ready to feast—as a female spider did with males.

Magic, she now realized, was overrated.

The real magic had been inside her all along.

Despite the gassy coachmen, the overheated stallions, and the seedy cushions, once Cinderella was delivered to Schönbrunn, she was so charming that she was able to gain entry without presenting an invitation; once inside, Cinderella had pulled out all the stops, waltzing and winning every eye, transforming her character to suit the taste of any and every man. It was something her stepmother had done to beguile Cinderella's father. While she'd always seen this as deceit, once at the ball, Cinderella found that every woman was doing it, changing her character depending on the partner; indeed, it seemed as standard as daubing on cosmetics or putting on an accessory.

The gowns, she had to admit, were part of her charm.

The Godmother had brought a gown with her each night so far, saying that she'd crafted three of them from a falling star. She'd gone on to say that such gowns, the kind that helped a good girl sparkle in this dark world, couldn't be whipped up in an instant. She'd worked her fingers to the bone making them. Cinderella had flinched at the sight of the old woman's hands. The bones of her knuckles had worn through her cobwebby skin. Such was old age, she supposed.

Cinderella could have criticized the choice of a material that dissolved into shimmers at midnight. But she'd quickly realized, even on the first night, that the gowns were merely gift wrapping on the true present. Cinderella herself. Furthermore, though the gown sparkled just fine, she would have preferred chiffon. Honestly, she now thought, if she only had a little money for a nice dress, and could somehow get to the ball in this storm, she could work miracles without the spinster.

Still, where was she?

There was a crash, a spatter of glass, a thud.

Cinderella recoiled from the object on the cellar floor—something the uninvited guest at the door had thrown inside. It was a rock trussed with twine, binding a sheet of rumpled butcher's paper to it. The visitor had made it from alley trash. She stared up into the street in fury as winds flooded from the street into the cellar, chilling her ankles and batting the raggedy hem of her dress. The visitor was lumbering back the way he came, past the other windows. Cinderella snatched up the sheet of paper. Its message was written in blood that was still fresh.

*Perchte sends her regrets.*

She saw a hair caught in the blood, dark and coarse, trailing from the *P* of Perchte to the *s* of regrets, stretched long and thin like a leech. Clearly, the disgusting hair had been either shed onto the scrawled message or yanked out in its making. Cinderella stared in revulsion at the crude lettering, the grotesque ink, even the stony envelope, but what stuck out most was the message itself. Perchte sends her regrets. It was, though curt, the language of society. She realized that, whoever the hairy stranger who'd thrown the rock in her window might be, he'd meant his every word to be taken not as politesse, but sarcasm of the most biting quality.

She wouldn't have it. Not sarcasm, not in her most desperate hour. She stormed up the cellar stairs, through the rooms of their home—now nearly empty—and undid the bolts of their front door. She leaped out into the street in her bare feet, and jolted by the cold, shouted so loudly that her voice succeeded in carrying over the keening blizzard.

Cinderella said something like this: "Return, sir! I have every intention of jamming that stone straight up your hindquarters!" Now, what she truly said was too vulgar to repeat here, but it was making her dearly departed mother in Heaven blanch and faint away.

In any case, she got what she wanted.

Huge as he was, the figure had nearly vanished into the white of the storm. He stopped, and then stood there, as if pondering a thing. Cinderella repeated her words, to make her threat get into his bulky head. She added more: she'd cut off every hunk of his nether regions, fore and rear, then stew them up in a pot, and serve it to—well, surprisingly, Cinderella went on and on, weaving a tale of regurgitation and fricassée that was making her father in Heaven run to the Pearly Gates to cover Saint Peter's ears, but the gatekeeper had heard plenty already, and he crossed Cinderella's name off the list in his big book. Though in truth, he'd crossed it off his list before.

The figure began lumbering toward her.

Cinderella pulled back to the doorway, then leaned against its frame, and made her observations as the stranger approached through the blizzard. He was tall as a man bearing a man on his shoulders, wide as a man carrying a man in each of his arms, and heavy as a man who'd eaten a man every day of his life. This last detail came to Cinderella as his face breached the heavy snowfall enough to become clear to her—his mouth, more a maw, was bloody. And his teeth, more like tusks, were festooned with intestines. His two horns were stubby and jutted from each of his jowly brows, and each had a man's skull mounted upon it. She supposed these, being demeated and bleached, were the stranger's idea of ornamentation. He was covered in great heaps of shaggy pelts—or, no—she now saw his meaty, clawed hands and cloven hooves.

He was a beast of some sort.

As he came the last few steps, Cinderella withdrew over the

threshold of the apartment, as if being the inch more inside would protect her. She remembered the Hungarian vampyr hysteria that her father had once said came to Vienna in his youth. Did thresholds actually hold any sacred power, to separate good from evil?

He did stop.

She stepped back again, revolted by his face, all jowls, from maw to brow. She searched these folds for any trace of eyes, trying to ignore the charnel house stink bladdering out his mouth. She finally found them, dark as beetles.

"You owe me," she said, "for the window."

His mouth opened, more it seemed to swallow her—head and torso in one gulp, the rest of her in the next—than to disagree. She held up a hand to interrupt.

"I will keep the rock," she said, "in case you come back. I may look lithe, but my arm is stronger than you'd think. So, before you dismiss me as a trifle, know that I can hurt you. You will make a meal of me, but I swear I'll dig my fingers into your eyes before you do."

The beast tried to begin again. She wasn't finished.

"As for your note? Perchte sends her regrets. Who is he, this Perchte—?"

"He?"

Cinderella was buffeted by a steaming gust. So, she thought, the jowly beast could speak.

"Mother Perchte!" he finished.

"And she is…?" Cinderella gestured for him to be quicker with his details, sighing as she rolled her eyes, but only a little. She wanted to be firm, not rude.

"The woman," said the beast, "who has been helping you with her magic for the previous two nights, and now realizes her mistake. That you are no diamond in the rough, but a chunk of charcoal like anyone else."

"You're saying that my Godmother isn't coming?"

"Godmother, you call her!" The beast shook his head, spattering the step with houndsome drops of slobber. "Visited by Mother Perchte? Who comes to a girl in mourning only once in a blue moon? She can barely get herself out of bed these days, and did so for you. And you didn't ask her name? Perchte, Godmother? Mother of gods, if anything, though that was long ago, when she was…? And I was…? Before all of…" His lapses were the sorts of pauses that would suggest centuries and disappointments, but Cinderella snapped her fingers to speed him along. "…this," he finished.

Of all the nonsense the beast had spouted, Cinderella latched onto only one detail. He knew the Godmother, which meant he could fetch her at once. There was still time to get dressed, find something that could be made into a carriage, plus some vermin to serve as steeds and coachmen. The ball was surely in motion. The first dance, starting without her.

"Get my Godmother." She grabbed the beast by his great hands, tried to shake urgency into them, but they couldn't be budged. "Tonight's my last chance to make my fate. I have to get to Schönbrunn. I have to dance my way into a better future. I refuse to spend one more day cleaning this house, cooking their meals."

"You're not listening. And I don't have time to explain." He lumbered off, grumbling. "I shouldn't even be here. I serve Nicholas, not Perchte. One last favor for an old friend." He lapsed again. "Likely the last before she turns into a star and leaves us all."

Cinderella watched the shaggy beast go off.

First a Perchte, now a Nicholas?

Two days ago, she would have been cowed by such mystical talk, but now she was blasé about magic shenanigans; what was important was what she, Cinderella, had to do. The only special thing about tonight was that it was the third night of the ball!

It was also December 5th. The night before December 6th. Saint Nicholas Day tomorrow. Tonight was his night. "Krampusnacht," she whispered, knowing exactly who he was, though she'd forgotten him since childhood. On Krampusnacht, her good father would dress up as the kindly Saint Nicholas, come a-knocking on the very door she stood at now, accompanied by her mother, soot smeared on her face, dressed in rags, with goat horns strapped to her head. Her mother—her lovely original mother—was the perfect accomplice for her father's Krampusnacht fun; Cinderella remembered how she stood in the street, acting the part of the goat-man, adopting a gruff growl, stomping her feet on the stones. Her mother—Krampus—tried to grab Cinderella's arm, to drag her off into the street, while Cinderella clutched her father—Saint Nicholas—for dear life as she wailed. Then her parents would drop the act, and Cinderella would drop the act, and they'd all laugh at how silly it all was. Then for a week afterward, Cinderella would apply salve to her mother's scalp, for the strapped horns scraped her head badly.

Cinderella began to sigh—a sound she'd grown to hate. Sighs helped as much as prayers. Her mother was dead. And badness, in the guise of her stepmother, had come to live in her good childhood home. Everything was upside-down and had been for years. No help ever came. At least until the Godmother had shown up. Finally, justice.

But once again, she'd been abandoned. Now, by her Godmother.

It was up to her now, as always.

"You, Krampus!"

"I'll warn you," he shouted over his shoulder, trudging off into the blizzard, "to speak to me with respect. You're lucky I pounded on your door doing her business, not Nicholas's." His words began to get lost in the blizzard, so Cinderella scampered off the step, into the street to follow him, wincing as the cold bit into her feet. She turned her ear to catch his every word, and found herself following him farther than she wanted.

"That saint," she heard him say, "will surely come out of the woodwork soon enough if I don't finish his bidding by midnight. One more person, that's all I have left. One skull to smash in. If only she was bad enough, that foolish girl, but she's only rotten and vain, which is nearly everyone these days."

Rotten and vain? Cinderella seethed to hear herself lumped in with the likes of her stepmother. This beast didn't know her. She tiptoed on in the snow, sure that she was close to eavesdropping upon something that would help. And then, there it was: "One more truly evil person by midnight," said Krampus, "but these days, it'd be easier to find a needle in a—"

"Krampus! You need to find someone?"

"Are you following me? Back to your cellar!"

"The most evil person in Vienna?"

"What do you know of such evil?"

She smirked. How little he really did know her soul. What she'd witnessed in this house. All its goodness and warmth, stripped bare by her stepmother.

"I have recently been to a place," said Cinderella, "where the most wicked creatures in all Vienna turn circles around each other with more abandon than witches and warlocks. They won't be disbanding until midnight. There you can do your Nicholas business quickly."

"Where? And I swear, if you're trifling with me, you will be my next kill."

"There's a cost."

"Of course, there is. When has any of your kind done something out of the goodness of their hearts? Why Perchte bothers is beyond me. I know why Nicholas gets involved, still trying to do good, despite his place in Hell, where many a saintly man has wound up, believing himself on the good path, and yet actually on the other. He's doing what he can, from where he is. Tell me, are there any truly good people these days? There are not. Only bad ones, spreading like bedbugs. Dead old Nick says I should scourge the worst, flay the rest with fear. That will get everyone in line, keep more people out of Hell. Do you want to be one of them? Be a good girl, and just give me what I need."

"Don't lecture me," said Cinderella. "If you knew me, you'd

realize that I've had everything stolen from me: my mother, my father, my home, my dignity. Why, I'd make a deal with the Devil himself tonight. So, you will get me into that ball, in a fashion that flatters me, then I will point out your prey. Come now, we need to be going to Schönbrunn Palace."

"You want me to take Perchte's place tonight?"

"That's the crux of it."

"You bargain poorly. I'll find the most evil person left in Vienna at Schönbrunn? You've given away the only thing you had. Good-bye, woman."

The beast began to shamble off into the blizzard.

"You, get inside? Past the gates, into the palace, into the dance? Certainly, the guards are wearing only ceremonial swords, but they'll hack you to pieces before you're three steps into the courtyard. Besides, there are hundreds of evil souls there, and I have not pointed out the most evil of them all, and there are so few hours left before midnight."

"All right. I accept your terms. I will get you inside. And then you must point out my prey. Do we have an agreement?"

Cinderella heard a note of cunning in his voice. She'd heard enough tales of devils making pacts with naive girls to know he thought he was being clever. But she was already damned as she was; being damned meant nothing as long as she could get to the ball. There she could remake her fate with a husband. A wedding, like the threshold, would keep Krampus at arm's length.

"Yes," she said, "we have an agreement."

Cinderella heard an unnerving noise—loud, out there in the blizzard—and it sounded like someone being presented with roast boar and tearing into the flesh with violence: the ripping of juicy meat, the tearing of tendons, the popping of joints, and the cracking of bones in half, as if the carnivore desired the silken marrow in those bones. Cinderella licked her lips, remembering all the dinners she'd had with her parents when she was young. How long had it been since her father or mother handed her a leg of lamb, like a scepter to a queen?

"Krampus?" she said, realizing the noises had faded. She craned her head to look down the lane and saw nothing at all, save for the blizzard. She stepped out into the lane, seeing that she'd been abandoned. "Damn you to—?!"

But before Cinderella could unleash a torrent of invectives that would have made even Satan himself genuflect, Cinderella felt a tickling around her feet. More viscid than wind. Wetter than slush. Warm as tongues. She looked down, expecting to see a slimy rat squeezing between her ankles, and saw instead a billowing mist of red and black. She shrieked, covered her mouth, and in stumbling backward, tripped over the threshold of the door and fell onto her back. She scampered crablike as the mist followed her inside.

"What is—?" She swiped at the mist to get it away from her feet, and she sent up eddying whirls of the stuff, which revealed itself to be pinpricks of blood, pinches of fur, and flecks of bone. "Get off of—!"

Her hand was now covered in an ermine glove. It was dark and lustrous, fit excellently to her hand. The temperature of the glove put her at ease instantly; it was like slipping into a tub of bath water heated to just the right temperature. The glove was the sort—or was becoming the sort, as she watched—that extended past the wrist, the forearm, almost to the shoulder. Her legs now too, enveloped in the mist, were becoming sheathed in the same material. If it didn't feel like such utter luxury, and more than a little sensual, Cinderella would have screamed bloody murder, knowing that Krampus was conjuring this.

Instead, she stood, closed the door, and went to the parlor.

There she found a wall mirror and regarded herself with a critical eye as Krampus finished dressing her. The mist was dutiful as a tailor, low as a toady; as more ermine garments coalesced on her limbs, hips, and torso, the mist exhausted itself until there was no more. At last, Cinderella wore matching arm-length gloves and a snug gown of the same.

"Not all that bad, Krampus." She turned once, the better to see how the gown moved. Though she was covered in fur, from her neckline to her ankles—no, she stood corrected—to her toes, as her feet were in boots of the same, Cinderella didn't feel smothered. One last lick of the mist, gone unseen behind her back, flowed over her shoulder, dipped under her chin, then rounded her face, all the while seeming to nibble her hair. Before she could recoil again, the work was done. Her head was now covered by an ermine cowl fit tight to her head, tailored to meet her cheeks, and her hair was braided pretty as buttered buns above her brow. She was so smitten that she couldn't stop the compliment from coming out.

"How perfect—superior to the Godmother's gowns."

"It's an odd woman," said Krampus, "who scorns a gown made of stars." His voice was near her ear. She glanced over her shoulder and did not see him. Even if he was half as tall, or a third as wide, Krampus couldn't be missed.

Cinderella then stared in the mirror, realizing as Krampus spoke—more intimately near her ear than any of the men she'd danced with at the balls—where he was. She was wearing him. She felt her stomach lurch, and through sheer will, governed her delicate sensibilities with an iron fist. Tonight was no night to vomit. Tomorrow, once she had her match, she could retch all the rest of her days.

"Well then?" she said. "What of my carriage? Do you expect me to ride to Schönbrunn in a vehicle constructed of guts and gore? Pulled by a dozen skeletal goats in mourning veils?"

"Don't be ridiculous," said Krampus.

"Then we finally see eye to eye."

"I'm all used up," he said. "There's no more of me to make anything else."

"Well? Then what?"

"I'd suggest," said Krampus, "you start running."

Schönbrunn Palace was as lovely as a wedding cake. Its main building alone, which rose up in alabaster tiers, would have made the case. There was a pair of white wings too, one to the left, another to the right, that made Schönbrunn look like a cake that could feed an empire. Though some—the French—said it was merely a Versailles in miniature, Schönbrunn had one advantage—though the French disagreed—in that it was walkable from Vienna, so every Austrian in the city could feast on the sight, even the poorest of paupers.

Cinderella made a shorter journey of this jaunt than usual. In her gown of Krampus, she found that her legs carried her in bounds, and her feet met the snow without slipping, and her body sliced through the wind. Some snowdrifts had grown high as country chapels; she had merely tilted her head, steeled her resolve, and rammed through them. Cinderella would have preferred to arrive in traditional style; on the other hand, this was power she'd never known.

But traveling in a gown of Krampus was not the same as arriving in said gown—and now she stood at the courtyard gate, wondering how to make her entrance. In the snow, Schönbrunn looked like even more of a wedding cake than usual; behind it, the great hill that lorded over the palace seemed a mountain of powdered sugar. The courtyard that she had to cross was so piled with snow that dozens of waiting carriages looked like teacups amid meringue puffs. She wondered how anyone was possibly going to get home.

Cinderella grit her teeth, thinking how best to make her way past the carriages with their carriage-men, and the palace doors with their servants. A woman—any woman—showing up in the night sans carriage would invite questions. Was she a courtesan, for instance? Was she a spurned lover? Or even, in this ermine gown and cowl, a woman from Russia?

This had to be done the right way.

"What are you waiting for?" said Krampus. "Midnight is only an hour away. Go now, woman. I have promised to get you inside. You have promised to point out the one."

"I am dressed in a gown made of Krampus. I'm not sure I will get inside."

"You thought it looked perfect before."

"Perfect for me," said Cinderella. "Not perfect for a ball."

"I'll warn you, woman. Do your part. I've done mine."

"I'm not sure you have. But I'll do what I can."

She made for the palace stairs, winding her way through a labyrinth of snowdrifts and carriages, finding her way blocked here by horses, and there by droppings, and yet in a third place by several carriage-men shooting dice. She was reluctant to let herself be seen. But finally, spying an impromptu boulevard through the mess, she hurried for the palace.

Cinderella heard coachmen as they caught sight of her. They uttered things, and not the usual vile trifles that men riding by women in the street might say; rather, one man called for the Lord Jesus, and another for the Holy Spirit, and another for God Above. A fourth carriage-man leaped down from his seat with his horse whip in hand, approaching her suspiciously, trying to make out exactly what he was seeing in the heavy snowfall. She did not shrink back, though he stepped into her path.

"What are you? Speak, thing."

Cinderella wondered what to do, spoken to so disrespectfully. Did he not recognize her as a woman of the highest quality? Krampus provided the answer: "Run, woman. Or else you'll suffer his whip. He sees me, not you. If you wish to get into the ball, swerve or defer!"

Run, swerve, defer? The invocations of the Holy Trinity had barely stirred her feelings, but those three words struck her to the core. She was meant to be inside that ball. Some carriage-man would not stand in her way. She approached him as she had any other man at the dance, meeting his eyes as if acquiescing. In his eyes, however, she saw fear. It gave her a giddy thrill, the likes of which were better than any sip of champagne.

She reached for one of his hands as if to give herself over to him for a waltz, but instead grabbed the whip in that hand, and then brushed him aside. Cinderella heard him whisper, same as before, now to himself, afraid to confront her. "What is she?"

Cinderella laughed. It was a good question. In the gown made of Krampus, she was projecting her newfound confidence differently, like a beam of light through a prism, but coming out a different facet, as a darker color. Violet, perhaps? She cracked the whip for fun, and found that she was a natural. The man called out the same of a saint, presumably his patron. She saw more men hopping down from their carriages, hearing their comrade's fear, and so she cracked the whip at them too—delighted to find how easily they leapt back, crossed themselves, and called out the names of sainted men.

"Don't get used to this," said Krampus. "I will be leaving you soon enough, and then what will you be? Little more than just another woman with petty ambitions."

Soon enough. There was the hitch in their agreement. He needed only get her inside, and as soon as she did her part, Krampus would abandon her. And likely leave her naked and shamed. But the moment of their parting was not yet upon her. She still possessed him by pact. "Perhaps I am just another woman." She approached the short flight of marble stairs that several men in silver and gold livery were sweeping of snow. "But until I point the finger, remember that you're nothing but a gown and gloves. All of those things never matter, unless they're a good fit for the woman."

One of the men, seeing Cinderella approach in the snow, stepped out of her way and snapped to attention. "My pardon," he said. "May I take your furs and—?"

"You may not," she said, going up the stairs, striding toward the double doors at the top of them, amused by how the men tripped over each other. Cinderella ignored them, proceeding like a chill wind; the servants fell into line, full of apologies, and two opened the great doors of Schönbrunn just in time.

"This really is something new, isn't it?" she said to herself, brushing the snow off her shoulders, proceeding across a foyer filled with servants waiting to attend to guests inside. "I am something new." She went for the inner set of doors, ready to make her debut.

She saw that the servants had not yet opened them; she shot them her most imperious glare and, raising her hands as if to make a cat's cradle, flung them apart with such violence, it would have shred the child's game to threads. Whether it was that or the whip flailing in her hand, the servants hopped to action. They opened the doors.

She glided inside.

The room was a surprising sort for a ball, like a lump of dough stretched long, and the waltzing pairs did not mass and circle, as they did in the cramped taverns where the dance had first found its feet, but rather went down one wall, rounded the bend at the end, and then came up the other wall. In the hands of unskilled dancers, the ballroom would have been inelegant as a sack race; but with these gentlemen, who knew how to work pliant ladies, and these ladies, who were eager to be worked, and plenty of champagne, which lubricated the whole affair? The ballroom was merry as a carousel.

Imagine it! The men in their suits, rotating, each on his own masculine axis. Medals on their chests tinkling. Epaulettes adorning their shoulders. And the ladies in their gowns, clasped tight to their partners. Silks and feathers fluttering. And where have they hidden the orchestra in this elongated hall? There it is, tucked at one end. Gleaming instruments. The silver and gold of flutes and horns. The chestnut glow of violins and cellos. Oh, and all of it contained within a place of mirrors facing mirrors, which given quintuples of candles in sconces and hundreds more in chandeliers, made this into a cosmos of light. And what is that above? A ceiling painted with pastel clouds, softest pinks and fluffiest blues. There—like the Apostles of old, or Philosophers who are older still, or the Muses older than that—are the new spirits of the age. Good Virtues and Shrewd Ambitions, wearing the robes of ancient empire, but celebrating a new era of Righteous Enterprise! Of course, no one sees the ceiling.

The chandeliers blind. The women, sparkle.

Cinderella entered.

She expected all eyes to be upon her, as they had the previous two nights when she was wearing a gown made from a star. But now, she felt as unnoticed as one's own shadow.

"I've done my part," said Krampus. "I got you inside. Now, point out the one."

"Patience," said Cinderella. "I'm inside, but I haven't arrived."

"I don't care for riddles. Just do your part."

She fumed. What was happening? Certainly, a gown crafted from Krampus was not usual for a ball, but it would still make her the center of attention. Had she miscalculated? No, she had not. She smirked to see a woman pass by, looking right at her with a confused expression as if the woman was seeing a breach in a dream—a dark spot amid the colors, a matte patch in the infinite light, a cold flame among warm candles.

Cinderella nodded her hello. The woman, whirling in her partner's arms turned this way and that, trying to watch her. Cinderella saw more ladies passing by, seeing the same, and thrilled to see confusion bloom on their faces. It was like each was seeing something out of their personal nightmares: a wolf, a murderer, a bear, a madwoman. She was delighted too, to see what her presence was doing to the dance itself.

These ladies were stumbling, recovering, stumbling. Their partners were doing their best to correct the steps, but Cinderella knew there was no stopping what she'd put into motion with her entrance. Chaos. And it was spreading. There, a woman shrieked. And there, a man apologizing. Over there, a couple falling to the floor. And then—what glory!—the whole of the dance, going down the drain. Hands in the air. Legs kicking. Contortions and flailing. Men and women, completely uncoupled. The crowd was in a roar. Instruments were silent, except for one flutist, in his own world, continuing to send his silvery notes winging until he too stopped.

Cinderella cracked the whip in delight. She smiled, and with the crowd mostly on the parquet floor, writhing in embarrassments, she caught sight of herself in the mirrored wall on the other side of the hall. She looked better than beautiful. She looked powerful. There was only one thing that spoiled the effect, and that was her pretty smile. She wanted a Krampus smile. But in lieu of fangs, she sealed her lips tight—a thin line. A scowl, she supposed.

"You," said Krampus, "are a wicked person."

"I did nothing but make an entrance."

"You relish the effect."

"I do, I'll admit. And who knew I would?"

"If only the Godmother could see you now. She'd be sickened."

"What do you care if I laugh at these fools, at this dance? Or even at myself? Now that I have had a taste of Krampus, what it must be like to be you, to frighten silly fools, I realize that I've been a fool to want anything less than that woman!" She curtsied across the hall at herself. "What would it take, Krampus? For you and I to remain together? I, the bride of Krampus? I swear I'll do anything."

"I don't care about anyone but my prey."

"Good luck finding your prey now." She surveyed the dancers all disentangling themselves. She wasn't even sure that she could find her stepmother if she wanted to.

"And now," said Krampus, "you're going back on your word?"

"Give me until midnight at least. Then I'll point the finger. That woman—" She stepped over fallen dancers, approaching the mirror on the other side of the hall. "—and this woman—" She gestured to her reflection; her reflection gestured back. "—we have only just met. Are you sure there's nothing I can do to stay with you?"

She put a purr into her plea, wondering if Krampus was lonely. Even if he would let her wear him once a week, she would dote on him for the other six days.

"I am already yoked to Nicholas," he said. "I would give anything to sever that tether. Except for one thing, to spend one more minute with you."

"But we have a pact," She switched tactics, from flirtation to fury, and cracked the whip. "You will not go back on it. And I will never point out the one—ever. I wonder, what happens to you if you fail to kill for Nicholas by the end of the night? Why would a monster as miserable as you serve anyone, if he wasn't holding something terrible over your head?"

"True."

"Then strike a new bargain with me. Or else I'll delay until midnight. Tell me what you want, so I can be her. Tell me, or I'll make you suffer!" She cracked the whip, and jabbed her finger at her reflection.

"You have pointed out the one," said Krampus, "which means we are done."

She heard and felt ripping and tearing, and Cinderella looked in desperation at the mirror, catching the bloody sight of something like a sausage being unmade, going up backward through the grinder, until there Krampus stood behind her, bloated and bloody, and she was worse than naked—left standing in her servant's rags. She heard the screams of men and women all around, but theirs were nothing to her own, revealed before the ball for what she was.

"Nicholas," said Krampus. "Another one, Hell-bound. I am done for the year."

The monster seized Cinderella, held her high, and thrust her at the mirror. Even in her final second, Cinderella scrambled in midair, trying to escape that reflection, seeing it loom large as her body hit the glass. Her last thought was: At least I tried.

Now, Schönbrunn was a palace on the site of a beautiful fountain, as the name translated from the German, and in imitation of Versailles, the palace had been built on the site of a royal hunting lodge, in a royal hunting forest. But Schönbrunn had one quality that Versailles did not. The beautiful fountain had, through shifts of time and tongue, once been known as the site of an enchanted well. The imperial family, in a more pagan age, knew it and held this possession dear as it did mystical objects in its treasury. But this empire, which had clothed itself in Catholic things, had forgotten about the magic of its lands, though curiously, still believed that they had the Holy Grail in its treasury.

The well was still there in spirit. As an idea more than a place. But sometimes, ideas are enough to save us in our darkest hour.

So it was down the well that Cinderella now fell, screaming her last, until she realized that she had not been dashed against the glass but somehow gone through it. She saw the notions of a well wall passing by as she plunged. Though faint, she could make out stones slicked with moss, veiny with lichen. She looked up and caught a glimpse of a chandelier, fainter than the rest, as if it had never been real at all. She looked down and—?

Cinderella fell onto a featherbed.

It should have killed her after such a long and fierce fall, but the mattress cushioned her softly, and instead spewed feathers out, as many as might have covered a goose. They billowed up, blinding her to her surroundings. But all feathers settle, and when these did, Cinderella saw that she was in a half-timbered house—a lodge that was just too darling, large enough for one, and adorable from the floor boards to its plaster ceiling.

It seemed to have been decorated by a woman with a tipsy grasp of color, or simply too much time on her hands. While one window was open to a starry night over alpine peaks, several others had their shutters closed. Their slats were painted all the colors of the rainbow, light and dark, plus more that were colors yet to be imagined, and more still, colors long forgotten.

Upon the fireplace mantle, hundreds of porcelain figures of children at play were crammed together, right up to the edge, to the extent that some had tipped off and should have fallen, but their limbs were hooked by those of other figures; the slightest tap could have brought them all crashing to the floor. As a fire behind the grate below roared, Cinderella caught glimmers of light around the ceiling. Its beams were painted with something like pentacles from fortune-telling cards, but they were more floral than that, more orchid than occult. She found her gaze lost to those symbols—owned by them, even—and could not tear her eyes away.

"All right now, you've had a busy night," said a woman who threw a heavy feather blanket over Cinderella. "Best you get some sleep."

Cinderella cringed, thrusting her head back, surprised to find she wasn't alone. The woman leaned over Cinderella to grab a pillow, and the night dress she wore, which was the color of snail shells, gave off the sorts of smells one caught in a gentle breeze: dewy grass at dawn, dandelions in the morning, sunflowers at dusk, lilacs in the night. The woman plumped the pillow, cupped the back of Cinderella's head in her hand, and then pulled the pillow under it.

Cinderella was suddenly so relaxed that she thought she might be dead.

But then the woman hobbled—it seemed one of her feet was deformed, with splayed toes like a swan's—over to the fireplace and dropped herself into a rocking chair. She began to rock back and forth slowly. "To sleep…" she said. "To sleep…to sleep…" As she rocked, the woman combed her long white hair with her fingers. "To sleep…to sleep…"

Cinderella sat up, recognizing the woman.

"Godmother!"

The woman smiled. "No more gods or mothers between us, my dear. From now on, we are friends, and you may as well call me by one of my real names. But which one? Your mother was from Kassel and knew me as Holle, and your father Vienna-born, so he knew me as—"

"Perchte," said Cinderella, remembering. "That's what he called you."

The woman stopped rocking, then sighed. "Ah, you mean my old goat." She began rocking again. "I am deeply sorry for sending him rather than coming myself. But I would have never guessed how poorly it all would have turned out."

"Tonight, turned out poorly?" Cinderella scoffed.

"Now, lasting friends—indeed, members of a loving family—should never speak in hooks and barbs, meaning to prick and bleed. This is a new start for you and me both. Besides, I meant the last thousand years. Had I known it would turn out so poorly, I may have done things differently. Like every caring mother, I had to let the child try its legs, find its direction." She made toddling motions with her fingers. The fireplace cast spidery shadows around the room. "When did it all go wrong?" The woman lapsed into deep thought.

It unnerved Cinderella. She remembered where she'd seen this before.

"Your Krampus did that too—faded off, all foggy."

"Did he?" The woman brightened. "Then he does remember better times, before the plague of cities, the felling of forests, the rise of steeples. He always was a good goat, back then. All the creatures of my garden have been lured off by hook and by crook, by saviors and saints, all of them promising to make the world into a paradise, offering the carrot of sweet trinity, even multiplicity, then beating my creatures with a stick until they were broken. Only Krampus still visits. All my other dearies are either dead…" She gestured uncertainly. "…or slaves like Krampus to pilgrims and progress."

"All right, this is all well and good," said Cinderella impatiently, pushing the blanket aside. "But I don't have time for you right now. I need to be leaving."

"Leaving?"

"The ball is not yet over. Come now, where's the third gown?" Cinderella swung her legs down to the floor, grabbed the tatters of her servant's clothes in her fists. "You can't expect me to wear this." She saw the Godmother staring back at her in bafflement. She clapped once, sharply. "Please, Godmother, no foggy thoughts. I'm right here, right now, and I have things to do."

"Even now, amid the peace of my home, you still yearn for the ball?"

"Look here. I'm not heartless. You need a companion to sit with you? To hold your hand while you share stories of bygone years? I'll come by as often as you need. Why, I'll not just lend you my ears, I'll slice them off and serve them on a platter."

"I don't have the third gown. I released it back to the stars."

"Then get me Krampus," Cinderella began to panic, feeling like she was trapped.

"Have you forgotten that he just—moments ago—tried to slay you? And dear, please put that down. The way you're handling it, I'm not sure what would happen. Tomorrow, I'll teach you all about my home. Best that tonight you stay very still, lest you unleash havoc."

"What?" Cinderella looked down at her hands and saw she'd snatched the feather blanket back to her lap and, in her anxiousness, was wringing it like a goose's neck. She bolted from the bed in her bare feet and went to the open window, and there looked out on the landscape. They were in the mountains, amid its most barren peaks. Below was a crumbling well. "I came by well," she said, sitting on the sill, "so I can leave by well."

She threw her legs over the sill, ready to jump down. The Godmother's bedroom was on the upper floor; directly below was rock, but farther off was a snowdrift. She might be able to jump to it, and then saw that she had the feather blanket still clutched in one fist. She snapped it over the sill, ready to tie it to something, and was startled by how many feathers came out of it, feathers that turned into the gusts of a blizzard.

Magic again, she thought. Frippery and foolishness—all of it!

"Put down that blanket," warned the Godmother. "It's seen enough beating tonight. Any more, and you'll bury Vienna under snow for the winter. There's nothing down that well but death for you anyway. In time, I'll teach you the ways of the well. You could visit Vienna again, or Heaven, for that matter, if you'd like to see your mother and father again, but first I'll teach you how to rock in this chair, to turn the world from night to day, and how to sweep the floor, to breeze the seeds in the spring, and how to stoke the fire, to warm fruits and wombs in the summer, and do all the cleaning of my house that keeps Nature going."

"No, no, no," said Cinderella, grabbing two fistfuls of the blanket and thrusting them against her ears. The old woman was talking about cleaning! Was she mad? And all this jibber-jabber about spring and summer and...

The blizzard.

Realization struck Cinderella, and her shoulders slumped. She looked at the blanket, then out into the night sky, which was clear and starry again. Cinderella leaned out of the room, outside, and punched her fist into the blanket.

Feathers fell, becoming blizzards, which flew off and away.

"You," said Cinderella, glowering at the Godmother.

"Yes, dear?"

"You dropped that blizzard on Vienna."

"Why, dear, yes."

"To stop me from getting to the ball!"

"No, dear—to stop the ball."

"Cruel hag! Why give me two wonderful nights, then cheat me out of the third? I was so close to being someone." Cinderella began to sob, but refused to give the woman the satisfaction of seeing her defeated, and covered her face with the blanket.

"I didn't want anyone to attend tonight's ball," said the woman. "There will be no more balls, ever again, if I can help it. You, of all the girls I've sent to balls, finally showed me the truth. Balls are no longer a celebration of women—not like the maypole dances of old. Balls have become a pyre upon which men load the wood, and women dance upon the flames."

"What? No more balls?"

"I have tried for years to send the best girls in the world to them in hopes of inspiring the best in everyone. But what have I done but merely fanned the flames? One girl, snatched from the pyre? While all the others stand in the fire—or worse, throw each other into the flames to escape the worst of the burning?"

"You couldn't have waited?" Cinderella raged from the sill, and loomed over the Godmother in the chair. "I don't care about any of this. You couldn't have had your change of heart after my happy ending?"

"Two nights, in today's balls, darkened your sweet heart. I can barely recognize the girl you were just days ago. Rest assured, I'll now do right by you. You will stay here with me, and we will serve Nature forever." The Godmother beamed up at her. "This is your happy ending, dear, the happiest a good girl can get in this evil world. Forget balls, forget Vienna, forget all the things that caused you pain, and embrace…"

Cinderella stared down as the woman prattled on. She was repulsed by a filmy mist in her eyes, cataracts as foggy as her thoughts. Even in her own rage, Cinderella could feel the woman trying to muster hope, that she had lived for a thousand years, or many more, and grieved deeply her mistakes. But whatever this woman had done, or not done, was none of her concern. The past was the past. The future—Cinderella's future—was her own.

She looked in revulsion around the little house where the Godmother meant to keep her. At the blanket in her hands, which made blizzards. At the broom next to the fireplace, which stirred up spring. At the porcelain figures of children, crowded to the brink of catastrophe on the mantle and needed dusting with a feather duster that did who knows what, and she'd probably get scolded by the old woman if she knocked a figure crashing to the floor. She would not be anyone's servant. Not the Godmother's, not Nature's, not anyone's.

She resolved to prove that she was serious.

Cinderella kicked the fireplace grate sideways, exposing the flames.

"Dear girl, no!" The Godmother shouted. "You don't know what—"

"I know enough," said Cinderella.

She tossed an end of the blanket into the fireplace, and smiled to see the flames quickly spread across it. She dragged it flaming across the floor, as the Godmother dropped to all fours and began trying to pat out the fire with her hands. But Cinderella whipped the blanket away from her, and leaning out the window, began flapping it outside—not hard enough to extinguish the flames, but rather to send fiery feathers gushing out. She wasn't surprised to see them transform not into a frosty blizzard, but a fiery maelstrom.

Cinderella marveled at the beauty of it all. Great tendrils of fire. Lashing the night sky. At risk of burning her hands, she gripped the blanket in two handfuls and ripped its fabric open, disemboweling it of its feathers. She threw handfuls of the stuff into the flaming night. By the time the Godmother reached her at the sill, Cinderella was basking in what seemed a ruby sunrise or a red-wine sunset.

The sky was on fire.

"You—!" said the Godmother, covering her mouth. "You have—! The clouds—! Girl, they cover the world, do you realize what you have—?"

Cinderella threw the last of the blanket outside, and then went calmly to the chair, where she took a cleansing breath, and began to soothe herself, rocking there. "If I must be here, with you, in this house, then there are going to be some changes around here. We're going to get things done. You didn't stop the ball, not even for one night. But I did. Just now."

The Godmother hurried to the window. "You've burned the world!" She looked at Cinderella in horror.

"Well, if things are truly as bad as you say…"

Cinderella waited for the old woman to correct her, to confess that she'd only been exaggerating.

"Then it's time that we start over. Why, if I remember what I learned in church, once upon a time, it's that every now and then mankind needs a little flood. You know, out with the bad, in with the good."

"But you don't have the years, or the wisdom, to make such a decision!"

"Three nights are more than enough," said Cinderella, "to learn that no one has the true measure of me—except for me. My eye is the clearer one, more than yours or Krampus's, to see the world for what it is." She looked outside to the seething sky. "Or, shall I say, was."

She shifted her gaze to the floor, where a few of the burning feathers had crisped black as tarantulas, and then put her feet closer to the flames in the fireplace, the better to warm her toes. She felt a steady tickling on the skin of her ankles. It was a brown dust sifting down from the mantle like cinnamon from a hundred teaspoons. The porcelain figures, those figurines of impossibly perfect children at play, were crumbling into dust.

"Don't mind that," said Cinderella. "We'll clean it up tomorrow. Now, you're upset and that's understandable, but you should get some rest. In the morning, I'll need you to teach me how this..." She motioned around the room. "...all works."

"But, dear girl!"

Cinderella squirmed to hear those words. "We'll need new names. You said there'd be no more gods or mothers between us. I'll insist on no more dears or diminutives." She closed her eyes and began to rock, turning the world a bit faster than it had been turned before. Dawn was going to break sooner. And why shouldn't it? She was a busy wo—! She cut herself off mid-word, recalling how eagerly she'd pressed herself, rib to rib, with every man at the balls.

She cast an ambitious eye to the mounds of cinnamon dust on the mantle and began to wonder what, with the right ingredients, she could make of it.

# HE SEES YOU WHEN YOU'RE SLEEPING

**Lissa Marie Redmond**

How do I get myself into these messes?

My name is James Jonah Fitzgerald, and a year ago I was broke, lonely, and living above the coffee shop I worked at in South Buffalo. That might not sound great, but I was content. Being a twenty-five-year-old, college educated, underemployed male suited my personality. Let's just say I wasn't a guy of big ambitions.

Then everything changed. There was a catastrophic winter storm last December that wrecked the coffee shop (my fault), and my boss decided to sell me the whole building for next to nothing, which was what I had in my bank account. After I fixed it up, I changed the name. Now I'm the owner of Once Upon a Java. It seemed fitting.

So now instead of passing off problems to the owner, I have to deal with everything myself. You might say: hey, you own it, they're your problems. The problem is, my problems aren't normal problems.

Today my buddy Peter, the mailman, stopped in after his route. It was snowing, of course. This *is* Buffalo and poor Pete had snot frozen to his bushy mustache, he was so cold. I set a large cup of coffee in front of his shaking hands and he scooped it up, savoring the warmth.

"Rough day on the route?" I asked, watching Ashley, my lone barista, out of the corner of my eye as she changed out some pastries in the glass case. Ashley liked to take things home without asking. I would fire her but she just got a new tattoo on her neck, and I know she's a little strapped for cash.

"Same old, same old," he replied, wiping his face with a napkin, for which I was grateful. The snot had started to melt.

I started to wash down the countertop (which Ashley should have done) and he went on, "Except there's this one thing."

The hesitation in his voice made me look up. "What thing?"

"You know how I had that little breakdown last year during the Christmas rush?"

"I do."

"And remember how I thought we saved a fairy queen in my mail truck?"

"Vaguely." It didn't actually happen in his mail truck, we used it as a getaway car.

"And remember how I imagined you had three little gnomes with nasty teeth here in the shop?"

"No, I don't remember you telling me that part." The three little winter elves with the gnarly teeth were actually in the back room baking apple turnovers at the moment.

"Anyway," he went on, "do you think that those kind of delusions can get passed on?"

Now I was concerned. "What do you mean?"

"My son, Myles, says there's a horned monster that's been coming in his room at night. Says it's hairy and carries a chain and stares at him. He hasn't been able to sleep in a week."

I dropped my rag on the counter and leaned forward, "What does it do?"

He shrugged, "He says it just sits there, like it's waiting for something, huffing and drooling. The poor kid screams in hysterics every night. We tried letting him sleep in our room, but he says he can still hear it."

"Has Myles ever suffered from nightmares before?"

"No. That's the thing. I was wondering if my delusions were catchy, you know? Because those things seemed so real to me last year. And Myles usually sleeps like an angel."

He might have slept like an angel, but his son was the biggest spoiled brat I'd ever come across. He was a bossy, nasty nine-year-old, prone to tantrums if he didn't get his way. And sometimes even if he did get his way. I cringed whenever Peter's wife walked into the coffee shop with him. He'd slop hot chocolate everywhere, throw napkins all over the ground, and demand another pastry heart because the first one he ate was 'crappy'. Myles is the reason I would faithfully use birth control if I ever had the chance again.

"It's probably a phase," I assured him. "Kids go through these things. Here," I reached into the glass case and pulled out a banana muffin. "On me. Don't stress, my friend. It's no good for you. It's only December fifth, and you've got a lot of packages to deliver."

He gratefully accepted the muffin of friendship. "Thanks man, I know I'm probably over thinking this."

I nodded, "Probably." Maybe not.

"I have to go teach a yoga class," Ashley announced, balling up her apron and throwing it on a chair.

"You're supposed to work until six," I reminded her. I hate being the heavy.

She shrugged, tucking her short blonde hair up under a knit hat. "It's dead in here. No offense, Pete."

"None taken," he assured her, eating the top off the muffin without removing the wrapper.

"You can handle it, James." The snake tattoo on her neck pulsed and intimidated me a little.

I tried to give her my best bossly smile, "See you tomorrow,

Ashley."

"Whatever." She pulled her parka on and waved as she slid out the side door. Ashley was into yoga, kickboxing, and boot camp aerobics. Never employ a woman who can beat you in an arm wrestling match.

Pete finished off his muffin and coffee, brushed the crumbs out of his graying beard, and headed for the door.

"Hey, Pete? Let me know how things go with you and Myles, okay?"

He turned with his hand on the knob, "Okay. My doctor says I need to talk about my issues."

"I've always got an ear for you," said the cause of all his issues.

The door slammed shut behind him and I heard a faint, "Tsk, tsk, tsk."

Sitting in the shadows, near the back at the repurposed door table, was Morrigan.

"What are you doing here now?" I asked.

Morrigan sat back against the funky painted wooden chair I had picked out of the garbage and repurposed, her wild crimson curls spilling over her shoulders like a big, red Brillo pad. She had a face like a baked apple and a personality to match.

"Myles' father is of the house O'Laughlan."

"So?" I prompted. Morrigan was trouble. Whenever she showed up something bad was about to happen.

She went on, "I keen for the house of O'Laughlan when tragedy strikes."

I came around the corner, locked the front door, and turned the open sign to closed. "What do you know, Morrigan?"

She put her tiny feet up on the table I had made from an old discarded door. "What your friend says is true. His son is in terrible danger. If anything happens to him, it's my duty to honor the family, as I have for centuries."

Morrigan was one of three sister spirits of war and destruction, along the line of Banshees, but higher up on the food chain. Each had certain old Irish families they were bound to. And with South Buffalo being the Irish Heritage District of the city, the old bags came in quite often.

"So what the hell is it?" She would beat around the bush all day if I let her.

"It's the Krampus. He was cursed by the High King eons ago for his sadistic ways toward your human children. He's set his sights on Myles O'Laughlan and when his time comes tonight, well, it won't be good for Myles."

"Why him? Why now?"

"Why him?" She mocked my voice. "You know why! You opened the door when you brought his father to save the Queen and now he has The Sight, only he doesn't know it. You let that poor man walk around thinking he's crazy. You know when you have The Sight and you can see us, we can also see you."

Didn't I know it? Ever since Cerena, the Fairy Queen, walked into my coffee shop the year before, I was besieged with all kinds of mythical beings, stopping in at all hours of the night, wreaking havoc in my coffee shop, dragging me all over town on one crazy errand or another. I never knew if I'd wake up and find five or six hungover leprechauns sleeping all over my floor.

"Can't you help him? If you're sworn to his father's house?"

"You know the rules. We don't kill each other, not in your realm."

"Yeah, you get us to do your dirty work," I spat out.

She chuckled, her wrinkled, gnarled face squishing up into something like a smile. "The Krampus is no easy foe. He's been feeding off of bad children for thousands of years. He's a powerful demon."

"So how do I defeat him?"

"Do your own homework, James the Hipster. It's December fifth. At midnight tonight the veil between the realms is thin enough for him to strike."

"Isn't it St. Nicolas's day at midnight?"

She snorted, "Nicolas is his brother. Welcome to the family feud. Now, if you'll excuse me, I feel a temper tantrum of Myles coming on. The more negative energy he puts out, the closer he draws the Krampus in."

Morrigan rose from the table and headed for the kitchen.

"How much danger is Myles O'Laughlan in?" I asked as she pushed the door open to visit with my three winter elves. I keep it locked, but locks don't stay locked for her kind.

Curly, Larry and Shemp started gibbering to her excitedly as she paused in the doorway, "Mortal, James. Mortal danger."

So I did what any millennial with a problem would do, I went upstairs and googled it on my computer. There were a lot of pages on Krampus, even a cheesy B horror movie with him as the star. Turns out this horned, black-tongued, cloven-hoofed demon has been punishing kids for centuries by hitting them with switches and dragging them off in baskets to wherever Krampi chill out. They actually still celebrate him in parts of Europe on Krampusnacht to this day, dressing up like him and getting drunk. Which goes to show that Europeans will use any excuse to party.

But every site I went to said the same thing. This guy was bad news.

I went back down to the kitchen to consult with my employees.

I have to keep the door locked so no one, especially Ashley, will stumble upon my trio of three-foot tall winter elves that looked suspiciously like garden gnomes with wicked teeth. Since they had taken up residence in my coffee shop, they had turned into master bakers. And when I say master, I mean they bake twenty-four hours a day. Nonstop. With only breaks to guzzle sweet cream straight from the carton. Their culinary skills are what saved my coffee shop because not only do I have the best pastries and goodies in town, every morning I drop boxes of treats off to other businesses for a very tidy profit.

Shemp wiped his four fingered hands on his apron and gave me a toothy smile, "James! Kaduba!"

"Kaduba! Kaduba!" Curly and Larry joined in. Curly was holding a huge mixing bowl, while Larry stirred it with a giant wooden spoon. They were both covered from head to toe with flour.

"Kaduba to you, guys. Hey, what do you know about this Krampus dude?"

"Ooooo," Shemp reached over and pulled a baking pan of strudel out of the oven without mitts. "Krampus ol guapno."

"Guapno," the other two agreed.

"How Guapno? Like if I try to interfere I might lose a finger Guapno? Or worse?"

"Ol Guapno, James. Nah vertum Krampus." Shemp gave a little shutter as he put his goodies down. I was getting pretty good at Elvish: Nah vertum = no good.

Then he shook his little knobby finger at me, "Nah vertum Krampus, James."

I put my hands up, "Okay, I get it. But I have to help Peter's son or very shortly he's going to end up get dragging away by Mister Krampus."

They all looked at each other and I knew what was going on under those ridiculous pointy hats they wore. "Come on guys! We can't let Myles get taken by the Krampus."

"So dum cul?"

"Yes, I'm sure, Larry. You should be ashamed of yourselves. I came down here to find out what I can do to help Myles."

"Nicolas," Shemp said taking a test bite of his latest batch. The other two nodded in unison.

"As in Saint Nicolas? Santa Claus? Do I have to go to the North Pole?"

"Nicolas," Shemp repeated, like I was a big dummy, "Ad im Blackthorn."

"I can find St. Nicolas in a bar?"

Shemp shrugged his shoulders, "Ad im Blackthorn, Nicolas."

Now all three were staring at me, meaning I was interrupting their work flow. "Okay, guys. Carry on. There's more sugar under the counter. Thanks for your help."

"Seeba, James!" They all called as I locked them back in.

"Yeah, Seeba later, guys."

I made sure the coffee shop was locked up tight and started walking to The Blackthorn. It was a local pub on the other side of Cazenovia Park that was known for its authentic Irishness. People love fake authentic Irishness around here.

It was cold, not as cold as last year, but there was a good two inches of snow on the ground. I could have taken my beat-up mini-van, but I tried to only use it for my morning pastry deliveries. I'm trying to lessen my carbon footprint. Which sucks if you live anywhere where it snows.

I shuffled my way through the park to Seneca Street, where the Blackthorn was located. It looked cozy and inviting after my brisk walk, and the first thing that hit me when I pushed the door open was the delightful smell of their homemade Beer Cheese Soup.

The bar was full of people drinking Guinness, eating wings, and watching the hockey game on the big screen TVs over the bar. The dining area beyond the bar was packed with people, shopping bags at their feet, winter coats piled on the hooks that lined the walls.

"Hey, James," Karen, the hostess, spotted me in the crowd and made her way over. "I don't have any tables right now, but you can have a seat at the bar, and I'll try to squeeze you in."

"That's okay. Actually, Karen, I'm looking for someone..." I scanned the bar. "You don't have anyone here, any regulars, who call themselves St. Nicolas, do you?"

She laughed, "Like Santa Claus? No. I think you mean Nick. He's over in the corner by the back bar. But he's in a bad mood tonight."

"Thanks, Karen. I'll find him."

Once she pinpointed the spot, I picked him out right away. Hunched over the back bar with a rather large beer in his hand was a portly gentleman of about sixty eating chicken wings one after the other. He was dressed in jeans and an old striped sweater that barely covered his beer gut, no red suit or shiny black boots. He did, however, possess an epic beard, the likes of which men my age can only dream about growing in their lifetimes. It was truly a masterpiece of facial hair.

I pushed my way through the crowd and approached him. He didn't look up from his plate of wings. "Are you St. Nicolas?" I asked in my most straightforward way, lest he not take my skinny jeans seriously.

He snorted a laugh. "No. I'm not Saint Nicolas. I knew him, though. Great guy. We get mistaken for each other all the time. I'm just Nicolas."

"I'm James Fitzgerald and I need your help, Nicolas. The Krampus has set his sights on my friend's son."

Nick took a gulp from his pint glass. "I know who you are. All of us Fair Folk do. James the Brave, Coffee Server. Do you have any idea what it's like to have to clean up your little brother's messes century after century?"

"The Krampus is your brother?"

"The thing that is the Krampus used to be my younger brother."

I shook my head, "I can't imagine…"

"No, you can't," he cut me off, slamming the glass down on the polished wood bar. Some Guinness sloshed over the side. "He gets cursed and gets me cursed too! What did I do? Now I have to spend eternity running around, rewarding kids with happy thoughts, counter balancing the anguish my selfish brother causes."

"Happy thoughts? No presents?"

"Typical millennial. Thinks everything worth having is a *thing,*" he said in disgust. "I got news for you, Mister brand new iPhone every six months, until very recently, and actually in a lot of the rest of the world, life is very hard. It sucks, actually. And good thoughts and hope and happy dreams are the best things a child can get. Not plastic trucks that live on in landfills for a thousand years."

"Hey, I'm sorry." I clapped him on the back, "Let me get you another beer."

He straightened up, "Damn right you'll get me another beer. Who do you think filled your dirty little mind with images of baseball games when you were twelve so you'd stop worrying you'd go blind? You didn't even like baseball."

I waved over to Kevin and he set two more glasses in front of us, "Uh, yeah. Thanks for that."

He chuckled into his Guinness, "I see you when you're sleeping, I know when you're awake…"

"Anyway," I tried to erase the memory of the Buffy the Vampire Slayer poster I'd had over my bed from my mind. "Back to the Krampus. What's going to happen to Myles?"

"My brother hasn't had much opportunity at kids lately, since so very few people have The Sight. It's almost been like a vacation since we decided to go underground, and not interfere with your kind anymore. But you had to drag his dad into your nonsense, and now my brother is chomping at the bit to get at another kid."

"So what do we do?"

Nick motioned to Kevin and called out, "Two shots of whiskey, please."

Kevin knew exactly what to pour into the shot glasses he lined up in front of us. Nick downed his in one quick gulp. I was a little more hesitant. He stared at me impatiently until I drank the whole thing. He rubbed his chubby hands together. "Okay, James Fitzgerald. Let's go take a peek in Myles' window and see what's going on." He pulled a set of car keys out of his back pocket and dropped them in my hand. "You're driving."

I just want it to be known, for the record, that Nicolas drives a bright red hummer. And he was hammered. All my innocent, childhood Christmas memories were crashing down around my Doc Martin's.

Nicolas was wedged in the passenger seat, belly smooshed against the glove box. I pulled the driver's seat up so my feet could touch the pedals. "How do you drive this beast with the seat all the way back?"

He folded his hands on top of his ginormous gut, "Because that's how I roll."

I put the behemoth vehicle into gear, and headed over to Peter's house.

"Don't get all sentimental on me. You Judeo-Christian types commandeered all our 'Pagan' holidays for your own. Saint Nicolas was a swell guy, but me and my brother were around long before he was born. I'm not him and he's not me."

I turned the corner. "It's just a little shocking, you know?"

"You know how many babes I get this time of year?" He gave me a wink, "The whole Santa thing works for me."

I pulled up next to the curb about four houses from Peter's. "I just threw up a little in my mouth," I informed him.

He grinned and looked out the window, "Don't hate the player, hate the game."

With that creepy image seared into my mind for all time, I dismounted into a snow bank. Fat Nicolas jumped down from his side and we made our way stealthily to the side of Peter's contemporary ranch. It was late and most of the lights were off in the houses we passed. The snow reflected the glow of the street lamps for us. I noticed when we walked, Nicolas didn't leave any footprints.

He noticed me noticing. "Trick of the trade."

I knew from having to build a bookshelf in Myles' room that it was the third window down. Peter and his wife's room was across the hall, on the other side of the house. Despite being a ranch, the window was still set high off the ground. "Okay," Nicolas said, hands on his massive hips, "make a step stool."

"Can't you just magic yourself up there?"

"Hands and knees. Now."

So I sank into the snow, my gloved hands going numb almost

immediately, bracing for the weight about to pulverize my torso.

He climbed on my back, knocking the wind out of me. "Ooofff…"

"Don't be such a baby," he scolded, grinding his work boots into my spine. "There you are, little brother…just as handsome as ever."

He jumped down with a heavy thump and made a basket with his hands, "Up you go."

I rubbed my back. "He's in there now?"

Nicolas motioned to the window with his head, holding his hands out to me, "See for yourself."

I stepped up, and he boosted me like I was a feather.

There was only a nightlight in the corner but it was enough to illuminate the nightmare in front of me. As Myles tossed restlessly under his race car blankets, a huge, horned beast stood over him, its black tongue lolling out obscenely. The thing was actually salivating over the little boy. His cloven hoofs shuffled around the side of the bed, like there was an invisible leash barely holding him back from devouring Myles right in front of me.

Suddenly, like he got a whiff of my scent, his head swung toward the window, red eyes blazing, his lips curled in a deadly snarl.

I fell backwards into the snow.

Nicolas collected me up, and took me back to the Hummer. As I tried to warm myself with the heater I asked, "How are we supposed to defeat that monster?"

"You can't defeat him. But you can trick him. Jolly old Nick still has a few cards up his sleeve." He readjusted his bulk. "Anyway, just drive back to the coffee shop. I've got a plan."

Cold, defeated, and disillusioned I drove back to Once Upon a Java.

My three little bakers were delighted to see their old friend. They danced around him and gibbered while I put a pot of black coffee on for my drunken Santa. He was now blubbery belly up to my counter, stuffing pastry hearts in his mouth one after another.

"So what do we do?" I asked, hands on my hips, trying to sound assertive.

"We create a diversion," he explained, showering me with half-eaten crumbs. "He feeds off negative energy. We need someone to draw him off while I go in and work my happy magic. Once Myles is happy and hopeful, my brother won't be able to touch him."

"So that's it? You plant some pleasant thoughts and the monster slinks away?"

"It's a curse, remember? He's cursed, and I'm cursed. He's bad, and I counter with good. We've been doing this dance for centuries."

"Does it always work?"

"Regretfully, not always. And my brother hasn't had the chance at a child in decades. He wants this child in the worst way. We need someone really awful to lure him away. Who's the nastiest person you know?"

"Ashley." I didn't even have to think about it. Nasty, rude, stealing, buff Ashley. The only person in the world who got angrier the longer she practiced yoga.

"Then let's go get Ashley and try to save the boy."

I glanced at my hip swinging Elvis wall clock, "It's eleven thirty at night."

Nick bounced off my stool and brushed the remnants of the pastry hearts off of his shirt. "You know how these things work. Midnight is always the witching hour. I didn't make the rules, I'm just bound by them."

As unpleasant as Ashley was on a regular day, I had no idea how she'd react when I showed up at her apartment at night with a guy who looked suspiciously like Santa Claus in a red hummer.

Her apartment was actually on one of the nicest streets in South Buffalo. It was decorated with strings of twinkling white Christmas lights and a gorgeous holly wreath hung on the door to the lower apartment. I knew her mother owned the house, but I had never had the pleasure of meeting Mrs. Krutz. As Nick and I stood on the porch

I could only hope from the cheery holiday décor that she was nothing like her daughter.

As soon as I knocked, I knew I was wrong.

"Who is it?" A voice demanded and then the door flew open, as if she'd been waiting behind it the whole time. A women in her fifties wearing a long kimono-type robe, cigarette hanging from her mouth, stood with her hands on either side of the door as if barring our entrance. "Yeah?"

"Hi, Mrs. Krutz. I'm Ashley's boss, James. I was wondering if I could speak to her? It's very important."

She turned her head and yelled up the staircase to the upper flat, "Ashley!!!" In a screech I was sure not only blew out my eardrums, but must have woken the entire street. The cigarette miraculously remained dangling from her lower lip.

"What, Ma?" The familiar stomping of Ashley's muscular legs came tromping down the stairs. She was dressed in military fatigues. "I'm doing my cardio up here!"

"You got some visitors." She ashed her cigarette out the door on my boot and disappeared down the hall.

"What are you doing here?" Ashley took her mother's position by the door.

"We have an emergency job. I need you to come in, right now."

"We sell coffee and muffins. What the hell kind of emergency can you have?"

"Just hop in the truck. I'll pay you overtime."

She raised an eyebrow.

"Triple time."

"I want the cash up front." She tugged her parka loose from a wall hook.

Nicolas held up a wad of bills, "I'm sure we can cover it."

"This better not be some sicko Christmas thing you two weirdos are into," Ashley said, counting the money and tucking it away as we walked to the hummer. "I see anything goofy and I'm out."

Nick held the door open for her as she eyed him up. "We just have to stop at Pete's house real quick and drop something off," I told her as we started rolling down the street.

"Listen, make it quick. I have to be up early for a kickboxing tournament."

"You're supposed to open tomorrow," I reminded her.

"Yeah, sorry. I'm going to be late. Where'd you steal this gas guzzler? I thought you were Mr. Green."

"It belongs to Nick. And, yes, I care about the environment."

She turned around in the front passenger seat to get a better look at Nick in the back. "You really need to work on your core," she said, glaring at his gut.

He slapped me on the shoulder. "She's going to work just fine."

Peter's house was barely a minute away. That close to midnight, all of the houses were dark, even the Christmas lights had been unplugged, making our undercover route even darker.

"Now listen, Miss Ashley, I need you to wait on the sidewalk while James talks to Peter. No matter what you hear, don't leave the sidewalk." Nick was already half out of the door.

"What are you two up to? Putting the squeeze on poor Pete for a bookie?"

Nicolas flipped her a hundred dollar bill. "Go stand on the sidewalk."

She snapped it up and tucked it into her parka. "You're the boss."

Ashley and I went to the front of the house, while Nick made his way towards Myles' window. I went up to the door and rang the bell while Ashley stood behind me, arms folded. A bleary-eyed Peter answered. "James, what are you doing here?" He glanced at the watch on his wrist, "It's midnight."

I pushed my way into the hall, leaving Ashley outside. "Listen, I've been thinking about everything you said about transferring delusions…"

"Can this wait? I have to work in the morning."

I steered him into the front room, which was one of those front rooms that's perfectly decorated but no one is allowed to use, and sat him in an overstuffed floral chair. "This will only take a minute. And you need to vent your feelings more, you said so yourself."

He pulled his green terry cloth robe around him a little tighter. "I guess you're right."

"Peter? Who's out there?" His wife called from their bedroom.

"It's nothing honey, go back to bed."

*Crash*!

From the front walk we heard a horrible ruckus. We rushed back to the front door.

Ashley and the Krampus were going toe to toe on the front lawn. Ashley had managed to shove the Krampus's wicker basket over his head so that his horns were sticking out. She had a horn in each hand, pulling the beast forward and was kicking him in his mid-section with her combat boots for all she was worth.

"What the hell?" Peter exclaimed.

"Go back inside," I pushed him in, pulling the door closed behind him.

Now Ashley had the Krampus on his knees, and was wailing on his basketed head. The creature roared an unearthly howl, and his left hand brought up his rusty chain to whack Ashley on her blind side. She was about to get clobbered.

Instinctively, I jumped on the filthy monster's back, grabbing the chain and pulling it around his thick neck. He smelled like a wet raccoon, with his black, matted fur and long, sharp claws. He tried standing up, to buck me off, but his cloven-hoofed feet slipped on the ice and we both fell back into the snow. He clawed at the chain around his neck, shredding the basket into pieces. I pulled as tight as I could, with him on top of me, bucking and snarling.

Then Ashley was there, parka ripped open, hands balled into fists. "I'll teach you to attack defenseless women, you dirty pervert." She proceeded to rain down a pummeling, the likes of which South

Buffalo has never seen, on his horned head.

The Krampus howled and spit and flailed against the chain, but I didn't let go. The links cut into my hands, blood dribbling into the snowbank, but I didn't ease up.

All around us, lights were snapping on. We were waking up the neighborhood.

He managed to get his hand up and rake his claws across my cheek. Blood poured from my face into his mangy coat. I pulled tighter. But I was getting tired, and the Krampus wasn't. Even with Ashley wailing on him, I didn't know how much longer I could last.

"It's done, Brother."

Nick was out on the sidewalk with us, looking sadly down at the Krampus. I felt the Krampus's body freeze underneath me at the sight.

"Go back," Nicolas said, almost gently. "The boy is full of happy thoughts and good memories. There's nothing for you here."

As if he could sense that his brother was right, that Nicolas had snuck in and done his magic while he was out here with me and Ashley, the Krampus gave one last tormented scream. His body pulsed with some unseen energy, and then melted away into the night.

I sat up, still holding the rusty chain. "Is he really gone?"

Nicolas nodded miserably. "At least until next year. Then it starts all over again somewhere else. It's our curse."

Peter came charging out of the house in his bathrobe and slippers, "What was that thing?"

Ashley stepped up. "It was some pervert wearing a mask that likes to attack lone women." She held out her bruised knuckles. "Thanks to me and James, he'll probably think twice next time."

Looking around at the blood-stained snowbank and sidewalk, Peter asked, "Where did he go?"

Ashley's eyes searched up and down the street. In the distance we could hear police sirens. "It happened so fast, I don't know. I think he was hiding in your bushes because all of a sudden he was standing in front of me with his tongue hanging out, drooling." She gave a shudder. "Then James came out of nowhere and throttled the guy with his own chain, like a knight in shining armor. I didn't think you had it in you, James."

"I have my moments," I huffed, still trying to catch my breath. Ashley actually smiled at that. A patrol car came careening around the corner, followed by an ambulance.

"I've got to go," Nick said, walking backwards toward the hummer.

"Thank you for all your help," I called, waving the bloody chain.

He just gave me a wink and hopped into the hummer. Nicolas revved the engine a little but no headlights came on. The whole truck vibrated for a split second, and just like his brother, he seemed to melt away into the night. The cops who were walking toward us never even knew he was there at all.

"You're bleeding," Ashley came forward and touched my cheek. I noticed she had really pretty brown eyes. "You're going to need stitches."

I reached up and put my hand over hers, "Cool."

This morning I woke up still in my blood-soaked clothes, with seventeen stitches in my face and Ashley's number in my phone. I looked up and there, above my bed, was a poster of Kim Kardashian.

Thanks again, Nick.

# SANTA'S LITTLE HELPER

## Beth Mann

"Salvation! Salvation through the good Lord at Christmas!"

I held out a soggy leaflet to the man in front of me, chin ducked into his coat collar, eyes on the ground, but he hurried past, his boots shattering the puddles at our feet and soaking me up to the knees. Another one missed. Not that I could blame him. If I'd been accosted by a grinning, bearded German in stripy tights waving holy papers in my face, I would have run like hell too.

I blew on my hands and stamped my feet in their ridiculous curly-toed boots. The costume was all Nic's idea. I'd wanted to dress as an angel, but he'd only laughed, said something in Turkish that I guessed was less than flattering, and thrust the elf outfit my way.

"Santa's little helper!" he teased.

Predictably, I'd had no response. So I'd squirmed my way into the tights, the green lederhosen and the red coat, and I'd gone out into the jolly Christmas market bustle and stinging winter rain.

This, I have learned, is typical of England. Winter does not bring snow, like it should—like it always does in the beautiful mountains of my fatherland—but endless sheets of rain, or variations on rain, in exotic degrees of solidity against which elf costumes are less than adequate protection.

I have very little time for England.

Shaking the water off my leaflets, I edged along the line of gaudy sheds that made up the city's Christmas market, which was billed, with more hope than certainty, as German. Across the square a lone accordion player with raw knees was looking longingly at the bar. I thought he had a point.

I stopped opposite the bratwurst stand. The sweet and sour scent of fried meat filled my nostrils, making me ache for home and, more immediately, for lunch. But I had come here with a job to do. If I screwed up on this one, Nic would kick me out of the flat for good.

A girl in a red duffle coat was watching me as she chewed on a gingerbread heart as big as her head. I shifted from foot to foot.

"Salvation through the good Lord at Christmas?" I offered, and held out a leaflet.

She turned and ran away into the crowd.

It's always the same. Hurtful, plain hurtful. I dug into my pocket, slapped down a handful of coins, and bought myself a bratwurst, a big one—with extra mustard.

When Nic had given me the assignment, coming to the German market had seemed like a good idea. All of the men and women we were hoping to snag were German, after all. People we'd been after for a while, who'd managed to slip under the radar and out of the country, hoping, maybe, that in England, they'd be safe. I'd thought that perhaps they'd be drawn to the market, drawn by the bratwurst and the wailing accordion and the gluhwein and song.

I'd thought that perhaps tonight I could go back to Nic a success.

The rain sluiced down my neck. Pigeons squabbled over crumbs of cake on the wet flagstones. I sat on a bench and ate my bratwurst, water soaking through my shorts.

I wished I were home. Not the flat, with its bare white walls and sleek black sofas, but real home: the mountains, the forests, crisp air and eagle cries and purling streams.

I finished my bratwurst and brushed the fragments on to the ground for the pigeons.

And then I saw her.

Tall, curvaceous, her blonde hair glowing in the grey morning like a halo.

Ach du lieber Gott.

My salvation.

I knew she was German without thinking. Even across the square I could smell it: a national fragrance, blend of sausages and beer, spiced with ingenuity and citrus-sharp notes of guilt. Under it was something else, heady, feral, curling off her like dark smoke. Wickedness.

No doubt about it: she was mine.

Palms sweating, I wove my way through the crowd towards her. Lise Hackelberg: that was the name on the file; thirty years old, wanted for embezzlement, theft and seduction. It was the last of the three, I think, that sealed her fate. Nic was always very hard-line on seduction. He had no sense of fun at all.

I stopped beside her, leaflets at the ready, wondering what to say. This was about more than offering salvation; it was about getting her hook, line and sinker. And she was the kind of fish who looked like she'd thrash.

I cleared my throat. "Excuse me."

"Oh." She moved aside to give me room to peer at the chocolate spanners and screws on the display before us, then registered my outfit. The smallest of smirks settled on her face.

Curse Nic. I knew in that moment he'd suggested this costume on purpose.

"You're…ah…not from around here, are you?" I asked, aware of the stall holder watching us with interest. "I mean. You're from Germany. Aren't you?"

"Really," she said to the stall holder, and nodded at the sign over the chalet, "English people who see an advertisement for chocolate tools and come here to find only spanners are going to be disappointed."

The stall holder and I exchanged glances of mutual sympathy.

"What I was trying to say," I continued, trailing her across the square, "is that...ah...I like your hair. Fancy a beer?"

She snorted. "Desperate, much?"

"A little," I admitted.

"Oh?" She looked at a young policeman standing on the far side of the square, and the child in the red duffle coat running into the crowd came back to me with unpleasant clarity.

"Not that kind of desperate." Clearly, I was making about as much progress as the England team in the World Cup. Nic's fault; he never let me date these days. I was rusty—too rusty. I tried again. "I've been out since seven shoving these leaflets at people. It's lonely. I just want a chat."

"A chat about what?"

"Ah...stuff?" I hazarded.

Another snort. "Are you drunk?" she asked.

"No."

"Lose your cushy, pen-pushing job?"

"No."

She looked over my outfit, and grinned. "Don't believe you."

"I am," I said with wounded dignity, "in full-time employment."

"Dressed as an elf?"

God, I was never going to live this down. "This is...ah...merely an attempt to get into the festive spirit."

"Festive spirit?" Amazingly, she laughed, and the laugh was not pure, unmitigated scorn. "Okay, you," she said. "Beer. But you're buying. And you have to take off that stupid hat."

"Willingly," I said. I stuffed it into my coat, and followed her golden hair to the bar.

❄

It took a couple of beers before she thawed enough to give me her name. Three before she slipped me her number. I'd been hoping for better, hoping that maybe I'd be able to entice her back to the flat and wave her right under Nic's nose, but no such luck. Still, the number was proof that I was making progress. I certainly needed to. Four people to get in the basket by the fifth of December, and it was already November the twenty-fourth.

"Is that really the best you could do?" said Nic, when I showed him the piece of paper—a little limp after being in my pocket all afternoon, its scribbled digits blurred with rain. "It's either fake or she'll get the wind up her at the first call and block your number." He gave me a jolly smile, one of those he'd been specializing in lately, with poison pills and whizzing blades at the back of it. "I would."

"The outfit didn't help," I said, feeling mutinous. "She laughed in my face."

"Something I feel the urge to do frequently." Nic sipped wine from a fluted glass.

I pushed out my lower lip. "It doesn't make it easy for me, you know."

"Easy? Easy?" Nic guffawed. "Oh, my dear boy. You surely don't still believe this job is supposed to be easy?"

"I had hopes," I said morosely. I knew what came next.

"You who are entwined with evil must suffer," intoned Nic, guzzling a mince pie. Same words, every time. He was big on tradition, was Nic.

I sighed. "So I suppose my dinner…"

"…is in your corner. Yes."

Dog food: chicken chunks, mashed up nicely in a steel bowl, with a dish of water beside it.

Arschgeige.

"Don't you think you're cutting this a little fine?" said Nic.

I poked the dog food with my finger. "I can do it, boss."

"Indeed." Nic turned up the speed of the spinning blades as he reached for another mince pie and shovelled it down. "Well, boy. I suppose that remains to be seen."

My knees shook all the next morning as I waited for a reply to my message. I'd decided to keep it simple: *Enjoyed our chat yesterday. Up for another drink?* I felt I could do with one or two myself, except that it was only lunchtime, and even I have standards. They were disintegrating with great rapidity.

When my phone beeped, I nearly took off with the pigeons.

The text read: *Sure. Six?*

It was like walking over the fluffy-cloud threshold of heaven. Sunlight spangled the rain on the chalets; a breeze blew the greasy smoke of the bratwurst stall away into the sky. Even the dog food churning in my gut seemed to slow.

One step closer to success.

We met at the bar, her looking sweet in a woollen peaked cap, me with my hat, in deference to her tastes, out of sight.

"You remembered," she said.

"One tries." I set a stein of beer in front of her on the plastic table top. "Good day at work?"

She shrugged. "So-so."

Maybe she was already embroiled in another embezzlement. Maybe she was planning something else; maybe she was hoping to get me in a back alley and rifle my pockets when my trousers were down. I didn't care. Anything as long as I could get this right.

"So," she was saying, over her stein, "what brought you to England? Work?"

"Work." I nodded.

"Me too."

I tried to look nonchalant. "And you are a…?"

"Financial advisor. You?"

Beer caught at the back of my throat. "I'm in…ah…criminal law."

"Oh." There was wariness behind her smile, but something else, too, which after a moment I identified as exhilaration. This was a girl who got a kick out of playing with fire.

Good.

"Been here long?" I asked.

"Three months."

I smiled. "You speak English very well."

She smiled right back, cool as you like. "You don't."

"Ah. No. Well." She was good at wrong-footing me, Lise; the sort of girl who in my younger days I'd have walked round in that ginger way a dog walks round a cat. "I don't get to practice much. Don't have many contacts here."

"Poor you." She leant across the table and ruffled my hair.

That, I have to say, was one of my best attributes: thick, black, and wavy. Girls liked it a lot. It was one of the reasons I'd been so peeved at having to wear that bloody hat.

"Tell me." Lise tweaked my ear, sending a bolt of shock through my body. "What exactly is a man involved in criminal law doing wandering the Christmas market dressed as an elf?"

The dog food in my stomach did an unpleasant back flip. I cleared my throat. "I told you. Just letting my hair down."

"You know there are better ways of doing that?" She grinned, drank, and pushed her stein away. "Do you have a girlfriend?"

Well, at least she'd had the good manners to ask first.

I cleared my throat again, and said, "No."

"Right." Her foot nudged mine under the table.

Oh, I knew what she was up to. She was an embezzler; I'd told her I was in law. Dancing with danger; it must have given her a real rush.

It was giving me something of one, too.

"Your place," she said.

I just managed to stop my jaw from sagging open. Finally, my luck was on the rise. Not the only thing, either; I adjusted my lederhosen.

"My place," I managed, and downed my beer.

Guilt mingled with my excitement. She was so pretty, so devil-may-care. I wanted to have her more than anything, and more than anything, I wanted to let her go.

I watched her swing her handbag over her shoulder, and decided. Nic could purse his lips and grind mince pies all he wanted. I was going to make sure she went out—the lovely, wicked Lise Hackelberg—with one hell of a bang.

I would have liked to have driven us back to the flat in a flashy BMW, but of course we had to take the bus. Lise looked put out to begin with, then settled into teasing, making noises of doom as I counted out the last of my change and passed it to the yawning driver with a sad sense of finality. Luck only held for so long, and it seemed I'd had my share for the day. When I unlocked the door to the flat, the first thing I saw was Nic.

The problem with a job like his is that you don't have to expend much energy on it unless you feel so inclined. Not that I'm saying he was lazy. He was a good motivator. A clip round the ear, one or two kicks in the behind; he was good at that sort of thing. Those, he had provided me with that morning, and now he had apparently decided that he deserved a rest. Nic's idea of a rest being to lounge on the sofa in his underwear, drinking gin and yelling Turkish obscenities at the TV.

"Friend of yours?" asked Lise.

"My flatmate," I replied.

Nic sat up and regarded me through bleary eyes. I gave him a tentative smile, and the eyes roved past. As soon as they battened on to Lise, they became bright as the fairy lights hung up round the walls. Brighter. Incandescent. I couldn't tell if it was pleasure or rage.

"Well," he said. "Well."

He slung his gin bottle aside and heaved himself off the sofa.

"Hello," said Lise.

Without answering, he pushed past her into his room, and

slammed the door.

"What a charmer," she said, under her breath. "Been living with him long?"

I pulled a face. "Feels like forever."

The door opened again, and I nearly bit off my tongue. Nic had good ears, and even better creativity when it came to punishments. At this rate, I'd be eating kibble for a fortnight.

Lise raised her perfect eyebrows. "Nice togs."

Dressed to the nines in his favorite white suit with the gold buttons, even his tie already knotted, Nic bowed and smiled. "Well, my dear. You mustn't think me a slob."

"Of course not," said Lise.

Nic beamed. "I shall be going," he said.

I recognised the voice; his plummy, come-and-sit-on-my-knee-for-a-present tone that he only used when he wanted to get people on his side. He'd used it with me, once. After that, it had been the corner and the dog bowl.

"Going?" I said.

"Going?" said Lise.

"I should think," Nic punched me none too lightly on the arm as he passed, "you'll be wanting some privacy?"

"Ah," I said. "Yes."

"How thoughtful," said Lise, tucking her golden hair behind her ears and giving him a dazzling smile.

Nic flinched, and backed towards the door. I could see that everything in him wanted to cross himself and run.

He beckoned.

"Ah…make yourself at home," I told Lise and, hating myself, slunk to his side.

"Now, listen," he said in an undertone, clapping a heavy hand on my shoulder. "No prevaricating this time."

I stared at the floor. "No."

"None. Understand? You know your job."

"Yes, boss."

"Certain?"

"Yes."

"Sure?"

He just had to string things out, make it harder; always. He couldn't seem to help himself.

"I said *yes*, boss."

"Good." Smiling, he put his mouth to my ear. "Santa's little helper, your duty awaits. Take. Her. Out."

Lise was watching us with narrowed eyes. I wondered what she was thinking.

Nic slapped my back with enough force to sink a ship, and brought out his happy voice again, all warm and glowing and cosy like a good blaze. "Enjoy yourselves," he said.

The door banged behind him. I locked it.

"Wine?" said Lise.

To my consternation, I saw she'd already raided the cupboards, and had set out two glasses of Nic's favoured 1989 Château Montrose and a bowl of crisps.

"Couldn't find much else," she said, plumping down on the sofa and stretching her deliciously long legs. "Maybe we could call for pizza?"

Confidence oozed from her, while I stood in the middle of the floor like an idiot in my tights and curly-toed boots and panicked.

"I'll order," she said. "What would you like?"

I felt my world crumbling around me. "Ham and pineapple."

While she dialed, I scooted into Nic's room, trying not to hyperventilate, and opened the drawer to his desk. I knew where he kept the petty cash; he'd taunted me with it on several occasions. As I palmed half a dozen notes, I went over the possible consequences in my head. I'd say I was anticipating my pay. He'd kick me round the house for a week. If he was feeling particularly nasty, I might not even get kibble.

The thought of ham and pineapple pizza had never made me so miserable.

"Should I change?" I asked Lise, when I returned to the living room. "I mean, this costume is a little…" There existed a large and interesting variety of words I could have used to finish the sentence; none of them polite.

"No," she said. "I think it's cute." She handed me a glass, and patted the sofa beside her. "Now, your flatmate is gone. Sit down, and relax."

I sat down.

"Kiss me," she said.

I sighed. So much for relaxing.

"Lise…"

"No," she said. "Quiet."

Since I failed to take the initiative, she took it for me—along with my boots, coat and lederhosen.

"You have a nice chest," she said after a while, running her fingers through the tangle of dark hair.

I blinked. It was the first compliment I'd had in ages. My tongue lolled out, like a happy puppy's; a bad habit of mine.

"Now you want to kiss me," she said.

Which was quite right. So I did.

"That was like *no* French kiss I've ever had," she panted, when we came up for air. "You're going to be on Santa's naughty list for sure."

"And you," I growled, "already are."

As soon as the words were out of my mouth, I regretted them; but she hadn't noticed. She was too busy trying to haul me upright, a task not made any easier by the fact that we seemed somehow to have drunk an entire bottle of the 1989 Château Montrose between us.

"Bedroom," she said.

I blanched. Even that, most private of all places, wasn't sacrosanct—not in my line of work. It was where I kept the tools of my trade, where later I'd have to take her, and…

"No," I said, pulling on her sleeve. "Here."

"Don't be stupid," she said affectionately, shoving me between the shoulder blades. "You want Nic to walk in on us?"

I froze. Nic. There was only so long he'd wait before he came to see how I'd got on; right now he might be lurking just outside the door, holding his breath, making plans involving sharp implements and the kibble diet.

"You're right," I said. "Bedroom."

Not waiting for an answer, I caught her by the wrist, and pulled her towards the door.

To be perfectly honest, my bedroom was something of an embarrassment. The iron rod—or, more specifically, crozier—of Nic's rule extended even into this, my own domain, resulting in a carpet that was mostly bald, a rusty bedstead, and a cast-off white duvet speckled with rosebuds. It was better than a dog bed—with which I had been threatened on several occasions—but only just.

"Don't take this the wrong way," said Lise, hooking her arms around me, "but I expected the bedroom of a criminal lawyer to be a little more salubrious."

I hid my face in her hair; it sang with the scent of oranges and ginger. "Never said I was a lawyer, exactly."

"Oh." She nipped my earlobe. "Naughty boy."

"Entwined with evil." My mouth, saying Nic's words, as usual. Sometimes I hated my mouth.

She laughed. "What?"

Before I could think to form a reply, she began to unbutton her blouse, revealing at first a plunging red lace bra, and then an awful lot more. My promise to myself to give her the best send-off possible suddenly returned to me with great urgency.

Teasing, she sashayed backwards, until her heel struck something that, in my idiocy, I had left poking out from under the bed.

My heart—and not just my heart—dropped like a stone.

"What's this?" She bent and pulled it into the light, spotted what was behind it, and dragged that out, too.

"It's nothing," I said, breathless. "Nothing at all."

"Really?" She grinned, and waved the things at me in playful accusation: a bundle of birch twigs, tied tight with twine, and two handcuffs joined by a length of chain. "I'd never have guessed you were into *this*."

"I'm not!"

"Oh, come on, you don't need to be coy." She switched the air experimentally. "This should spice things up a bit."

"Lise..." I edged backwards.

"You can tell me what a naughty girl I am, if you like," she said.

"You are a naughty girl."

"With a little more conviction?" she suggested.

Mutely, I stared at the floor.

"So you're taking the submissive part?" Her mouth was full of teeth, perfect and white; in the uncertain light, they looked longer than they should. "That's fine."

I had no time to stop her. My own mouth opened; closed again, as if I was a fish. She stepped forward and clicked the handcuffs round my wrists.

You can never pinpoint the exact moment of change. I've tried it over the years, hundreds of times, without success. It's like breathing; something so natural that it goes by unnoticed, completely unmarked. Lise noticed, though; I could tell.

Mostly from the shriek.

It's always the hair first. As I looked down in despair at the iron manacles on my wrists, I saw it thicken, furring my arms, spreading like a mold, black and dense. Bone cracked and skin split: my horns budded, branched out and dipped into their familiar curve. A pain in my left leg told me that foot now sat uncomfortably alongside hoof. I shifted my weight. There was an unpleasant ripping sound, and I became conscious that my tail had just burst through the seat of my tights.

Heat filled my face.

"Sorry," I said, and my tongue unfurled and hung there looking, as I well knew, like a fresh chilli pepper.

It was some comfort to see that Lise wasn't much better off. Her eyes were as round as potato dumplings.

"Krampus?" she said.

Introductions: they were always so awkward. Relieved that I'd trimmed my claws the day before, I held out a hand.

She took a step back. "You're the *Krampus*?"

I forced a smile. "I'm flattered you've heard of me," I said, wondering if I should be. "I've known about you for a while, Lise. You see, you were on my list." I waited for the tears and the pleading with a hollow stomach. I could never stand this part of the job. Never.

There were no tears. Instead, Lise's face was rapidly going the same shade of scarlet as her bra. "You decoyed me here?" she said. "Is that it? Pretended to like me just so you could get me in your sodding basket?"

"Well, I…"

Put like that, it did sound less than adorable. I tucked my tail between my legs.

"It's my job, Lise."

"Your job? You know what I think of your job?"

The birch twigs hit me with a crack right where it hurts. Gasping, I dropped to the floor.

"Lise, please"

"Arschloch!" she yelled, and whacked me across the head. Pretty soon she had a good rhythm going. I put back my ears and tried to curl into a ball.

"Going to send me to hell, were you? Is that what you had in mind?"

"I don't have any choice!" I yelped. "Lise, I only get paid commission. If I don't get you in my basket tonight, I won't even be able to pay my share of the rent!"

There it was; admission of my total abjection. I sniffled on to the back of my hand.

"Commission?" Lise sat back on her heels with the birch twigs across her knees. "I thought this was your *calling*, or something."

"No. I told you." I risked untucking my tail, and rubbed the tassel on the end, where she'd yanked out a fistful of hairs. "It's just my job."

A job I'd never wanted; a job I'd come to hate.

"When the new god came," I said, reaching for the box of tissues on the bedside table, "he brought a lot of vacant positions that needed to be filled. None of the saints wanted the dirty jobs, did they?"

For once, I didn't bother to hide the bitterness in my voice. Everything the saints didn't want to do had been loaded on to us: the older kind. We were told from then on we were to be terrifying; no longer spirits of the wild, but things that frightened Granny into fits, or grinned through the windows at naughty children, who promptly wet their beds and had to be grinned at again. God, it was tiring, scaring all the men, all the women and the children, and then Uncle Heinz's dog just in case the saints felt like awarding an extra mark.

"We're all on contracts," I said. "They have us by the short and curlies, Lise."

She shook her head. "Why did you sign?"

I blew my nose. "Why do you think? We trusted them. Most of us came from rural backgrounds, we couldn't read or write. We put our marks down without having a clue."

"Ich glaub' mich knutscht ein Elch," muttered Lise. "You can't be serious."

I tugged another tissue from the box; my chains rattled. "Do I *look* like I'm joking?"

"And Nic is…? Oh." She looked thoughtful. "Oh."

"He makes me eat dog food," I said. I couldn't help it: a fat tear rolled down my face and plopped off the end of my beard. "Chicken chunks."

Nic had seemed so approachable at first. Unthreatening, you might say. Short and bald with a pot belly and a grey beard, he had given me a mug of beer and some sticky sweetmeats. I'd been as happy as a child at Christmas. I could still remember the day he'd tricked me, standing at my shoulder making encouraging noises as I splodged a clumsy mark at the bottom of his contract. Another tear splashed down to join the first on the threadbare carpet.

"Oh, Schatzl," said Lise, and put her arms around me again. That girl had fortitude, she really did. "You can't let him treat you like this."

I scuffed my eyes. "What else can I do?"

"Quit?" she suggested.

"Quit?" Hope flared, then died again. "I can't quit, Lise. These contracts are written in holy pen. The notice period is ridiculous. Anyway, I have no pension scheme."

"Are you kidding?" She sounded angry; angrier than she'd been when she hit me with the birch twigs. I got my legs under me to run.

"Do you know where he keeps this contract of yours?" she asked.

"Yes." Like the petty cash, it was hidden in plain view, in a small drawer at the back of Nic's desk. After all, what could I do with it? The paper was practically bomb-proof; even the fires of hell couldn't have burnt that.

"Can I see?" Lise was asking. "And bring me the pen. I have an idea."

"An idea," I said dryly. The set of her mouth warned me not to say any more. I crept into Nic's room, feeling like a thief; even though all I'd come to steal was my own life.

"Good," said Lise, when I handed her the papers. "Let's have a look." She read. She read some more. "Schatzl," she said, after a few moments of silence, "you've been screwed over."

I grimaced. "You don't have to tell *me* that."

"What did you say about the pen?" she asked. "Holy?"

"Yes." I shrugged. "Whatever is written, will be. That's how Nic put it, anyway."

"Well." She chewed her lip. "Wait there. I need to get my handbag."

"For what?" I asked, but she was already gone.

While I waited, I peered at the sheets of vellum that were my fate, crinkled and crumbling at the edges with age. The scrawl was as meaningless to me as ever.

"Here we go." Out of nowhere, Lise was back, pulling a small bottle of something out of her bag.

"What's that?"

"Correction fluid." She grinned. "We're going to rewrite your contract."

My heart bounded like an Alpine goat. "What?"

"It's no big deal, is it?" she said. "Just replace a few words, change this and that. What is written, will be. That's what you said, right? Oh." She tapped the second sheet of paper I was holding. "That's Nic's."

The thing seemed to scorch me; I dropped it like a burning potato. "I must have picked it up by mistake."

"Well, that's all right." That thoughtful look came over her face again. "Why not rewrite his contract, too?"

"Lise! That would be—"

"How would you like Nic's job?" she interrupted. "With a few perks on the side, of course. Whatever you'd like."

My ears pricked up. "Give presents to the kids?" I said.

"That's the idea."

"Every year?"

"It's traditional."

I squeezed my hands together so hard that my claws dug in

through the fur. "Me?"

She smiled. "I'm going to take that as a *yes.*" She uncapped the correction fluid.

As I watched, my mood fizzled like a firecracker in the rain. "But Lise," I said. "I can't. It's Nic's job."

"Nic who makes you eat dog food?" Her brow creased. "Krampus, come on. This is your chance to be *free.*"

The word reverberated through me, right up into my horns. Freedom. I could have *freedom.* Save for one tiny, trifling matter: "It's not just that," I sighed. "If I took his job, Lise, who'd do mine?"

"Yours?" she said. She glanced down at the contract in her hand. "I'll tell you who'll do yours." Without a pause, she looked me bang in the eye. "Me."

"You?" I gawped.

"Listen," Lise said. She dipped the brush into the correction fluid, tapped it to remove the excess, and began dabbing it on. "I'm on your wanted list, aren't I? Which means sooner or later, I'll wind up in a basket, right?"

"Right," I conceded.

"This way, you get off the hook—and so do I." She swirled the brush. "I can do this job, Krampus. You know I can."

I could smell her confidence, how sly she was, her wickedness smooth and dangerous as dark chocolate.

"I know you can," I said. "But the terms …"

"Are now mine to dictate." She fanned the paper, and then, satisfied the correction fluid had dried, she unscrewed the cap of the pen.

My whole being filled with admiration. The woman was a criminal mastermind—she was perfect for this job. Perfect.

And me?

I picked up the contract I'd dropped, and, lifting it to my nose, inhaled the scents of cinnamon and laughter.

"Krampus?" said Lise.

I held the paper out to her.

"Please," I said.

I'd never meant a single word so much.

She swiped the little brush smoothly across Nic's scrawl, obliterating it forever. With the same coolness, she set the holy nib to the paper, and began to write.

Eventually, she passed me the pen.

"Sign," she said.

She was a cheat, a liar, she was slippery as hell. Yet for all that, I trusted her. She had never tried to hide from me who she was.

My fur on end, I fumbled the pen over the paper, leaving a snail's trail of ink.

"There," said Lise.

A shiver ran through me. The handcuffs around my wrists groaned and creaked. Then, with a soft sigh, almost as of regret, they broke open and fell gently to the floor.

We celebrated with pizza and another bottle of wine.

Lise brought my basket into the living room and sat on it; she was determined to do her job properly.

From the look of things, she'd been rooting in my clothes cupboard, and had found the slinky red dress I'd used once when my weekly quota rendered it necessary to seduce and bag a randy Munich businessman with a background in fraud and lane hogging on the autobahn.

It looked an awful lot better on her than it had on me.

"Also, I have these." She rummaged through her handbag. "I bought them for the office Christmas party."

Out came a pair of horns; not the usual cheap plastic tat, but proper ones, just like mine, heavy, ridged and black. She slipped them on.

I grinned. "Devil," I said, and settled back into the sofa, chewing a slice of pizza.

Nic had never let me on the sofa. He said my claws would spoil the upholstery.

A key rattled in the lock.

"By the pricking of my thumbs," Lise murmured, "something wicked this way comes."

The door swung open, and there, silhouetted by a streetlamp glow that could have been the light of heaven, or the fires of hell, stood Nic.

"You."

That was the first thing he said. Not "hello" or "good evening" or anything like that—oh no. But that was typical, you see. Typical of Nic.

His voice curled and tightened around me like a python. "You filthy little creature. How often have I told you to keep off my sofa?"

"Nic." I flattened my ears. "Don't."

"Don't?" He didn't even seem to have noticed Lise. "How dare you speak back to me like that? I'll geld you, I swear, you little—"

"Evening, Nic." Lise, in her tight red dress, her horns catching and spinning the light, slid off the basket with the grace and fluidity of a cat.

Nic's sentence ended in stumbling bluster as he caught sight of her; then he looked at me.

"So," he said, with a flicker of poisoned tongue. "It's going to be the whip."

More pain. More humiliation. Fear grasped my throat.

"No." Lise's face had changed; hardened, though she was still smiling. She picked up the birch twigs from their resting place on the arm of the sofa and gave them a swing.

Nic, resplendent in white and gold, stared. The metal buttons on his suit seemed to tarnish as I watched.

My heart lightened. Pineapple popped under my tongue.

Lise Hackelberg: devil, avenger; punisher of the wicked.

My salvation.

"Oh, Nic," she said. "You've been a very naughty boy."

I picked up another slice of pizza and made myself comfy.

"Not to worry," said Lise, in her sing-song voice; and the smack of her birch twigs on Nic's fleshy arse was like the sound of justice. "Santa's little helper is here."

# THE BUSINESS OF CHRISTMAS

ANYA J. DAVIS

The sled rattled and juddered as the huskies raced across the packed snow. Petra Krampus gripped the wooden strut beneath her, although she knew it wouldn't help if the contraption tipped. The line of snow-clad firs that had taunted her for the last few miles, beckoning her onwards with the promise of a journey's end, were within walking distance now.

Petra felt the driver shift behind her and the sled slowed. The dogs pulled up and raised their heads to the skies. A cacophony of whimpers and high-pitched barks filled the icy morning air. Petra clambered off the sled, nodded to the driver and clapped twice, motivating herself to move, her thick gloves making a dull thud each time they connected.

She trudged towards the tree line. The only tracks in the snow were imprints made by the hooves of deer, a random pattern of directionless markings, but Petra didn't need a trail to follow. She knew where she was going and the quickest route to get there. She'd been there many times before.

The light began to fade, the sky turning a filthy grey, as she slogged on. She tugged her hat down and pulled her scarf up to cover the tip of her nose, but the cold stung her cheeks. Fresh flakes of snow fell, and she quickened her pace. She couldn't afford to get caught in a blizzard. If the weather worsened, there was no guarantee that the sled driver would wait, and every chance he'd settle for the money that Petra had paid upfront. He'd be content to lose half of his fee in return for being somewhere warm. She was almost there now though. The energy radiated from the place.

As she plodded on, she saw the protective barrier: the violet, electric blue, neon pink and luminous green lights swirling like the aurora borealis. The wall was invisible to travelers without Petra's capabilities and heritage. Any hunter or hiker that strayed too close would experience a sense of discomfort, a foreboding that transformed into overwhelming dread as they moved towards it. By the time they reached it, no matter how urgent their business or strong their desire to continue had been just half a kilometer ago, they would be compelled to turn back or veer off in another direction.

For Petra, however, the sensation as she passed through it was comforting. The energy crackled like popcorn, and the small sparks that shot across her form made her skin tingle. The barrier hummed, although the sound wasn't audible to humans. It had never been linked to alarms, but she caught her breath as she exited the light. Had extra security systems been installed without her knowledge? Did someone suspect her?

The only sounds were those of branches cracking in the distance and the crunch of the snow beneath her boots. She strode deeper into the forest. Finally, she slowed, focusing on the glow that was now visible through the trees. Its warm tone made the freezing conditions seem even colder. She hugged herself and shivered.

She reached the edge of the clearing and surveyed the log cabin in its center. The light emanating from its window flickered and flared. Petra knew it was no ordinary fire. The flames that danced in the cabin's hearth were fueled by magic, not by wood or coal.

She waited for what seemed like hours, concealed by the trees, nervous of moving or making a sound. Nothing stirred inside the cabin. She was taking a risk, but she had to be sure. She crept towards the building and peeked through the window.

There he was, fast asleep beneath a pile of reindeer skins, on a gigantic bed in the middle of the single room. Petra smirked. She could fly to England and execute her plan. Santa was snoring loud enough to wake the dead. He wouldn't rise until just before the big event. Nobody could stop her now.

A week later, in a narrow side street close to Covent Garden, London, Krampus Enterprises opened its doors for the first time. The owner wasn't expecting any customers, however. The only advert that she'd placed was for a job vacancy: a single postcard in the window of a nearby newsagents. The company had nothing to sell and no services to offer. There would be no income, and she would be paying all the bills herself. She'd manage the bookkeeping and cleaning on her own.

She'd only had one application for the post, but she only needed one employee for the job, so that had worked out perfectly.

*No point in having more of anything than you need. That's how everything got into such a mess in the first place.*

She trailed a finger along the table she'd bought for the cramped second floor room. She'd need somewhere bigger eventually, of course, but nothing as glamorous as Santa's business premises. His head office, in New York, was a hive of activity, filled with pompous men and women in suits who shouted about costs and deadlines, as real-time updates on the nice and naughty lists flashed up on the screens displayed in every room. There were regional managers, weather experts, legal teams, and marketing and PR gurus everywhere. Anyone visiting the place would have thought that Santa Co. was one of the most productive businesses in the world. Petra, however, knew the truth. It was all a façade.

The only part of the organization that did any real work was the marketing department, and even they didn't have a great deal to do nowadays. Santa rarely had PR disasters and he had the monopoly on the market, so he didn't have to worry about competitors threatening his brand. He didn't even have to deliver the toys anymore, or oversee a host of delivery sleighs, as he had just a few decades ago. Somehow, Santa Co. had convinced grown-ups that the big man didn't exist, so they'd buy toys for their children themselves and slip them under their Christmas trees when the little ones had gone to bed.

It was a work of genius. As the world moved on, and children in its wealthier areas demanded bundles of luxurious gifts and pricey electronics devices, rather than the traditional paper dolls, oranges and nuts that had kept their ancestors happy, it was the parents who had to pay for it all. Santa's toy factories had shut long ago. He'd reduced his overheads so that he could run things on a shoestring, allowing him to retire.

He'd make an appearance in early December to make sure everything was operating to schedule, then he'd circle the globe in his sleigh on Christmas Eve, landing on a few buildings in every town, just for show. On Boxing Day, he'd fly to the Seychelles to bask in the sun for a week or two, before heading to his cabin, where he'd spend most of the year asleep. Even the nice and naughty lists were computerized now, with the help of a little magic. Santa had no responsibilities and a lifestyle that would make the laziest of people feel industrious.

It was Santa all over. Only the people who really knew him had any idea how sneaky, manipulative and greedy he was, and there were few who got close enough to him to find that out. Petra Krampus had, however. She'd discovered what he was capable of the hard way—and she was going to make him pay for what he'd done.

The knocking startled her. She patted down her dress as she walked to the door, and transformed her scowl into a beaming smile.

"Good morning, Amy. Welcome to Krampus Enterprises. I'm

looking forward to working with you."

Amy Meadows had been sure the advert in the newsagent's window was a scam when her boyfriend had pointed it out to her.

"Oh, come on, Mark. You know what they say. If something sounds too good to be true, then it probably is. Well, this sounds far too good to be true. That salary's way above average and genuine companies don't advertise high-paying illustrator's jobs in shop windows."

Mark nudged her with his elbow. "If you want to base an argument on clichés, then you could just as well choose 'if you don't try, you won't succeed,' or 'you make your own luck.' What have you got to lose? Just ring them."

Amy wrinkled her nose, but took her phone out of her pocket nonetheless.

"What if it's one of those things where you ring a number and it charges you a fortune?"

"What if it is? Your phone isn't on a contract, is it? What's the most you can lose? Ten quid?"

"I guess so. I don't know. Doesn't it sound a bit weird to you though?"

Mark peered at the advert again.

> **WANTED IMMEDIATELY:**
> Talented Illustrator for a Children's Book
> The successful applicant will possess the ability to draw exquisite snowflakes, candy canes and bundles of birch twigs. A passion for Christmas is also desirable.

The salary and contact details followed.

"Okay, so it's a bit unusual. It's not that strange though—and I'm pretty sure you can knock up a snazzy snowflake if you put your mind to it."

Amy glared at him and tapped the number into her phone. “Fine. But if it’s a scam, then you’ll be paying for my next phone top-up.”

One phone conversation and one face-to-face interview later, and Amy was officially Petra Krampus’s first and only employee. She still wasn’t convinced the woman wasn’t going to relieve her of every penny she had or involve her in something illegal, though. There were some things about the business that just didn’t add up. When Amy had asked her employer where she was planning to sell the book they’d be working on, for example, Petra had laughed.

“Oh, we’re not going to sell it anywhere, dear! I’m going to give it away.” She’d leaned forward and patted Amy on the knee.

“Don’t worry, it won’t affect your pay. In fact, I’ll give you a month’s wages in advance on the day you start, just to reassure you.”

Amy didn’t find it reassuring at all. It made it seem even more like a con. The job seemed perfect though. She just needed to produce the illustrations for a book that Petra had already written. She’d be given an idea of what to draw, but would be able to make suggestions and execute the pictures in her own style. She’d have plenty of time to work on them, and could come and go from the office as she pleased.

Petra’s only rules were that she was never to discuss the project with anyone, and mustn’t take the story or her sketches home. Those conditions sounded fine to Amy, and it wasn’t like she had any other job offers, so she accepted the role.

Amy hadn’t expected her first day at her new job to be the traditional whirl of introductions, training and meetings, which was just as well as, if she had, she’d had have been disappointed. Instead, Petra showed her where the kitchen and toilets were, and handed her a pile of papers and some keys.

“This is the manuscript and my notes for the pictures. Here’s a set of keys to the office. I'll be back to see how you're getting on in a few weeks. Have fun!"

The sound of her employer marching down the stairs and the slam of the front door caused Amy's heart to flutter. She'd be working on her own. She'd have no guidance or support, and nobody to help her if anything went wrong.

There was nothing she could do about it, however, so she made herself a cup of coffee and settled down to read. As the rain splattered against the window pane and the March wind howled outside, the words on the pages transported her to a snow-topped wooden cabin in an Alpine village, and immersed her in a magical tale of a kind-hearted woman with the power to change children's lives.

Forty-eight hours later, Petra was in a coffee shop in the Big Apple, having a clandestine meeting with an elf. This wasn't just any elf, either. This was Henrik, the highest-ranking of the handful of elves that worked for Santa Co.

Most self-respecting elves wouldn't have anything to do with Santa now—not after the way he'd treated them. The long hours, unrealistic targets and ridiculous outfits had been hard enough for them to tolerate in the old days, but even elves have to make money somehow. Despite their magical abilities, the Ancient Guild of Elves wouldn't tolerate its members whipping up homes, food and cash out of nothing. It required them either to remain in their traditional, isolated forest communities or, if they wanted to co-exist with humans, to work for a living.

It was the job losses that had been the final straw. When the plan was drawn up to shut the toy factories, Santa Co's board members opted to keep their decision a secret from the workers. They couldn't risk them all leaving at once. While parents were doing most of the present buying, some toys were needed for the families who were slow to change their ways, and others for store Santas to hand out to kids while the corporate contracts were still in place.

The executives decided to make the transition over the course of several years, reducing output gradually. They searched for ways to get rid of the staff in a controlled manner without paying them severance packages. That's when the firings began.

Elves who'd been loyal to Santa for centuries were hauled into managers' offices and accused of everything from laziness to theft. Whole teams were shown the door for failing to abide by rules they'd never heard of—usually because the rules didn't exist. Rumors of factory closures circulated, but nobody could get to the bottom of what was going on, because anyone who questioned it was always the next one to be fired. Finding other work was difficult too. Store elf jobs were limited, seasonal and poorly paid, and most real elves found the occupation humiliating. By the time the final factories closed, Santa's name was a curse word within the elf community. One or two unscrupulous traitors were given high level jobs at Santa Co., but most elves wouldn't go within three states of New York now.

Despite appearances, however, Henrik was not a traitor to his kind. Although he'd accepted the job as "Head of Magical Technology" the second he was offered it, the first thing on his "to do" list had been to contact Petra, and, together, they formed a plan of action.

Petra sipped her steaming hot chocolate and tried not to stare at her companion as he nibbled away at a cinnamon chocolate chip cookie. She'd been around elves all her life, but she still found their ears enthralling.

"So, everything's going to plan in the UK?" Somewhere, beneath his New York accent, lay a hint of his old one. It reminded her of pine trees and fresh mountain air. Just for a moment, she was home.

"Petra?"

"Oh…sorry. Yes. Right on schedule. As long as the illustrations are up to scratch, the book should be ready on time. I've found a warehouse that's big enough for our needs, at least for now, and I have a meeting with the letting agent about it next week."

"Great. Well, I have a gift for you." He handed her a small, silver tablet and winked. "Don't forget to check it twice."

"Oh my, Henrik, is this it?" She stroked the metal casing, the feel of it sending shivers through her. "You managed to do it!"

He raised his eyebrows. "Sure I managed to do it. I'm kinda good at this stuff, you know."

"Sorry." Petra laughed at his mock-offended tone.

"Anyhow, yeah, that's it. Just switch it on, click on the Christmas stocking icon, and pick your list."

"And the updates…will it…?"

"Sometimes I wonder what you think I am, Petra." Henrik shook his head. "Yeah, it's linked to the mainframe and yeah, it works in real-time. Every time some little terror pinches his sister or uses a cuss-word in class, his behavior scores get recalculated. If they tip the scale, his name will shift from the nice list to the naughty one."

Petra leaned across the table and kissed Henrik on the cheek.

"Hey, quit it!" The elf pulled away from her, but his lips crinkled into a smile.

"You're a star, Henrik. An absolute star."

"Yeah, well, I hope that doesn't mean you're planning to stick me on top of a Christmas tree when this is all over." He shoved the last piece of his cookie into his mouth. "So, what's next on the list for your festive preparations?"

Petra drained her mug, slipped the tablet into her bag and pulled her jacket on. "I'm heading off to Europe to find someone who can supply me with enough bundles of birch twigs for every child on this naughty list."

Amy had sketched out more than half of her illustrations for the book by the time Petra returned from her travels. She handed them over and chewed on her thumb nail as her employer leafed through the pages.

"These will be wonderful when they are finished." Petra's eyes sparkled.

"Thank you." Amy hoped her tone didn't reveal just how relieved she was. After Petra had called her the day before to say she was heading home, Amy had spent the afternoon and evening worrying that her work wasn't good enough. She'd been awake most of the night too.

It wasn't simply that she didn't want to lose her job, although that was one of her concerns. It was more that she didn't want to disappoint Petra. She wanted to create something that did justice to the story that the woman had created, a tale that had touched Amy's heart.

It was a strange story, but then, in Amy's opinion, most good children's stories were. Written in rhyme, it told of a witch who wanted to ensure that the children in her village who had a tendency to misbehave didn't continue down that path. Concerned that being labeled naughty would cause little ones to become even more disruptive, she decided to take action.

One year, in early December, while Saint Nicholas made his annual journey through the streets, delivering gifts to those who had earned rewards, the witch trudged through the snow to the houses that he'd left out, the homes where those deemed undeserving slumbered. Using the ancient magic her mother and grandmother had taught her, she entered each property and laid a bundle of birch twigs by the fireplace, where the Saint's gift would have been. Upon each mantelpiece, she placed a note which read:

*"Sadly, you have not been visited by Old Saint Nick this year*
*But in twelve months' time, you could be full of festive cheer,*
*Just take this as a sign that it's now time for a fresh start,*
*Use these twigs to sweep the old year out and purify your heart,*
*Listen to your parents and try not to annoy,*
*And next December, you'll be the owner of a brand new toy."*

Her efforts brought success. Several of the village children, who had previously been written off by the residents as "never likely to amount to anything," stopped tormenting their teachers, swore never to disobey their parents again, and set about sweeping their rooms with gusto. As a result, their names were soon reinstated on Saint Nicholas's list.

Each year after that, the witch made the journey through the village, a sack of birch twigs and elegantly written notes in hand. Eventually, she and Nicholas met on the doorstep of a house where a well-behaved boy and mischievous girl resided and, from then on, they decided to walk the route together, to ensure that no child was ever forgotten.

Amy had been brought up in the belief that naughty children got nothing from Santa. She much preferred Petra's vision. The tale was filled with hope and she adored the idea that nobody was beyond redemption. That, as far as Amy was concerned, was the true essence of Christmas.

She flashed Petra a smile as the woman handed the sketches back to her.

"I'll get the rest finished as soon as I can. Then I'll start on the final versions. I should have everything done well before the deadline."

## Three Months Later

Amy laid her paintbrush down and squinted at the wall clock. Three o'clock. Perfect timing. Petra would be there in half an hour. She ambled into the tiny kitchen, made a cup of tea and then made her way to the top of the stairs, to gaze out the large window that overlooked the street. It was quieter than many streets in the center of the capital. There were no shops lining it, just offices and a few apartment buildings, and it didn't lead to anywhere of interest. Nonetheless, there always seemed to be something going on.

Today, some of the workers from an office opposite were clustered on the steps outside, chatting and soaking up the sun. Their laughter carried up to the window, and Amy felt a sudden pang of longing for company and conversation. Petra was absent most of the time and, although she appreciated the peace while she was working, sometimes she wished she had someone to go to lunch with or to say "Have a great weekend" to when she left on a Friday night.

Maybe she should search for an office job. Now she'd completed her final illustration, her days here were numbered anyway. Perhaps she and Mark should take a holiday first. They'd managed to save some money since they'd both been earning, and it would be good to spend some time together. They could escape the city and head to the coast, or even splash out on a week abroad.

A familiar figure appeared around the corner and crossed the road. A few seconds later, the front door slammed and Petra made her way up the stairs.

"Good afternoon, Amy. What a glorious day. A little warmer than I'm used to, but beautiful, nonetheless. How are you?"

"Very well, thank you. I've got something to show you too. Something I hope you're going to like."

Petra stopped halfway up the stairs and stared at her. "You've finished them?"

Amy laughed and cocked her head towards the office. "Come and have a look."

She strolled towards the easel and, as Petra entered the room, she pointed at it. "That's the last one. The rest are over there." She gestured to the table, where a large, black folder lay.

Petra stood at the easel in silence, surveying the scene before her. Two figures trudged up a steep, snow-covered hill, past cuckoo-clock style houses adorned with white lights. Each of the walkers was cloaked, carried a large, hessian sack, and clasped the other's hand. Amy scrutinized her employer's body language, waiting for a reaction. When Petra finally faced her, Amy was horrified to see tears glistening in the woman's eyes and her brow furrowed in distress.

"Petra? Oh my goodness, whatever's the matter? Don't you like it? I'm so sorry. Don't worry, I'll do it again."

She reached for the clips on the easel, but Petra laid a hand on her arm and shook her head.

"No." Her voice was husky, as if she was struggling to speak. "Don't. It's beautiful."

"Really? But I've upset you somehow. What is it? What have I done?"

"Nothing." Petra wiped her eyes. "It just brought back some memories, that's all. I tell you what, why don't you pop over to the bakery and get us a cup of coffee and a cake to celebrate?" She rummaged in her bag and pulled out her purse. Unzipping it, she took out a ten pound note and held it out.

"Are you sure?" Amy paused, unsure whether to leave or to stay with the woman.

Petra nodded. "I'm fine."

Amy noticed the quaver in the woman's voice. She took the money, sped downstairs and strode down the street towards the bakery. The quicker she got there, the quicker she could get back to Petra and make sure that she really was okay.

When she returned with the coffee and cakes, Petra seemed to be her old self again. She was flipping through the illustrations in the folder.

"These are even better than I imagined." She took her cup of coffee from Amy. "You are exceptionally talented."

Amy felt her cheeks burn and mumbled a protest, as she placed her cup on her desk and opened the bag containing the cakes.

"I know that you've finished the pictures now, but would you like to stay on, just until the end of the year? I'd like to create some gift tags for the books, and there'll be plenty of other administrative tasks that I'll need help with."

A host of thoughts rushed through Amy's mind, churning like a river. Staying on would mean she'd have a steady income until Christmas, and she and Mark could do so much with the cash. They'd have to forgo the holiday she'd been dreaming of, but they could have a longer, more extravagant break next year. Did she want to be stuck in this office on her own doing admin, though? Perhaps she'd be better finding another illustration project—but jobs like those didn't come along very often. No, she couldn't afford to turn this down. And she was fond of Petra, although she didn't see very much of her.

"Yes." She placed her cake on the lid of her coffee cup and handed the bag containing the other one to Petra. "I'd like that very much."

"Well, that's settled then." Petra put the cake bag down on the table and beamed. "Now, I hope you won't be offended, but I think these just need a little something extra." She marched over to the easel and picked up one of Amy's brushes.

Amy stared at her in horror. She reached out to grab Petra's hand, but her body seemed to freeze. Petra raised the brush to the paper and muttered something in a foreign tongue. As the woman placed the tip of the brush onto the painting, the paper rippled like the water in a pond.

The movements got larger, becoming waves, spreading until the room itself seemed to undulate. Tiny lavender and ice-white lights appeared and disappeared like twinkling stars. The spicy aroma of cinnamon filled the air, quickly followed by the rich smell of chocolate, and then the fresh scent of pine. Amy heard a crackling sound, like flames licking the logs in a hearth, and the faint jingling of bells in the distance. The desk, the table, the easel, Petra...all of them faded and suddenly she was outside, in another place, knee-deep in snow. Before she could take in her surroundings properly, however, she was back in the room again, and everything was just as it had been before Petra had picked up the brush.

Except that it wasn't. The painting. There was something different about it. The colors seemed more vibrant, the lights on the houses seemed to glisten and the people seemed more realistic.

"If I gazed at it for long enough, I could step inside their world," she said.

"Not quite." Petra's tone was laced with amusement. "But the magic has added to its charms. I'm sorry. That must have been disorienting. Perhaps you'd like me to do the others when you've left?"

Amy stared at her, unable to formulate a reply.

"It's old magic. Powerful magic. It's not dangerous, in case you're worried. It won't harm the little ones who read the book. It will just make it a more fulfilling experience for them. They'll want to come back to it again and again."

"What...what are you? How did you do that?"

"I'm a witch, dear. Not just any witch though. A very specific witch." The woman picked up Amy's portfolio and waved it at her.

"The book...the witch in the book. It's based on you?"

"She isn't just based on me. She is me, Amy. It's my story. Well, part of my story. The bit that's been corrupted over the years."

"Corrupted? How? By who?"

"Well, I was turned into a monster, that's how. By Santa."

Amy fled from the room, darted down the stairs and left the building. She had to get as far away from Petra as possible. The woman was clearly insane. She'd only got a few streets away, however, when an image of her paints and brushes popped into her head, swiftly followed by one of her bag hanging from the back of her chair. She stopped dead. She'd have to go back.

Perhaps she could sneak in later, when Petra had gone home? But what if the woman took her bag and paints with her? She didn't want to speak to her employer again but she was going to have to.

Amy retraced her steps. She ought to explain things to Petra and make it clear that she wasn't planning to return. The illustrations were complete, so she wouldn't be leaving her in the lurch. There were plenty of people who'd be happy to take on the rest of the tasks that Petra wanted done before the book launch.

She turned into the road where the office building stood and pressed her fingertips into her palms, trying to muster up the courage to go back inside. Perhaps the whole thing had been a misunderstanding? Maybe Petra had been joking or about to explain that she was writing a sequel to the book, and that was the tale it would tell? But the rippling air, the lights, the aromas—they were so vivid. She hadn't imagined them. Something strange had happened; and suddenly, the thing that Amy wanted more than anything else was to find out what it was.

She entered the building, marched up the stairs and flung the office door open.

"Who are you? And what the hell is going on?"

## December 5

It was bitterly cold. The meager heating in the warehouse, which was tucked away on an industrial estate on the outskirts of the Essex town of Harlow, didn't seem to take the edge off the chill at all.

"They're forecasting snow tonight," Amy said, as she attached a gift label to a book and popped it on top of the others in the box beside her. "Let's hope that doesn't mean the deliveries will get held up."

"You think a little snow can slow this down, do you?" Henrik nodded towards the sled. "What kind of amateur do you think I am? Of course it won't affect deliveries. This baby was built using the most technologically sophisticated magic around. Nothing will stop her in her tracks. Well, apart from using the brakes."

"Sorry, Henrik." Amy stifled a laugh at the elf's indignant expression.

"So you should be. You're getting as bad as Petra. Have some faith in me, will you?"

"Hey, I do have faith in you." Amy winked at him. "Everyone knows you're the best."

"Damn right, I am." Henrik puffed his chest out a little. He picked up a box of books and loaded it into the sled.

Amy glanced at the huge pile of boxes on the floor and then at the sled. "Are you sure there's enough room for all these?"

The elf glared at her and emitted a noise not unlike a growl.

"Ok, Henrik." She raised her hands. "I know. It's not some ordinary sled. It's magic and everything will fit just fine."

Before the elf could reply, the door banged open and Petra entered, dragging a huge sack behind her.

"It's going to be freezing out there tonight, so I got a few more blankets and skins, just to be on the safe side." She pulled the bag towards the sled and began to unpack its contents, placing them in the vehicle.

"Henrik, they're saying there's snow on the way. You're sure that won't cause any problems?"

The elf let out a howl of fury and Amy burst out laughing. "Probably not the best question to ask at the moment, Petra. I think he's feeling a bit sensitive." Henrik's face was puce.

"Sensitive?"

Henrik opened his mouth to complain but the air was suddenly filled with an electronic rendition of "Jingle Bells." The color drained from his cheeks and he pulled a pager out of his pocket.

"I need to get back to New York." His tone was edged with panic. "Santa's awake."

With the help of a few spells, Amy and Petra had all the boxes on board by nightfall. Amy helped her employer into her seat, and arranged the blankets and skins to protect her from the frosty air.

"Are you sure you don't want to come with me? I think it will be an experience you'll never forget."

Amy shook her head. "Like I said, I'm not fond of heights. And I think this should be your moment, after all the years you've waited."

The witch clasped Amy's hand, her eyes glistening as she spoke. "Thank you for everything. I couldn't have done this without you."

"Just go, will you?" Amy tried to hold her own tears back. "Get it done before Santa finds out."

Petra nodded and released her grip on Amy's hand. She read the incantation that Henrik had written out for her, pronouncing each word as he'd taught her to. In front of the sled, eight ghostly huskies appeared, howling and barking, ready for the off. Petra shook the reins and issued the command. The sled and its occupant, together with the dogs, disappeared in a cloud of glitter.

"Flash, Henrik." Amy smirked. "Very flash."

She grabbed her coat and bag, and headed out the door, just in time to see the huskies pull the sled across the night sky and disappear into the distance. "Safe travels, Petra Krampus," she whispered.

The following morning, Santa was far from jolly. Henrik's office was directly below the boss's and all he'd heard so far were roars of rage. There hadn't been a single ho-ho-ho.

The elf fixed his gaze on his computer, pretending to work, as another harassed PR executive hurried past the glass door in tears. He'd had to use a cloaking spell just to get past the gaggle of reporters that lined the sidewalk and make his way into the building.

It had already become more than just a scrolling "Breaking" item on the 24-hour news channels. Interviews with excited children had been playing every ten minutes for the last few hours, and experts had been hauled in to discuss topics such as "Witchcraft—Is it Evil?" and "Is this the End for the Man in Red?"

Part of him wanted to flee, to head back to his homeland to hide out with family and friends. It wouldn't take Santa long to discover what he'd done. If there was one thing Henrik wasn't though, that was a coward, and when there was music to be faced, he'd stand up and pay attention to the tune.

Besides, he was proud to be working with Petra—and he deserved some of the credit for the plan's success. It was an impressively clever operation. They'd used Santa's own PR tricks against him to clear Petra's name and sully his. Henrik had rung the press, hinting at

Santa's betrayal of his former friend and recasting Petra as the hero of the story, while she'd been making her deliveries. He'd met her just outside the city when she'd finished and concealed the sled in the workshop he'd constructed it in.

The book had been Petra's idea. After all, it was a poem that had helped Saint Nick to become an All-American superstar, so it would be fitting if it were literature that brought his lies to an end. None of it would have worked without Henrik's technological expertise, however. They made the perfect team.

He glanced at the telephone on his desk. He wished it would just ring already. He wanted it over and done with. He'd take whatever verbal assaults were coming to him, listen to Santa's threats of legal action and then, when the shouting was over, he'd walk back out of the building, head held high, and take his place at the board table of Krampus Enterprises.

His desk phone didn't ring. Instead, his cell phone vibrated, alerting him to the arrival of a new email. As soon as he saw the sender's name, his heart pounded. He opened it to find that the message consisted of a single line:

"He wants to meet me in Central Park at 11."

Henrik put his coat on, slipped his cell phone into his pocket, recast his cloaking spell, and headed out the door. Petra could take care of herself, but with the mood Santa was in, he wasn't taking any chances.

Santa was already there when Petra arrived. She scanned the area for signs of concealed security operatives. Satisfied that he had come alone, she perched on the bench beside him. He continued staring out across the lake.

"I should sue you. You stole the idea for a book from me. You said terrible things about me too."

"You're hardly original yourself, Nick. You based half your act on Odin's. And I haven't told anyone anything that wasn't true."

There was silence.

"It didn't have to come to this, you know," she said. "This was never how I wanted it to be."

A couple strolled past them, arm in arm, oblivious to their presence.

"We used to be like that. So close, so happy. What happened, Nick? What did I do to make you hate me so much?"

Bewilderment was etched across his face.

"I don't hate you. Although you seem to dislike me enough to want to destroy everything I've worked for."

Petra studied him. He hadn't changed a bit. He'd dropped the enchantment that made him portly enough to satisfy the general public. His hair and beard were back to their original shade too, rather than the white tone he'd affected over the years.

"Destroy you? Nick, you're the one who destroyed me. You turned them all against me. You spread rumors that I was a demon. You said that I'd whip their children with my birch twigs, throw them in a sack and drag them off to hell! You even told them that I was a man! Why?"

He shrugged. "It seemed like a good idea at the time?"

"Oh, come on, Nick, I deserve more of an explanation than that."

Santa fiddled with his watch strap and kicked his heel against the ground. Petra waited in silence. Finally, he cracked.

"Okay, fine. I wanted more. More than the village, more than you and me. I wanted the world. I wanted fancy restaurants, cruises, fast cars and money. I wanted to be appreciated, to be the guy that everyone loved."

"I gathered that, but did you have to make my life a misery to do it?"

"Yes."

Petra curled her top lip in disgust.

"There wasn't room for both of us in the business. I had to be number one. Everyone I spoke to, all the experts, said that if I wanted to make it to the top, I had to ditch the dead weight."

She cleared her throat pointedly.

"I don't mean that I thought of you like that. Those were their words. They thought they could brand the business more successfully if we just focused on a single personality. I was going to tell you, really I was, but it was just so difficult to find the words."

He bit his lip and shot her a pleading look. Petra steeled herself. He was almost sounding convincing. Less like Santa and more like the Nick she used to know.

"I wanted to make it work for us, so that we could reap the rewards together. But the PR guys decided to give you a bad name, so people forgot about you quicker. It was too late by then. I knew you'd trace the stories back to their source and you'd never forgive me. So I thought it would be better to just go. Make a clean break of things."

"I see." She adjusted her position. They sat in silence, the awkwardness bristling between them.

"I miss you." His voice was small, like a child's.

"Nonsense," she said, although she felt like something inside her was about to snap like a twig. "You just want me to stop what I'm doing. Let you have Christmas back."

"That's really what you think of me?" He laid his hand on top of hers. Instinct told her to pull away from him but she didn't.

"Yes. No. Probably."

"If we compete against each other, the chances are we'll just ruin each other's operations," he said. "So yes, I'd like to see if we can come to a compromise. But I'm not lying about missing you. I do. I always have. It would be good if we could at least be friends again."

"I'll think about it. No promises, mind you."

"That's all I ask." Santa gave her hand a squeeze, rose and left.

As the sound of his footsteps faded into the distance, Henrik emerged from behind a tree and jogged over to her.

"Is everything okay? What did he say? What is he going to do?"

Petra tapped the seat, beckoning to the elf to join her.

"The thing about that man," she said, "is he never *has* been able to admit when he's been a fool."

## Christmas Eve

Any child who'd ignored his or her parents' pleas to go to bed early that night, and had gazed out of the window instead, would have seen two magical vehicles streak across the skies: one pulled by reindeer and filled with toys, and another laden with bags of birch twigs and drawn by huskies.

Santa took the lead position, but Petra had only agreed to that so that she could see what he was up to at all times.

"I still don't trust him as far as I could throw him," she confessed to Amy, as they were loading up her sled, "but it wouldn't be fair not to give him a chance."

Amy put a hand on the woman's shoulder. "Nobody's beyond redemption. You're the one who taught me that."

"I'm not sure that includes Nick. He's going to have to work a lot harder to get his name off the naughty list as far as I'm concerned."

Amy laughed. "Henrik is definitely on the nice list though, right?"

Petra scowled at her. "I have no idea what you're talking about."

"If you say so. I must have imagined the way you two have been looking at each other the last few weeks."

Petra muttered something and, for a moment, Amy wondered if she was about to be transformed into a rat. Thankfully, nothing happened. It must have just been a regular curse, not a magical one.

"I think we're done. Almost time for you to fly, so I guess it's time for me to say goodbye." Amy waited as Petra settled herself into the sled. "Have a safe journey. I'll see you in the New Year."

"You've not changed your mind about taking the job then?"

"No, I'm looking forward to it. Head of Magical Art. It sounds so impressive. I just hope I'll do you proud."

Petra cocked her head. "Of course you will. I wouldn't have

insisted on you having the job if I didn't think you were up to it. Your artwork is already superb, and Henrik and I can teach you the magic side of it in no time." She huddled up beneath the reindeer skins.

"Enjoy your holiday, Amy. You deserve a break after everything you've done to help me."

"It was nothing. And thank you again for the tickets. Well, thank Santa for me when you speak to him."

"No need. They'd have only gone to waste. I don't know where he'd got the idea that we'd be going to the Seychelles from in the first place. Apart from anything else, we've got far too much work to do. This company merger won't just organize itself and we've got factories to reopen."

Petra grinned. "Just think, in a few weeks, Santa Co. and Krampus Enterprises will be no more. Next year, all anyone will be talking about is Yule Co." She grasped the reins and shook them firmly.

Amy took a step back as Henrik spoke the words to prepare the sled for take-off. A puff of glitter and it was gone. Petra Krampus was on her way to help lost children find the right path once more.

# SCHADENFREUDE

## E.J. HAGADORN

I don't think we've met before. Good for you.

Krampus, they call me. Oh, you've heard of me? Good. I can't tell you how many times I've had to explain my job to people. Or justify it.

Oh yes, I love my job. You'd like it too, if you had a chance to try it. Don't believe me? Wait until you see a kid having a meltdown in public. They'll scream and whine and make a mess, and I guarantee you their parents won't do a thing. You'll be stuck there wishing someone would set that kid straight, and then you'll remember Krampus.

Now don't get me wrong; it's not that I hate these kids. On the contrary, I love naughtiness in all its forms. Remember, this is me we're talking about. So why do I do this job? Two reasons: one, the dental plan is great for a guy with fangs; and two, the tears and misery of children, naughty or nice, fill my black heart with glee.

You know the Germans have a word for that, right?

It's not all fun and games, though. If you've ever dealt with an evil child, you know what it's like. Imagine dealing with all the baddies. It can get ugly.

How ugly? Tell you what, I'll tell you about one of the worst imps I've ever met.

This was a long time ago, back in 1820. Or was it 1920? There weren't any Nazis yet, I know that. Anyway, I was relaxing at home with a glass of Riesling and a copy of *David Copperfield*, when an old associate knocked on my door.

"Saint Nicholas. Shouldn't you be spying on little kids like the creep you are?"

"Krampus, you are the most despicable, asinine, soulless bastard I've ever met, and I hope you burn in a thousand hells!"

We laughed and gave each other a big smack-on-the-back hug.

"Good to see you again!"

"You too, Krampy."

"So what's up?"

"Believe it or not, I've got a problem, and it needs your kind of…intervention."

"Are the elves on strike again?"

"No, nothing like that, thank God. It's actually a child."

"Since when is a child too much for you to handle? Don't you deal with the good ones, anyway?"

"Yes. And I've noticed a lot of good ones getting hurt recently."

"I'm listening."

"His name is Rolf; one of the worst I've ever seen."

"I like him already."

"He makes bodily noises in church, he puts snails and frogs in people's pockets, and he ties flaming rags to dogs' tails. And that's when he's not being creative. He once tripped a girl and knocked out her two front teeth!"

"Can I adopt him?"

"No. But you can pay extra special attention to him this year. Take an entire night if you have to. I don't want to have to bring his victims any bandages and ointments this year. Give him hell, okay?"

"Shouldn't be too hard."

"Don't get cocky. This kid's no joke. I want you to be careful, you understand?"

"Oh please, I once scared a kid so badly she stopped wetting the bed. I think I'll be fine."

I was so eager to get the jump on Rolf that I spied on him a month before the big night. I found him crushing snails in the schoolyard with rocks, looking bored out of his mind. Then the girl came running by, the same girl he'd tripped. Her new teeth were well cared for. She ran away when she saw him, but then she tripped over a tree root and knocked out her front teeth again.

Rolf laughed while the girl ran screaming to the schoolhouse. He didn't even bother denying it when she accused him. The teacher punished him severely at the head of the classroom, and even under all that pressure, and the hateful gazes of his classmates, he was still laughing. When his punishment was complete, he promptly made a rude hand gesture at the teacher and it all started again.

I had to admit, I was impressed. Not many kids I encountered were that disruptive or antisocial without having some kind of condition. Not Rolf, though. He was different. He loved to inspire anger in others. It made him feel powerful.

The joy I felt at finding a kid so like myself was unprecedented.

Fast-forward to December 5th, and I was making my way to a certain little village in the German Alps. I surveyed the town from a cliff. I breathed the snowy air, felt the pale moonlight on my skin, and listened to the still streams.

With my fur and my Christmas cloak swishing, I rode upon the wind and tramped from rooftop to rooftop, clattering the shingles with my hooves and awakening children in fear. I heard them crying and cackled. What a night to be Krampus!

Finally I reached Rolf's house. It was a big one, up on a slope in the hoity-toity part of town. They had their own well out back and an elegant snow-banked garden. I grinned. Rich kids' tears are sweeter than any other.

I crept over to the dormer window and lingered over the edge. The window was open. Gripping the roof, I swung my hooves out and down, and landed silently on the boy's carpet.

I saw an empty room—and then a sharp crack on my horned head knocked me back. A fire log fell to the floor. Somewhere at my ankles a string pulled tight, and I fell hard on my back.

A sack of flour tipped over a shelf.

"Oh no."

There was a fall, and an explosion, and I sat coughing in a cloud of white dust. I stood up and shook my fur loose like a dog. Next thing I knew, a broom came flying out of nowhere and started beating me around the face.

"Take that, Krampus!" cried a high-pitched voice. "Cower before me! Feel the wrath of Rolf Schmidt!"

I was more startled than hurt, but the kid was so fast I could barely keep my senses. I raised my clawed hands, bared my snarling teeth, and did everything I could through the relentless beating. Finally I pulled the broom out of his hands and snapped it like a match.

There he was: short, pudgy, and spoilt, three-feet-nine-inches of nasty, with slick black hair and a wicked smile on his baby-fat cheeks. The perfect image of evil.

"You little hemorrhoid! Look at me! Do you have any idea how much shampoo I go through in a single day? It's gonna take me forever to get all of this out! I swear, by the time I'm done with you—"

"You'll have to catch me first!"

He ran over to the dark fireplace and grabbed another log, but before he could chuck it I seized him by the scruff of his nightshirt and hurled him into his headboard.

Then I advanced, ready to punish, but when I reached into my robe to draw my weapon, it was gone. Nothing but an empty pocket.

Rolf stood up. In his hand he held a knobbly wooden stick.

"You won't be taking me away tonight, Krampus! I don't care what Papa says! I'm not going anywhere!"

"Kid, you put that down!"

"No one tells me what to do!"

"You give me that rod or I'll—!"

"Get back!"

He pointed the rod at me, and I was lifted off my hooves and thrown against the wall. The house began to wake up.

Rolf looked down at the weapon he held. An expression came over his face that I'll never forget as long as I live.

"Looks like I have a new toy to play with. Tell Saint Nicholas I said thank you."

"Rolf!"

He swung the rod around himself, and in a gust of blizzard wind he had vanished.

Sounds from the house below brought me to my senses, and I swung myself out the window before the bedroom door was open.

By now you're probably wondering what it was that Rolf had gotten his hands on. Some people call it a switch, but for lack of a better word, it's a magic wand. Laugh if you want to, but that's pretty much what it is. I call it a rod. With one wave I can fill a girl's bed with cockroaches or freeze a boy's bath water. I remember one time I enchanted a kid's parents to make them think he was a demon, and they chased him around the house with a Bible and crucifix. The rod packs quite a magical punch.

And Rolf, the most evil waste of sperm I'd ever met, had just taken it out into the night.

Naturally, I was not in a good mood. I sat sulking on the roof and listened to the drama unfolding down below. Rolf's parents and maid were frantically searching the wreck of the bedroom and calling his name out the open window. His mother was wailing like an opera diva. Soon they all retreated downstairs, and took their search out into the street.

Now, like I said before, I usually like naughty children. They're my kindred spirits. However, this was a new low. Rolf had robbed and humiliated me. An impressive feat, in hindsight, and maybe even praiseworthy, but I wasn't about to congratulate him. If I didn't set this straight, Nick would never let me hear the end of it. But to do that, I was going to have to take my punishment techniques to a whole new level; not just scare tactics or pranks, but an honest-to-God personalized nightmare. Rolf was going to get the absolute worst of Bartholomew J. Krampus.

I decided to start Rolf's punishment with a little Saint Nicholas flair. I went back into his room, where a line of shoes sat at the foot of the bed. Snickering, I left a shiny little surprise inside each one of them. Something to get my point across.

Just as I finished, a tumble of noise startled me from behind. I turned. There on the floor was a pile of gingerbread: soldiers, sheep, elephants, and figures of me and Nick, all decorated with icing and marzipan.

Then, with a puff of smoke, an entire gingerbread Noah's Ark jumped out of the air and shattered on top of the others. Again and again the gingerbread popped up and littered the boy's bedroom floor.

I grinned. So that's where you went to, eh Rolf?

Typical child.

I jumped out of the window, ready to fly on the wind and catch the boy in the act, but instead I plummeted headfirst into a snowbank. Hooves kicking, I pulled myself free and cursed. Without my rod, magic was off the table.

Then I saw a toboggan leaning against a nearby tree. Hoisting it over a shoulder, I raced to the edge of the yard. Rolf's parents were across the road, rallying the neighbors to their search. Two other households were shivering in the snow beside them. It wouldn't be long before the whole town was awake.

I sat down on the sled, my knees coming up to my bovine ears. I'm not usually one to get embarrassed, but at that moment I was glad grown-ups couldn't see me.

I pushed off and raced down a long line of palatial estates. I leaned into the wind as the toboggan scraped over the cobbled streets and into the village.

As I sped down the road, I noticed that a nearby tailors had had its windows smashed open. I was hot on the trail! Unfortunately, because I had my eye on the window, I wasn't watching where I was going. I crashed into the statue in the town square. What a night to be Krampus.

With stars in my eyes I tossed aside the toboggan wreckage and made for the shop. It was dark and silent, but it stank of smug entitlement and rich kid soap. I followed the scent (and his tracks) to a gingerbread shop down a side street.

Pausing to strip a branch off a nearby young tree, I peeked through the shop's broken window. Rolf, bedecked in a stolen coat and boots, was heaping bits of gingerbread onto the floor. Every now and then he'd stuff a handful in his face. Then he would wave my rod over the sugary piles, and in a puff they were gone. I could only imagine what his room looked like now.

I waited. Finally, Rolf turned around to take another piece off a shelf. I quickly eased through the hanging-open door and stomped the floor hard. Rolf jumped.

"You!"

"Me!"

"But…I took your wand! You can't be here! Go away!"

"Silence, mortal child! No one commands Krampus! You think you can best me by stealing a stick? Behold!"

I held up the branch I'd taken. It was bare and leafless, and completely dull, but it was bigger than the rod in Rolf's hand, and in the poorly lit shop, that was all that mattered.

"This," I continued in my best theatrical voice, "is true magic, greater and more powerful than anything you could ever wield! How else could I conjure myself in your midst?"

The look in Rolf's eye told me my plan was working.

"Is it really that powerful?" he asked.

"Yes. Far more powerful." Do it, kid!

With a wave of the rod, the branch flew out of my hand and into his. He tossed the rod aside, and I lunged for it. Rolf was too enamored with his new prize to notice.

"I win again, Krampus! Now I'll be the one to do the punishing, and I think I'll start with you!"

The boy swished, but nothing happened. He tried again. The branch quivered uselessly in his pudgy hand. I waved the rod and it fell to the floor in a heap of cinders. Then the truth sank in, and Rolf looked up at me with fear in his eyes. It was beautiful.

"Please don't kill me!"

"Relax, kid. I'm not going to hurt you."

"You…you're not?"

I dusted myself off. "No. In spite of what you've done, I kind of like you."

"No you don't. Krampus doesn't like anyone."

"Is that what Papa told you?"

"Yes."

"And since when do you listen to Papa?"

He couldn't say anything.

"From one trickster to another, I promise you, I'm not your enemy. Look, I'm putting the rod away. See?"

Rolf unballed his fists.

"You're really not going to hurt me?"

"No. Truth be told, I'm actually a fan of your work."

"My work?"

I helped myself to a gingerbread Saint Nick. "I've been keeping an eye on you, Rolf. I've seen what you can do, and I must say I'm impressed. That thing with the girl's teeth was amazing, and that trap you set for me was genius. You're so devious and cunning. I don't think I've met anyone like you before."

"Wow. Thank you, Krampus."

"Say Rolf, how would you like to help me play a trick?"

"What kind of trick?" Ah, that face. So eager and hopeful.

"Right this minute, your parents are running around town waking everybody up. Listen."

He held a hand to his ear. Sure enough, the voices were growing in number and volume, with his parents at the lead. They were all calling his name.

"They are going to be so mad!"

"They probably think I've captured you. But we know the truth, don't we Rolf?"

"This is the best trick ever!"

"And we're going to make it even better."

"How?"

I whispered in his ear. When I was done, he was wearing a smile as evil and devilish as my own. I almost felt guilty.

We made our way across the town square and ascended the broad church steps. The bronze statue stood frozen below us.

"Are you ready?" I asked.

"Yes!"

"Good. Hide over there."

"Wait. Is that my toboggan?"

"No. Now hide or I'll turn you into coal."

He ducked behind a pillar and waited. I jumped up onto the roof and climbed the steeple.

All around me the little German town was waking up. Rolf's mama and papa, bless their hearts, were half out of their minds wondering what had become of their little angel, and one by one their miserable neighbors had joined them. I could even see some policemen in the mix.

I stood on my tiphooves and held up my rod like a baton. With a graceful curl, I conducted my orchestra. Every bell in the town, be it church bell, school bell, clock bell, servant bell, or police bell, started ringing. Without rhythm or rhyme, as fast as they could go, every bell beat itself violently, screaming to the stars and lighting up every window in town.

People spilled out of their homes, their nightshirts dangling around their pale ankles. Meanwhile, horses and livestock added their own agitated screams to the din, so that everyone had their hands over their ears.

Then the bells were silent. All except for one church bell, clanging high over the town square. Everyone followed the sound, confused and hopeful for answers.

At the forefront were Rolf's parents. Perfect.

I stopped the bell, and all that remained were the clamoring voices of the crowd.

Then Rolf jumped out from his hiding place.

"Rolf?" cried the townsfolk.

"Was this you?"

"Where have you been?"

"Rolf!"

"Son!"

Rolf threw off his coat.

"Ladies and gentlemen, I present to you—" (I made a grand flourish of the rod.) "—my ass!"

And with that, Rolf presented his bare hindquarters to the entire town.

Nobody said anything. Nobody did anything.

Except for Rolf, who stood up and blinked at them, wondering what was wrong. Before he could try again, his parents embraced him.

"Rolf, why did you run off like that? We were so worried!"

"Come home now, son. If you stay out here too long you'll catch cold."

Rolf, looking fearful, desperately opened his nightshirt and presented his front to the audience. Nothing.

"What? But I…! What's the matter with you?"

"Rolf, is this your coat?"

"No! I stole it! See? I broke those windows over there!"

"Goodness!" said one of the spectators. "What a terrible storm that must have been, to do so much damage."

"Indeed," said the shopkeeper from the crowd. "It'll cost me quite a lot to replace them."

"It wasn't a storm!" Rolf cried. "It was me! I did it all! It was me!"

But it made no difference. Whenever he spat in someone's face, or said a rude word, or heaved a rock at a window, no one took any notice.

Rolf was escorted back up the hill, and I made sure he heard my maniacal laughter every step of the way.

"Spare the rod and spoil the child!"

That was ages and ages ago, and to this day it still tickles me pink. I'll never forget the look on Rolf's face when he found those thumbtacks in his shoes the following morning. Priceless!

And that was just the beginning. Whenever Rolf misbehaved, desperate to elicit anger from his parents or teachers or peers, he failed. It was like being invisible, and it lasted all throughout his childhood. While the rest of the village went on cheerfully with their lives, he sulked away in the background, powerless and miserable. And seeing him miserable made me very happy indeed.

You know the German word for that, right?

# FAMILY TRADITION

## S.E. Foley

Laney Marshall realized what she had done. Intending good, she'd done something pretty damn bad.

The trailer was on fire.

She spun around, looking for the way out, her electric guitar slung over her shoulder and her little brother and sister clinging to her arms like shrieking monkeys. Out presented itself as an unlikely hole in the wall, left by the invaders. Lungs already burning from held breath, she made the dive through billows of smoke towards what she hoped was life and not… something else.

### A Few Days Before

Laney shuffled out of her closet-sized room. Morning sunlight seeped through the thin drapes, forcing a nocturnal squint from her. She turned, the brightness driving her to the couch where she flopped, hip dipping towards the center. In a previous life the couch must have belonged to a boulder, and she was reasonably sure it had liked to sit in the dead middle of the thing.

Her siblings, the fraternal four-year-olds Taylor and Jayne, were sitting in the middle of the floor. They were too close to the small TV, huddled in their pink blankets. They were waiting for cartoons to resume, their cereal bowls cradled in the hollows of their crossed legs.

"What stupid thing are you watching today?"

"Gemma Genius," the twins replied in the tandem way to which they were partial. Taylor added, "Not stupid, Laylee."

Neither of them could say her name right for anything.

Laney looked for a spot to put her feet on the coffee table. It had the usual junk on it. Legos, a sticky bowl, a soda can, and some old bills. On top of the paper mound was a permission slip. She swept it up to read. She hooked the edge of the table with her toes and her skinny knees banged together painfully. A soft grunt left her. She lifted accusing eyes to where her mother was wiping down the counter. She flapped the paper, the sound traveling to her mother over peeling tiles and chipped formica.

"Ma, are you gonna sign this or what?"

Her mother looked up from a gap in dark hair and it was there. It. The look that showed up that time of year. Pinched. Strained. Laney imagined that someone forced onto a tightwire by a cattle prod would have the expression that her mother wore. A convict's air of desperate, miserable acceptance. That was what met Laney's question, along with a tired sigh.

"I'm sorry, I forgot," she sounded like she was reading flat, tired lines from a script.

A commercial for *It's a Wonderful Life* came on. Their mother walked over and poked the channel button randomly. The twins protested until she grabbed a disc and popped it into the player. "Here, watch this instead."

"They want Taylor for baby Jesus for their preschool play, ma. Come on, he'd love it." Laney pushed, feet dropping off the coffee table. She sat forward with the slip of paper in her outstretched hand. Her mother walked back to the kitchen as if she didn't notice.

Laney was used to it. She knew she would get nowhere, but her mouth persisted. Skinny legs stiffened. She flipped the paper back to the cluttered surface. She leaned up and spat angrily, "Why do you have such a problem with..."

"I'm going to work. Your father won't be home until late, so you have to put the twins to bed."

Laney sat slackjawed. A moment of annoyed silence passed and then she barked out, "Seriously? Did you have me so I could babysit the rest of your spawn? Cuz that's how it feels..."

Her mother didn't grace that with a response. She straightened the cuffs and collars of her white work shirt, checked her hair in the mirror by the door, and grabbed her coat and purse. In a jingle of keys looped through fingers, she blew kisses to her three children and said with a hint of the energy that had been lacking before, "I'll be late if I don't go right now. Love you, be good."

Then she was gone. Laney got up to peer out into the overbright glare of snow and sun. The short driveway was a sheet of rutted ice. The constant melt and freeze had shaped it into a winter hazard. Just outside, her mother's old Grand Am backed carefully away from the trailer.

"Eff this dookie," Laney muttered, turning to look at the tiny boy and girl. Her arms crossed, she trudged over to her room. She pulled her one treasure down from the hooks over her headboard: her Fender electric guitar. Before she left to walk herself and the twins to school, which were both in walking distance to the trailer park, she strummed the instrument and sang her favorite Blue Oyster Cult song, "Cities on Flame with Rock and Roll." She liked it because she had a Fender, and her name was Marshall, just like the words in the song.

Later, when the three siblings were walking back from school, Jayne asked Laney, "Why are there lights on the houses?"

Taylor was quick to pipe in, "We should have some."

She didn't answer right away, instead ducking her shoulders

enough to get her nose close to the collar of the jacket she wore. It was one of their father's, too big and comfortable.

"Lights, lights, lights!" The twins were pointing and shouting as they shuffled along in their pastel colored layers, mittens on strings flopping around red fingers, and ends of scarves dragging, collecting snowballs in the fringe.

"Oh, you can ask Daddy about that, squirtlings. I'm not touching that one."

"Why not?" Tandem question, the rise and fall of their high voices just off enough to create an eerie dissonance.

"Because I'm not."

Laney's black boots, patched with copious duct tape, crunched and squeaked as she walked through the snow. The twins shuffled alongside her, heads down against the nippy air. The three tromped up to the door. Laney unlocked it.

The door swung open to reveal a dark interior. A rage began to build within Laney as she stepped through and ushered the twins inside. It grew as she stood glaring around the dimness at the slumping couch, the ancient carpeting, the dull colors of the place they most recently called home.

There was a lumpy blanket on the recliner. A pair of work boots hung off the raised leg support and rhythmic, rumbling monster noises came from beneath it. The twins looked at each other and then squealed, running to make a flying leap onto the blanket. They landed, and the thing beneath it cried, "Jumpin' Jezzzussss you two tryin' to kill me?"

"Daddy!" the twins crowed in unison.

Laney leaned back against the door, arms crossed. She didn't realize how hard she glowered until she rolled her eyes enough to see her own reflection in the cruddy old mirror. The glare in her dark gaze startled her. It's his fault, she thought. I don't know why, and somehow he always wiggles out of giving a real answer, but it is his fault that we don't get to do the Christmas thing. No tree, no cookies, no gifts, and worst of all, no real explanation.

"But whyyyyyy?"

Laney's attention snapped back to her family. Though the twins were still in their thawing winter gear, Alan Marshall held them close. He wasn't that clean, himself. It looked like he collapsed for a nap straight from work. While she was lost in her own little mirror world, the twins had bugged him about the lights. He was feeding them the same line of steaming crap he'd given her.

"Because the lights draw the Tom-men and their bad news boogieman boss," he was explaining.

"But whyyyyy?" Taylor wailed, arching dramatically in his father's arms.

Jayne leaned towards her father's narrow, bearded face, "Who is their boss?"

At the same time, Tayor asked, "Why is he their boss?"

"Can't say his name, or he'll come knocking," their father explained. He booped his daughter's nose, and blew a raspberry on his son's cheek. "And I guess he is their boss because he is bigger and meaner than the Tom-men. The man with the plan, so to speak. He is the one that takes naughty children away, after all."

Taylor persisted, grabbing his dad's scruff and got up close, too. Tiny forehead pressed to his father's larger one, the child begged, "But whyyyyy?"

"Me and their boss had a falling out when I was just a little bigger than you. Oma… my grandma, used to leave porridge and butter out for the Tom-men, and a glass of homemade beer for their boss. Every day, without fail, if the spirits get their taste of butter and beer, the family has good luck, but if not, all havoc breaks loose and their boss comes for the mortal children," Alan explained, tickling both their sides at the same time. The children giggled.

"One winter's night I was mad about something, I don't even remember what. I kicked the bowl and glass she left for them off the back porch. Oma saw the mess the day after and sent my family away. She said the spirits would be angry at me, and we had to leave the farm. The boss isn't nice to naughty kids. He stuffs them in his bag and sends them away for ever and ever. Since then, things from the old world have been after me. My mother and father saw to it that we never stayed anywhere they could find us, or did anything that would call their attention to us. I gotta watch it, or they'll get me!" Alan chuckled as he said it, as if it was some long gone old joke that no one but he understood.

Laney rolled her eyes and snorted loud enough for everyone to hear. Her family ignored her. She clenched her fists and chewed on the inside of her cheek as she took off her winter things. She almost kept her mouth in check, except… she didn't.

"Ma said you were working late," she started with an accusatory tone.

He looked up from the squirmy duo with a consternated look. "Not enough work. They cut me loose early today, and won't need me until tomorrow night."

Laney stared at him, her irritation rising upon a wave of something that felt ugly and helpless.

"Whatever. We don't do Christmas things because we're poor, not because of some stupid boogieman boss," she said, headed at a fast walk for her door as she spat her last words. Fast, because she knew what would come next.

She heard the recliner creak, and the twins get dumped into it. She heard his steps behind her, and knew what she would see if she turned around. His face would be florid, his gaze changed from cheerful to a flat, alien anger. His knuckles would be white where they weren't engraved with black grease stains in the creases.

She shut her door before he got there and leaned her back against it. She felt the heavy thud of his angry fist right behind her head. It resounded, her skull bouncing away at the impact. The wood was pathetically thin, and it would have been easy for him to punch right through it. He didn't. Probably never would.

She felt the rush of blood from her heart to her head, vision sharpening to take in all the meager details of her room. The dust cobweb in the corner. The ratty edge of her dull green blanket. The scraped metal of her bed frame. The guitar pick on the floor. The sag of the dark blue blanket she nailed over her window and where the color was fading, bleached by light at its center.

"Watch your mouth, girl! Do not sass me, do you understand? You keep your ass in there until you remember how to be respectful!"

His words were followed with another thump of his fist on the door. The sensation of the strike through the wood traveled, less of an angry impact this time. Merely a punctuation of his demand. She pressed herself against the wood and felt it to her bones.

She listened to his heavy footsteps, heard him return to the recliner and put the TV on. Her arms tightened around herself and she whispered to the air, "Yeah. Just what I thought. Too poor, but we can't admit that, can we? Nope, gotta make up stupid stories about it."

She flung herself belly first onto her bed and stewed in her anger. All his fault. All their fault. Never have anything nice. Always have to move. Always promise to find better jobs, better homes, and it always ends up like this—some crap trailer in some podunk town and minimum wage, dead end jobs. Schools full of strangers, and just when things become familiar… wham.

One parent or the other got a new, supposedly better job somewhere else, and it was time to move again. She got to where there were no more words, just an ugly, soupy dross of bad feelings pooling around her like so much psychic scum. Somewhere during that toxic, bubbling rumination, Laney came up with a plan. As soon as she got that defiant plot settled firmly in mind, she felt much better.

She got up and grabbed a school notebook, pencil, and scissors from her backpack, and started designing ornaments. Crafted with the kind of awkward care only new enthusiasm can have, there was soon a scattering of things on her bed. The sick anger had faded into focused industry. Paper balls and cut-out snowflakes, snowmen with crayon eyes, and the most ambitious ornaments were four-legged creatures with protrusions from a thick necked head. They were supposed to be reindeer, but they ended up looking more like inbred cows. The delicate antlers tore off easily. She taped them back on, so then they looked like inbred cows who were wearing fake antlers. They all looked awful, but she didn't care.

She would do more than that. She had to wait until her dad wasn't so pissed off, so she could leave. She could just make it to the library before it closed. She sat up and pulled her Fender off the wall and started to pick away, singing softly to herself.

"Cities on flame with rock and roll…"

When the moon rose high and small in the sky she prepared to escape the trailer, empty backpack over her shoulder. Everything from the floors to the door creaked at her passing. Lucky for her, her father's snoring was loud and rhythmic. It paved the way for her to grab hold of the squeaky door knob and ease it open.

Her boots crunched ice at a run, her breath billowing outwards in majestic, pillowy clouds. She felt her insides sing the dark mischief of midnight freedom when she got to the sidewalk. She pulled her hood up, stuffed her hands into her pockets and stalked with purpose into the night.

There was a tree in someone's yard that would be easy pickings for a string of lights. There was another place where plastic critters were touching each other in a mad rave of snowmen, elves and reindeer. There was yet another place she'd noticed on the way home from school that had pitched their old, busted-ass fake tree to the curbside. She was sure it would still be lying there. She intended to give the things back, but for the time she had them, they were victims of petty larceny. Her backpack was filled with all that she could take, which in the end wasn't a lot. A few elves and a coil of lights.

The tree scraped and bumped along as she walked backwards as swiftly as she dared. The bristling branches groaned, metal and plastic instead of proper fir. She hustled the thing all the way down two blocks and around the corner, to the access road where she stopped to catch her breath. Laney stood up straight and looked at the cold, distant eye of the moon.

"What are you lookin' at," she mumbled. It felt like it was watching, judging her. She hated the feeling. It was just the moon. The shadows it cast were deep black on pale snow, reflecting a strange starkness. Robbed of vibrant color, the world around her slept, but felt still aware in its dreaming.

She shook off the nameless shame and continued to drag the tree around behind the trailer. She hoped no one would look out and see it tucked against the siding. The snow that was banked up around the skirting crunched and hissed under the tree. Her teeth gritted harder, and she prayed to go unnoticed.

She entered as she had left. Her cold things were shed and her sheets warmed up around her. She drifted off to sleep, but it felt like the moon followed her deep into her dreams. She didn't feel rested when she woke.

That morning there was cereal, squabbling over the TV, and a brief argument with her mother about what she could use to feed the kids. Then it was mom going back to bed for a nap before work. While her mother was sleeping, Laney checked the backpack stashed in the corner of her room, stuffed beside the bed. All of the ill-gotten goods were still there, just as she left them.

Later, both parents got up and went about their routines. A visit with the twins, a tense circling of their teen daughter, and then off to work. Engines turned over, rumbling in protest, creaking with the cold. They were gone, again.

Laney came out into the living room to see the twins sitting on their blankets, playing with stuffed dolls. A sudden sense of icicles dragging up her spine caused her to hug herself tightly. She turned around and looked through the open door of her room. It was the same as always with the Fender on the wall and her bed with rumpled blankets. Her gaze fell to the backpack. It had to be a side effect of stealing things. She shook her head. She was only borrowing. They would all go back tomorrow: Christmas Day.

"Hey guys. I have some special plans for us for tonight. You be good and keep playing. I'll only be outside for a minute."

The twins barely looked at her. They were deep in some construct of life as they viewed it. One doll was helping another one get up on the edge of the coffee table while a bunch of other dolls were standing back and making horrified noises at this death defying feat.

"Oh no, don't fall!"

"I won't!"

"Oh no you're gonna fall!"

"I can fly!"

Laney stomped into her boots and bounded around the trailer to where she'd hidden the tree. It was even more pathetic looking in the watery gray light of day. She grabbed the base and dragged it inside. The children watched while Laney pulled the thing in. It lay on its side on the floor, reaching up with hinged metal limbs. Finger-like plastic green bristles jabbed at the stained ceiling, falling far short of brushing anything at all.

Laney looked at the children triumphantly. They stared back, looking between her and the thing lying there on its side. She put her fists on her hips and guessed they didn't know what it was, so she explained, "It's a Christmas tree."

"We know it's a Christman tree…" Taylor began.

"Christmasss tree," Laney corrected, drawing out the mass part of the word.

"Christman tree," Jayne said firmly. She hugged her dolls close. She looked down at them, rubbing her chin into their yarn hair. She glanced at Taylor.

He frowned back at her and asked very cautiously, "What about the Tom-men?"

"Fu-uuuhhhget about the Tom-men. They're a load of doggie poo," Laney growled, narrowly avoiding a swearword. She was so done with her father's stupid tales. He had warped the whole Christmas elf thing into some wacko gaggle of bad minions for some evil Santa Claus. All because he was a cheap jerk.

The twins looked doubtful. That just pissed her off even more. She yanked the tree up and fixed the base so it would stand. It teetered, so she dragged it to the corner of the room and propped it against the wall joint. It leaned there petulantly. Brushing her hands on her jeans she huffed, "There."

The twins spectated, tensely squeezing their dolls. Laney flung up her hands. They would see, it would be fun. She went to her room, not letting her frustration get in her way.

"Jeez, guys, everything is gonna be alright, okay? Here, I got a movie from the library. You'll love it. It's called *Rudolph the Red-Nosed Reindeer.*"

She brought her pack out, retrieved the movie and popped it into the disc reader. She let it play while she got the paper ornaments, lights, and the lawn decorations she had taken. The kids were watching the movie with fascination. Having not seen the movie before then, Laney found herself distracted by it as she fumbled around the tree. First, she pulled the strings of colored lights out from the bag in tight coils.

Laney tried to put the lights around one way, and then another, before finally getting them on from the top, around and around the tree to the bottom. Next came the misshapen snowmen, cow-deer and cubist snowflakes. She grumbled the whole time she decorated, holding back the curses that she wanted to unleash upon her Christmas monstrosity.

She waited to plug the tree in. She lifted the hand-sized elves, each holding a colorful present, from her bag, and set the resin figures on the carpet in a circle around the tree. When she was done, she frowned. They looked more like guards than gift-givers. She turned them so they were all facing one way, like they were dancing around the tree. She plugged the lights in. The lamp in the corner flickered briefly, and she gave it a threatening look. Nothing else happened, so she relaxed.

Taylor looked over his shoulder when the colored lights flickered on. The gentle shine of blue, green, red, and gold had caught his attention. The tree didn't look half bad with the lights shining on it. Taylor gasped. Jayne took longer to glance about from her enrapt TV trance.

"Ooohhhh, pretty."

"Aww, it's our very own Christman tree. Are those the Tom-men?"

"No, Jayne, they are Christmas elves. Sometimes they bring presents all wrapped up and put them under trees. Lucky boys and girls get those," Laney felt a drizzle of shame dampening her pride. She hadn't been able to get them anything.

"So, who wants SpaghettiOs?" she covered her feelings with an offering of food.

They both cried, "Me!"

Laney went to the cupboard to pull out a couple of cans. She found the stuff gagworthy, but it was food, and when she was hungry enough, it worked. As she prepared dinner, the twins made their first adventuresome move towards the tree. She had expected them to joyfully embrace this rebellious celebration, and it was just not happening. Instead of embracing it, they were sneak-crawling over, looking up at the kaleidoscope light cast from the tree to the ceiling.

When she looked up from her task, she saw Jayne picking up one of the elves and felt an edge at her nerves. She warned, "Be careful with that, kiddo. I have to return him in the morning."

Jayne looked up and nodded, then went back to running a finger along the tall red hat. She tickled the yellow clogs the elf was wearing, and pressed her finger to the tiny red nose peeking through a white beard.

"Boop," Jayne smiled. Soon enough she and Taylor were making the figures climb the tree, and having them talk to each other about the gifts stuck in their tiny elf hands.

"What's in your box?"

"I have a polar bear in mine. What is in yours?"

"A diamond crown."

"Do these boxes come out?" Taylor yelled, pinching the shiny red box that was in his elf's hand.

"No! I told you to be careful…Jeez…"

Laney carried bowls out to the living room. She finished watching the movie with the twins, who had settled down with an elf each among their dolls. When it was time for bed, she had to make the children give up their new buddies and put them back under the tree. They were cheerful as they went about their bedtime routine.

"Silver and gold… Silver and gold…" They sang over and over, the only words they could remember from the song in the movie. She tucked them into their tiny little toddler beds and snuggled dolls up against them.

"Goodnight, and merry Christmas, squirtlings."

"Merry Christman, Laylee," they both said, at the same time.

She turned to leave and flipped the light switch on her way, drawing the door shut behind her. Down the narrow hall past her door she went, to the open space where the kitchen spilled out to the living room.

She stopped, a hand falling to one of the twin's high chairs. Something felt wrong, like needles tickling over bare skin. She looked at the tree. It seemed to have gotten bigger. It loomed in its corner, the top brushing the ceiling. That was wrong, she knew. Fake trees don't grow. It must have always been that big. She also noticed that the twins had arranged the elves around the tree in a half-circle facing it, all their presents seemingly offered up in supplication.

"Creepy," she mumbled to herself. The sensation of wrongness remained. As she cleaned up, she found herself keeping her head turned so that one eye would always have the tree in the corner of her vision. She decided to catch a nap before the quick run out to return the borrowed things, trash the broken old tree, and get away clean with having a flippin' Christmas. She may not have been really pleased with the results, but she felt pretty good about her choices, overall. And so, she took herself to her bed, set her alarm for an hour and curled up tight.

Smoke.

She woke up to the unmistakable scent and instant panic burned her gut. Limbs flailed in the twist of blankets. She flung herself upwards to grab her guitar. Her first thought was *Fire? Save the guitar!* And then it was…

"Twins!" she screamed, slipping the strap over her head and rolling off her bed to hit the floor, tearing her door open. Her legs were hit with instant sensation. She expected heat, but instead she felt prickling, bitter cold. Gaze whipping about, she saw that the door to her sibling's room seemed undisturbed.

The other way was very disturbed. The place where the tree was, wasn't, anymore. There was a gaping hole, as if something took a big bite off the corner of their trailer. All that was left of the tree was a torn wire dangling from the wall socket where she had plugged the lights in. The cord threw sparks on the frayed carpeting.

She would have run for the fire extinguisher if not for the elves.

They all turned and looked at her, beady eyes glaring over their white beards. Her throat was too dry to utter a croak. She blinked and thought, *Stop*.

They were still there when she opened her eyes. Creepy little elves in clogs of wood, wool tunics and pointy hats of red, no taller than her ankle, staring at her. The colorful presents were gone from their calloused little hands.

And then IT came through the hole. Freakishly tall, it crouched in, all soot-smeared fur and cloven hooves. Rusty chains jangled, draped over it like jewelry. Crooked horns gouged into the ceiling, causing debris to dust its ice-crusted head. The whole trailer creaked and shuddered as it drew itself inside. Its gaze was colder than the frost that clung to it. The black void of space could not be as cold as that compassionless visage. A long, stained burlap sack swung limply from its malformed shoulder.

Right beside it was her father's chair. The thing stooped low to sniff the cracked surface. A long clawed hand caressed the top of it. A serpentine, blood red tongue lashed out of its bristle-toothed mouth, slurping the air. Chains rattled, slithering over the fake leather. It had a bundle of slender birch branches, which it shook at her.

It spoke. She heard languages in its voice, warring for supremacy, as if it spoke all the words of every known language in one breath. Dialect of Babel, the sound of madness, but one she could understand.

Through hands she'd unconsciously plastered over her ears, she heard, "I smell the blood of Alan Blaine Marshall. A debt long owed and mine to collect. Give me a child!"

The babies. She pivoted and ran. Fire was starting behind her. She could smell it grabbing onto the exposed materials from the hole, taking hold, making itself comfortable, eating her house like hot, ravenous maggots after the monster had taken its first bite.

She burst into the twin's room. The trailer shuddered as the invader followed, the sound of its hooves on linoleum sent the burning taste of half-digested SpaghettiO's up her throat. It stooped low to fit down the narrow hall, reaching for her.

The Fender was in her hands. She twirled and swung that thing like it was an axe made for chopping down giants. Fear gave her slim arms strength and a new level of panic gave her back her voice. "Get OUT, d-bag!"

The trailer groaned when the monster fell. She grabbed the twins out of their beds. They began sobbing instantly. There was one horrible second where Jayne fought back, and then clutched her big sister as tight as her frightened twin brother. Laney spun back around, her guitar knocking her hip. The monster was lying face first on the floor between her and escape. She scampered between the creature's sprawled, goatish legs.

The madness that was the beast's voice cried out, "Tomte! Take a child!"

The Tomte had scattered around the trailer, most congregating around the door. Fire was crawling along the insides of the trailer, consuming the couch, flowing up the thin drapes. It ringed the place where the tree had been, but it was still passable. There was only one angry elf in front of it. Laney dashed that way. As she ran, she hooked a foot around a kitchen chair and kicked it.

Her hasty aim was good; the chair struck the Tomte in her path, knocking it through the flaming gap in the corner. Chains scraped, rattling against the floor. Laney looked back to see the big monster getting up. The trailer was on fire all around her. The walls were orange and black, aflame, the smoke thickening. She ran for the hole.

From behind, she felt stripes of stinging pain bloom across her back. The children shrieked again, watching wide-eyed over her shoulder. It had hit her with the sweep of an unnaturally long arm and the switches it had carried. She stumbled at the edge. She fell to her knees, skinning them on the raw cold snow.

The night was fathoms black. Her arms were empty. Her lip exploded blood when her face hit the cold hard packed snow. The air felt viciously unforgiving. Her heart remained in her chest, but she felt it begin to tear away when a black cloven hoof came down beside Taylor. Chains hissed over the ground.

Taylor was so far away. How had he fallen so far? She couldn't move. Her limbs felt attached to the burning cold ground.

"NO!" she screamed, bubbles of blood popping on her lips. She rolled, but she was all elbows, no fingers. She flopped as she watched a large clawed hand scoop her little brother up off the snow.

The monster's sack fell open to reveal a gaping black nothingness. Laney was sure she could hear the faraway cries of children coming from that awful burlap vessel. Her little brother screamed from where he dangled. Jayne let out a horrific wail, her tiny, chubby arms wrapping around herself where she lay on the yard in powder blue pajamas. The creature spoke again, "He will repay the debts of his father."

"Take me instead!" Laney sobbed, her voice wet and nasal. She saw Tomte jumping out of the hole, scattering around the yard in a wide circle around them, as if she or her siblings were in any shape to try to run away.

The monster shook its head, arm sweeping away the idea with a gesture. The ominous portal swung wider. It stuffed the little boy inside.

Laney shrieked wordless fear, fumbling, grasping, finding her beloved Fender and flinging it at the creature. The guitar tumbled end over end to strike its hand. The one with the sack. The evil portal fell to the snow.

She wasn't sure how she got up and scrambled for it. The bag felt sooty slick in her grasp. The monster swung about to grab at her. Thrusting her hand inside was an agony she had not expected. She felt something in her numbing grasp. She screamed with pain as she tossed the sack away from her, and into the burning trailer. Flames roared upwards. All around, Tomte threw tiny hands over their mouths in shock.

The monster turned and stared as the bag went up. It seemed more shocked than the Tomte at what had happened. Laney fell, curled around what she'd pulled from the bag.

From around the other side of the trailer came the sound of a car engine and tires crunching to a stop. Further back, sirens echoed. Laney heard her father's voice, but she had never, ever heard his voice sound like it did that night. "Oh, God, oh dear sweet Jesus..."

Taylor gasped a sob. He was caught against her, face red streaked, streaming tears and snot. His pajamas were torn, his skin showing signs of frostbite. When he opened his eyes to look at the sound of his father's voice, they were pure white, unseeing.

The monster stood there, looking between the Marshall family members as Laney scooped up her brother with her one good hand. Her other seemed seized around his arm, and she saw a frost burn so bad it scared her. Her father ran to take Jayne up into protective arms. The creature seethed, bristling, glaring a look fit to give a demon nightmares, "Next winter, Marshall family."

Men in firefighting gear came tromping around while the beast called its minions with a ragged bark and vanished into smoke and mist shadow.

She heard her father say with a guilt she'd never heard in him before, "What have I done?"

Numbly, Laney felt heavy gloved hands guiding her, saw them do the same with her father, away from the fire, towards the flashing lights of the fire truck. As she went, she saw one of the little elf statues she had stolen standing in her yard, holding a shiny present, smiling through its beard with next year's promise.

# KRAMPUS: THE SUMMONING

BRAD P. CHRISTY

Tucked away in the Eastern reaches of Bavaria, the sun set as the town clock of Fluchstadt chimed six times on the evening of December fifth.

Heavy snow muffled the sounds of tubas, accordions, and laughter that filled the air as locals and tourists danced and sang along with a lively polka band. Couples huddled together against the cold as they meandered through brightly lit stalls of the Christmas market that lined the village square, selling their handcrafted goods. The surrounding forest lent its scent of evergreen to the robust smells of cinnamon, apples, hot mulled wine, roasting meats, and the many steins of beer being guzzled and spilled as they clinked together with a boisterous, "PROST!"

On any other night of the holiday season the quaintness would have gone uninterrupted until the lights went out in the market and everyone nuzzled into their beds. But this was no ordinary night. On this night, people dressed in fur and horned masks prowled the streets, making their own kind of merriment through mischief and mayhem. They howled, barked, and laughed as they chased children and pretty girls with switches, all in the name of Krampus, a creature that represented the counterbalance to Saint Nicholas's rewarding nature.

It was a new tradition that had gained popularity with each passing year.

A scream cut through the music and howling as a boy, with his scarf and clipped-on-mittens trailing behind him, was pursued down the snowy street by a couple of older boys in Krampus masks.

A hand grabbed him from the side of the street. The old woman, gray hair hanging disheveled around her face, pulled the boy in against her.

The two ruffians slid to a stop in front of her. "Give us the naughty boy, crone!" growled one of the boys in his most demonic voice, laughing and holding his hands over his head as if he were about to strike.

Her wild, wide eyes met his behind the mask and he took a step back.

"Come on, Johan," taunted the other boy hesitantly. "You can't hide behind old ladies forever," he said and poked at Johan with a stick.

The old woman snatched the stick out of the boy's hand. "Old lady? Crone?" She swung and slashed the stick at the ruffians with the precision of a swordsman, striking them both several times before they tripped and ran off into the night.

"Disrespectful hooligans! We know who you are!" she yelled and threw the stick at them. "This isn't even a proper switch!"

Johan squirmed out of her grasp. His knitted hat was pulled so far down over his blond head that he couldn't really see who had saved him. He adjusted his hat and scarf and wiped his red nose on his sleeve. "Thank you," he said sheepishly, embarrassed he had to be rescued by an old woman.

"Oh," she said and shushed him. "Don't worry about a thing. I'm sure you will have plenty of chances to prove your bravery in the future." She smiled. "Johan, is it? That is a very good name. I have an ancestor whose name was Johan. He was the bravest man I have ever heard of."

Johan sniffed and smiled back.

"My name is Petrissa," she said, brushing snow off of his shoulders.

Johan, like all children of the village, already knew who she was. She was the eccentric woman who lived alone in the woods. He could have said this—he could have run away after what he had heard about her—but instead he put out his hand for the shaking. Hopefully the rumors were only rumors.

Petrissa looked down at the hand as if expecting him to be holding a weapon, but then smiled and shook it. "You seem like a very polite young man, Johan. Why would those boys call you naughty?"

Johan shrugged.

"Well, Johan, they don't know anything about this blessed night—"

"Krampusnacht," Johan interrupted.

"Yes, Krampusnacht," she said, excusing the interruption. "If they did, they wouldn't dare act that way."

She knelt down to his level. "Let me tell you a story about a little girl who lived in this very same village a long time ago, and how Krampus came to be. It was a thousand years ago, when our ancestors had finally driven the marauding Quadi tribesmen out of our lands and back to Bohemia. There was to be a great celebration…"

It was a harsh winter, and the snow had piled waist deep. Game was hard to come by, and many men of the village of Fluchstadt had been killed in battle against the Quadi; even more were still recovering from their wounds.

The snow picked up and the sky grew dark as Johan, the spiritual leader for those who remained loyal to the pagan gods, sat with his daughter, Basina. He could see villagers looking at them queerly as they passed by on their way to the village square. Nobody looked directly at them. Even a group of children huddled in an alleyway, whispering amongst themselves. It was an increasing trend in the years since the Roman missionary came to Fluchstadt.

"Father, did the Christ lord really defeat the Quadi?" asked Basina, breaking Johan's nervousness.

Johan smiled at his inquisitive child. "No, my dear. We defeated the Quadi."

"Then why is the Roman saying it?"

"I believe this is a test. And if we did receive divine help, it was from Nerthus, in retribution for the bloodshed at her Feast of Peace."

"Then why do the villagers believe otherwise?"

"I am afraid the village has lost faith in Nerthus, but do not worry about your neighbors. She who has dominion over nature will restore the balance of the world."

Basina's eyes sparkled, "It was Nerthus who helped us?"

"If you are ever in need, you should always beseech her," said Johan, pinching Basina's nose.

The voices from a large gathering roared through the streets. Flickering torchlight cut through the shadows as villagers gathered in the square. "Come, Basina. Let us see what this is about."

As they approached the village square, they could hear children laughing and shouting with joy. The Roman, Manlius, stood in the center of the crowd with his arms outstretched. His red robes looked like the wings of a bird.

"Little children, Christ loves you so very much," said Manlius in a loud, but sweet voice. "He offers you peace and salvation." The children looked at the brightly-clad speaker with wide eyes. "And we will celebrate his charity tomorrow morning. We will have a merry feast in his honor to give thanks for the ousting of the Quadi." Adults in the crowd cheered. "And as a special reward for your love and faithful devotion to the one true God," said Manlius to the children, "Saint Nikolaus will visit the good and righteous children and bear them gifts."

Many of the children covered their mouths as they gasped in delight. Excited, they argued amongst themselves about who was going to get gifts from this Saint Nikolaus. Those who had not converted to Christianity looked back at their parents with tears in their eyes.

Basina looked up at her father. Her face tensed in confusion and her brows furrowed, which was a reflection of her father's expression.

Manlius pointed at Johan and Basina. "Ah, Johan! I was hoping you would be here," his voice echoed off of the small shops. "I was just telling everyone about the bounty of God's grace."

Johan looked around at the villagers, friends, and neighbors who he had known his entire life. Johan took a deep breath and clasped his hands. "My friends, the Roman has poisoned your minds against our gods. You must not risk angering the great god, Woden. I beg of you, stop this blasphemy and return to the sacred grove."

"To do what, Johan? Christ has brought the faithful this victory and promises peace, which your pagan gods have failed to do for generations." Manlius turned to the masses. "Where was Woden when the Quadi invaded your lands from the East? Where was Nerthus when her Feast of Peace between the tribes ended in death?"

"It is not for us to question the gods."

"Of course," said Manlius. "I remember overhearing you once telling people that if a god had forsaken them, it is acceptable to call upon another."

"I did," said Johan. He addressed the crowd, "That is our way, but is not our way to cast aside our gods completely in favor of this Roman invader. We must sacrifice to regain Woden's favor and that of Nerthus. The balance will be restored."

Hushed voices rolled through the crowd.

"It appears not every member of our village is as eager to join your congregation as those bribed children," said Johan.

"So it would seem," said Manlius. "It has been the same for

hundreds of years in hundreds of villages. Some cling to the pagan ways. They deny Christ and therefore deny salvation. It would be a pity if you were to stop our Lord's grand work here in Fluchstadt and cause all of those delightful children to burn in eternal flame."

Johan looked about the very concerned faces of his neighbors. "Do not listen to this stranger from the south."

No one would look Johan in the eyes.

"Oh dear. It looks like your heathen tongue will not stop this village from being saved," said Manlius as he admired his fingernails. "But our Lord opens his arms to even to the most unrepentant of heathens, such as yourself, Johan." Manlius addressed the crowd once again, "In a dream, an angel came unto me and showed me the way to peace, a sign to bring those who have not accepted God into their hearts."

Manlius nodded a signal to someone out of Johan's sight.

Johan hid Basina behind him. "What is this, Roman?"

"We are simply beginning the festivities in Christ's honor early," said Manlius.

A sickening feeling fell over Johan. He ducked down and looked Basina in the eyes. "Basina, I need you to run home and lock the doors. Do you understand?"

Basina looked over her father's shoulder. Her heart pounded in her chest and she had trouble breathing.

"Basina! Abide your father's will," said Johan, shaking the girl. And with that, Basina ran around the corner and stopped to watch, to make sure her father was alright.

"Do not worry for her soul, Johan. Christ will accept her even after you are gone."

A brushing noise raked along the dirt street.

Behind the crowd, men dragged a large birch tree attached to chains. The men lifted and dropped the birch beside Manlius. Johan recognized the tree, as he had tended to it since he was a boy. It was the tree of Nerthus from the sacred grove.

"What have you done?" screamed Johan, dropping to his knees.

"Consider this your Christmas gift. With these pagan idols you so foolishly cling to out of the way, you can now accept Christ as your savior."

Tears welled under Basina's eyelids. The tree of her faith was gone, taken from her by the Roman and the villagers that had turned their backs on her father. Her father's screams broke her heart.

A rock hit her in the back.

"Pagan!" yelled a young boy named Willeic, standing at the front of a mob of children.

"Because of your father we are going to burn like the Roman said."

"Yeah!" yelled a few more children.

"Because of your father, we will not get gifts from Saint Nikolaus!"

Another rock hit Basina, then another until she ran, pursued by children and a volley of rocks.

"No!" yelled Johan. He rushed at Manlius, who raised his arms to shield himself.

Johan did not make it far before being tripped and pushed to the ground. He skidded to a stop on his now bloodied hand. A boot to the ribs knocked the air out of him. As Johan lay on the snow-covered ground, more feet came down on him. He was yanked to his knees and large snowflakes fell on his swollen face.

"Repent, heathen, and disavow these pagan gods," said Manlius, holding out his ring for Johan to kiss.

"Never," growled Johan before spitting blood on Manlius's robes.

"How dare you!" hissed Manlius, and smacked Johan's face with the back of his hand. "Bind this devil in chains!"

Heavy chains draped over Johan's shoulders and arms. His skin was pinched, and the weight of the chains was hard to bear. He fought as the chains were tightened, constricting his breathing.

"Repent," said Manlius in a much calmer voice.

Staggering, Johan got to his feet. With all the energy left in him, Johan kicked Manlius as hard as he could in the chest. Johan fell backwards as the Roman landed in the thick branches of the birch tree.

Villagers broke into laughter.

Johan collapsed.

Manlius fought to free himself from the tree. So enraged was he that he snapped off a branch and stripped it down into a crude switch. The laughter stopped as Manlius whipped it again and again at Johan's face, leaving slices and welts with each strike. Bound in chains, Johan lay helpless in the snow.

Basina ran as fast as she could. The rocks became fewer as she outran the mob of angry children. Soon all she could hear were incoherent shouts and curses.

Out of breath, she leaned against a shop. The oddest sound caught her attention coming from the village square. She crept up to the corner to investigate, making sure she wasn't seen.

Basina gasped in horror as the switch whizzed through the air and snapped on her father's face.

"No!" she screamed and ran straight for Manlius, who seemed just as shocked as anyone in the crowd that this young girl was interrupting the enraged Roman. "Get away from him!"

Manlius stood over Johan, who was almost unrecognizable.

Basina grabbed the switch out of Manlius's hands, and he slapped her to the ground. She ignored her burning cheek and cradled her father's head.

Johan was no longer breathing. Her whole body shook in great sobs.

Basina took a final look at her father before running from the square. The crowd parted, making no attempt to stop her as he passed them. They only watched, stunned and unwilling to help her.

The cold blurred her vision and choked the air from her lungs as Fluchstadt fell into the distance. No torches followed her. Soon her legs stiffened as she trudged through the deep snow.

Then the snowstorm stopped completely. The eerie silence of the winter night closed in. The full moon, ringed with ice crystals, shown down on her brilliantly. She knew this place; it was the sacred grove of Nerthus. Basina sniffed and wiped her numbed face.

"Great Nerthus. Mother of all nature, please hear my cries. I am your humble servant," she began to pray, but the words fell short as the cold set in. "They took my father from me," she said meekly.

A ram appeared before her in the sparkling, virgin snow. Though the ram did not speak, a woman's voice echoed from it. "I am here, my child. What is it that you ask of me?" asked Nerthus.

Basina wiped her eyes again and smiled nervously. "Restore the balance."

"What have you to offer, child?"

Basina presented the bloodied switch to the ram. "I offer you the blood of my father, the same blood that is in me, and the weapon that was fashioned by the Christian priest from your sacred tree."

The ram slowly walked up to Basina and knelt down to smell the switch.

"Restore the balance," said Nerthus. "I see your heart has more to ask of me."

Basina looked at her hands. "Make them know my pain and the pain of my father."

The ram looked up. "I accept your sacrifice. It will be done, child. Your father's blood will bring about balance on this night and for all nights that follow. As my servant, I will protect you and your offspring until the end of days. Your father's blood will be the vessel of balance."

Basina's head swam and she fell unconscious.

In the village square, the shadow of a ram stalked along the walls. The sound of hooves on the packed dirt streets broke the silence, though there was no ram to be seen outside of its shadow until it appeared beside Johan's freezing remains. The bloodied switch was between its teeth.

"Your daughter is a remarkable child who will grow to do remarkable things, Johan," said Nerthus.

"Your blood will be the instrument of balance in this new world." The ram's shadow fell over the chained body of Johan. "Rise, my Krampus. Rise and bring balance!"

The earth trembled, shaking snow from the branches of the birch tree. The chains rattled and Johan's body shook. Tufts of wild hair and fur sprouted from Johan's flesh as it cracked and stretched. His bones broke and shifted. The chains buckled and snapped and his clothes ripped into shreds as his body grew. Claws tore out from under his fingernails. Horns cracked through Johan's skull.

Johan's eyes opened, now a vibrant yellow. A monstrous groan let loose from his belly, revealing rows of jagged teeth. Standing on his hoofed feet, Johan embodied nature's wrath.

"Krampus," said Nerthus. "On this night of each year, you will seek out those who are wicked. Where they find merriment, you will bring torment. Where their families are brought together, you will take from them."

A deep laugh, like the cracking of a tree branch bending in a storm, spilled out from Krampus. He picked up the switch and wrapped his long tongue around it, savoring the taste of the blood that fueled him.

"Go now," said Nerthus.

Krampus sniffed the air, catching the scent of the naughty. It was intoxicating and he shuddered in ecstasy. But two scents rose above all the others, the smell of the man who took Johan's life and that of a little boy who had tormented and attacked Johan's daughter. He flashed his jagged teeth in a malevolent grin and stomped down the streets of Fluchstadt towards the small church where Manlius resided.

His beastly shadow passed over the stained glass of the sanctuary. Chains rattled against his broad, hairy shoulders and hoof prints pressed into the snow. His yellow eyes focused on the source of such delicious wickedness.

Standing at the rectory door, Krampus dug his claws into the wood. The lock unlatched itself from the inside. The door burst open, ushering in a gust of freezing wind and snow. The black-horned silhouette of Krampus stood in the doorway, blocking out most of the full moon's light behind him.

Candles blew out and papers scattered around Manlius's office, where the priest had sat in contemplation. He frantically grabbed the Christmas sermon he had been writing to address the death of the pagan. As wind swirled around the room, he abandoned his scrambling and made his way through the moonlit rectory to close the door.

Given the events of the night, he walked cautiously, investigating every turn for any villagers who might be seeking revenge. He relaxed when he made it to the door unharmed.

Manlius stepped outside and squinted against the wind and blowing snow to see if anyone was there. He saw no one. He stepped back inside and shut the door, making sure it was securely latched this time, figuring he must have been too distracted at the time to check the lock.

He exhaled and pulled his robes tight against the cold. It was odd that his hearth had been extinguished. He again dismissed it as him being too distracted to tend to the fire. He lit a candle, which filled the rectory with shadows.

Shuffling to the darkened hearth, he struck a flint tool to relight the tinder. Sparks flew and bounced off of something inside the hearth. A low growl rumbled from the dark. Manlius fell backwards and grabbed the candle, expecting a wolf to have snuck in while the door was open.

A pair of clawed hands came out of the dark, each grabbing a side of the hearth. Two large horns appeared and curled up and out of the hearth followed by a set of yellow eyes. Krampus growled again, twisting it into a chuckle. A cloven hoof extended out and stomped down in a puff of ash as he pulled himself out of the hearth.

Krampus towered over Manlius, who sat shaking in the candlelight.

"You cannot be here, demon," Manlius managed to say.

Krampus sneered and snatched the priest by his ankles in a loop of chain and hung him upside-down from a rafter beam.

Manlius went into a flurry of prayers. "Demon, in the name of Christ the savior, you will go back from whence you came!"

Krampus bent down to get within inches of the priest's face. "I have always been here, Roman," said Krampus.

"What?" said Manlius, signing himself with the cross.

Krampus laughed and pushed the priest, spinning him around. When Manlius stopped, Krampus was tapping a blood-stained switch in his hand.

"What is this, demon?" said Manlius.

The switch sliced through the air and opened a deep cut across Manlius's cheek.

Manlius held his face and waved his hands defensively against the switch. The switch came down again and again. "Mercy!" he cried out.

Krampus grabbed Manlius by the hair and lifted the writhing man to his eye level. In the shabby light, Manlius could see the many cuts on Krampus's face through the hair. "Mercy? Why should you receive mercy when you cannot give it?"

Manlius's jaw quivered. "Johan?" Blood dripped down his cut face and soaked into his hair.

Krampus laughed and struck Manlius mercilessly until Manlius was too exhausted to defend himself.

"Not anymore, Roman." He picked up a large sack that had been filled with gifts for village children, and emptied it into a pile beside the priest. Slinging the sack over his shoulder, Krampus looked back at Manlius, "Consider this your Christmas gift."

Manlius shook and sobbed as he watched, bleeding from dozens of cuts, as Krampus walked out into the night. A blast of cold air blew out the candle.

Krampus drew in a deep breath through his nose. The air was saturated with the scent of wickedness. But one scent stood out from the rest. The rest of Fluchstadt would have to wait. His stomach growled. The children who attacked Basina with rocks made his mouth water.

"Willeic," Krampus said, sniffing the air greedily.

Ouside the house, Krampus could hear Willeic's parents arguing about the demise of poor Johan. His mother scolded his father for leaving Johan's body in the street like trash. His father countered by saying they would be cursed if he touched the body.

Krampus thought it was funny, and crept around the side of the home to Willeic's window. He opened his sack and gently pawed at the shutters.

Inside, Willeic was awakened by scratching at the shutters. Rubbing his sleepy eyes, he went to investigate. He had been told by Manlius that Saint Nikolaus would visit all of the good boys and girls. With a smile, he unlatched the window and stuck his head out the window.

Petrissa stopped her tale and blew a strand of her gray hair from her nose.

Johan stared at her in stunned silence. He licked his lips. "What happened after that?"

"Oh," said Petrissa. "Things did not go so well for Willeic or the rest of the villagers, and it would be many years before they recovered."

"And Basina. What happened to her?"

Petrissa stood up straight and smiled. "She lived a very full life and had many children of her own, who had children of their own, and so on, and so forth. In fact, there is at least one descendent of Basina's who still lives in a small cabin just outside of Fluchstadt."

Johan gasped and took a step back. "It's just a story, though, right? Krampus isn't real, is he?"

The shadows behind Petrissa darkened and stretched. A pair of clawed hands slid over her delicate shoulders. "That would depend, Johan, on if you have been naughty or nice."

# THE OUTFIT

## Ross Baxter

Karl looked his friend up and down and frowned. He shook his head in disappointment.

"You look really lame," he muttered.

"I know," Paul sighed, squeezing himself into an old fur coat discarded by his younger sister. "But this is a really lame idea."

"We agreed on this; we look our age so there's no way anyone is going to sell us any alcohol tonight unless these costumes completely disguise us," replied Karl stubbornly.

"Well, your costume certainly disguises you," said Paul, casting a jealous look at Karl's costume.

"Yeah," Karl agreed, a smile returning to his boyish face. "But you look more like a cross-dressing canine rather than Saint Nick's demon alter-ego. And you smell of mothballs."

Paul nodded, despondently reaching for his cheap plastic Halloween mask. The mask, like the rest of his mismatched costume, did not really capture the true essence required for the revelries of Krampusnacht. But Karl's outfit, in stark contrast, was perfect. In fact the attire was more than perfect; it was the best and most realistic

Krampus costume the boys had ever seen. Neither could believe the paltry sum that Karl had paid for it in the dingy second-hand shop in the backstreets of their native Mittelberg. Although the Austrian town was a relatively inexpensive backwater, the asking price of just twenty Euros was still ridiculously cheap. Made from some sort of real animal skin and complete with bone-like horns, tusks, claws and wickedly-sharp teeth, it appeared to be the deal of the century. The ancient shopkeeper had seemed surprisingly happy to sell it to Karl for a fraction of its true worth.

"Hopefully we'll be able to beg some alcohol from some of the other party-goers," Paul grumbled, silently cursing Austria's strict licensing laws.

"Or steal some," Karl shot back, his voice strangely distorted by the close-fitting, scaly, black mask.

"Jesus!" Paul gasped in amazement at the change in pitch of his friend's voice. "You even sound the part."

"Don't use that name in front of me!" Karl commanded, opening the front door of his parents' house and stepping quickly out into the cold dark December night.

As they walked, they could hear laughter and the shouting of people thronging the main street of the town ahead, the voices mingling with the heavy bass of music blaring from the various hostelries and bars. The shadowy side street they were on soon opened onto the central thoroughfare, the bright lights of the busy shops and public buildings illuminating the cheerful townsfolk and tourists. Costumed revelers laughed and joked, fooling around and boisterously taunting each other. Paul was pleased to see that his outfit was not actually the worst, and smiled with relief as the many dressed as Krampus mingled with Darth Vaders, zombies, vampires, and even a solitary Spider Man. Karl seemed less impressed with the non-Krampus costumes, refusing to acknowledge their shouts and greetings. Instead he steered Paul across the street to a side road where a small general store sat.

"Just do what I say when we get inside and we'll have plenty to wet our whistle," Karl ordered.

"There is no way they'll sell us any alcohol," Paul groaned. "We've been over this a dozen times; they'll just ask us to take out masks off and show our ID, and then they'll see we're just seventeen."

"Stop whining!" Karl snapped. "Just do what I say."

Paul made to protest but was forcefully bundled through the entrance. Inside the store was almost empty, most people having already done their shopping before the Krampusnacht celebrations had begun. The shopkeeper stood alone at the single till, idly looking out of the window at the street beyond. Karl stalked over to the shelves of beer and cheap wine, greedily eyeing the cans and bottles.

"Here!" he hissed. "Put this under your coat."

Paul stared at the proffered bottle in disbelief.

"Quickly!" Karl ordered.

"No!" Paul shot back, turning back towards the door.

Karl growled and placed the wine under his armpit, the coarse hair of the costume swiftly hiding it from sight. He followed Paul out of the store, the theft unnoticed by the shopkeeper who gave them a friendly nod as they left. Paul ran quickly back to the main street with Karl laughing loudly behind.

"What the hell was that?" Paul demanded, turning angrily to face Karl.

"Something I won't share with you!" Karl replied, holding up the liter bottle of cheap Liebfraumilch like a trophy.

"You've got to be out of your stupid mind," Paul grumbled. "What if we'd got caught?"

"You're just a wimp!" Karl shot back.

"We're here to have a good time, not to get arrested," warned Paul.

"So let's have a good time," said Karl dismissively. "Lighten up and follow me."

With growing uncertainty, Paul followed him back to the noise and bright lights of the main street and the throngs of revelers. In his ill-fitting costume it was hard to keep up with Karl, who moved lithely through the crowds, doing a little jig every few yards. With a hand on the waistband of the baggy oversized trousers, Paul jogged along, feeling hot beneath the old moth-eaten fur coat. The plastic mask kept slipping and obscuring his vision, and the coarse wig itched and irritated his scalp. As he passed a waste bin he discarded the Halloween mask, which made his progress slightly easier. He lost Karl a couple of times in the crowd but finally caught up with him by a row of carts selling snacks. The alluring smells of roasted chestnuts, nougat and donuts competed with each other, punctuated by aromas of hot chocolate and the lemony tang of spiced olives.

Karl appeared to be studying a table laid out with fudge and chocolate. As the vendor turned to serve a customer he surreptitiously stuck out his foot to trip an elderly tourist, sending the old man crashing headlong into the wooden counter. The stall collapsed and the plates of confections and treats flew in every direction, the steel trays clattering noisily to the cobbles. Stall-holders and passersby ran to help, and in the ensuing confusion Paul watched in stunned surprise as Karl stealthily filled his pockets from the untended stalls. By the time Paul waded through the crowd, Karl had finished and stood watching as a couple of onlookers helped the shaken tourist to his feet.

"Don't you just love the irony?" Karl leered at the red-faced Paul.

"What irony?" Paul answered angrily.

"That the first to come to the old man's aid are Freddy Kruger and Jason Voorhees!" Karl laughed.

Paul glanced backwards, seeing the costumed party-goers dusting down the retiree.

"Now that is funny," Karl continued.

"It's as funny as a normally sane guy turning into a psychotic kleptomaniac as soon as he puts on a lousy Krampus outfit!" Paul derided.

"Lousy?" Karl sneered. "You're the one in the crappy outfit. Krampus wouldn't wipe his ass with what you're wearing."

Paul made to reply, but spotted three girls from their college walking over. None were in costume and all were dressed like they were going to a party. His heart leapt; this could be the chance to improve the night a hundred-fold.

"Paul, that has got to be the worst Krampusnacht outfit ever," laughed Trudy, her flowing blonde hair shining in the bright lights of the stalls.

Paul blushed and shrugged, knowing she was right but unable to come up with a suitably witty reply.

"And who is your hirsute friend?" she continued, peering at Karl.

"I'm Krampus, you stupid idiot!" Karl yelled.

The three girls stared horrified at the outburst, then turned, with looks of disgust, to walk off.

Karl quickly darted round to stand in front of them, holding out his large hessian bag. "Hey, why don't you ladies check out the contents of my bulging sack? You know you want to!"

"In your dreams!" Trudy uttered dismissively, swerving around him.

Again Karl dashed round in front of the trio. "If my bulging sack doesn't interest you, then get a load of this bad boy."

Out of his mouth shot a huge red pointed tongue, quivering and throbbing grotesquely in front of the three girls.

"This reaches parts that other tongues simply cannot reach!" he declared proudly.

Trudy yelped and tried to bat the glistening protuberance away, but the tongue swerved and dodged as if it had a mind of its own.

"Come on," Karl leered, "you can't lick this!"

"Get lost you creep!" Trudy shouted angrily. "Both of you!"

With a looks of utter revulsion the girls barged past and disappeared into the crowd. Paul felt his anger rising again and grabbed Karl by the arm, pulling him away from the stalls and down a dark alleyway between two shops. Karl willingly followed, still chortling.

"Hey," Karl laughed, "you're just jealous because I gave Trudy the chance to inspect my bulging sack instead of giving you that offer. I've always had my doubts about your true sexual orientation, Paul."

"You just made me look a complete idiot in front of the best-looking girl in town, someone I had a real chance with!" Paul scolded.

"You?" scoffed Karl. "A schmuck like you would never have a chance with someone like her. She's leagues above you; it's me she dreams about at night."

"Just stop this stupid act, Karl!" Paul demanded, pushing him back against wall of the dark passageway. "It's not funny, and it's going to get us into some serious trouble. You've spoilt everything with this damn charade, you've ruined the whole night before it's even started!"

"It's you who's ruined it!" Karl snarled back.

"Krampusnacht is only night in the whole year where I get to go out and play; and I have to spend it with a boring killjoy loser like you!"

Paul continued to push but Karl suddenly straightened up, moving away from the wall to face him squarely. Paul made to push him back again but the shaggy form stood unmoving. He doubled his efforts, pushing much harder this time but Karl stood as firm as a rock, his body feeling like iron under the fur. Surprised at the resistance Paul took a step back, unsure of what to do next. The glassy yellow eyes regarded him mockingly whilst the snake-like tongue weaved and bobbed hypnotically.

"You're just a nut job," Paul mumbled uneasily, noticing that the yellow eyes seemed to glow malevolently in the darkness of the back alley.

"I'm so much more than that," came the hissed reply. "But I never try to hide it. You, on the other hand, try to hide everything, keeping every sick aspect of your personality bottled up inside to ensure your life is just one big lie. Don't think I don't know about how you sexually fantasize about your cousin, about how you enjoy cyber-bullying anonymously, even about your sadistic pleasure when you torment your neighbor's cat. You may to try and hide it from yourself, but you can't mask any of it from me."

"None of that is true!" Paul gasped in shock. He took another step backwards, his mind reeling at truth of the revelations.

The hairy figure remained silent, the sickly eyes fixing him with their ghastly stare. Paul turned, suddenly desperate to get out of the dark passageway.

"Stop!" the voice growled behind him.

Paul turned just in time to see the heavy chain fly towards him. It struck him a sickening blow to his left temple, the force pitching him sideways. He sprawled down heavily into the discarded garbage bins and empty boxes, his consciousness departing as his head thudded hard into the dirty cobblestones.

Paul woke up abruptly, conscious of a searing pain in his head which gripped him like a tightening vice. He felt a sense of utter confusion; it was dark and he was bunched up in some sort of restraint. He reached up to his scalp and felt the slickness of blood, wincing as his fingers traced the jagged cut from temple to crown. With rising panic he felt the rough cloth which seemed to envelope him, desperately searching for an opening but finding none. Nausea rose in his throat as he was bumped and swung, and he suddenly realized he was moving, being carried in some sort of large sack.

"Hey!" he shouted groggily. "Let me out!"

He heard no reply, all sound seemingly muffled. He desperately tried to push out the sides of the confining material but was unable to move his bunched-up legs and cramped arms. The jostling sides would not budge an inch, and he started to sense a growing heat beyond hessian bag's constraints.

"Karl!" he yelled hoarsely. "Help me. Stop and let me out. Karl!" But Karl was long gone.

# FAMILY NIGHT

## NANCY BREWKA-CLARK

"Elton?" Krampus slammed down the goose quill. Red ink splattered over all over the blank page of the ledger. He was way behind in his logging of rotten children but did anyone care? Not in this household, apparently. "Elton, stop that infernal screeching."

Marching over to the foot of the spiral stone staircase leading to the castle's north tower, he shouted, "Young man, did you hear me?"

Of course he hadn't, not over that abominable caterwauling.

Whose bright idea was it to give Elton an electric guitar for his tenth birthday anyway? Not his. No, that was Malignity's doing. His wife was the wiliest witch ever. The problem was that more often than not he didn't even know she was manipulating him until he was twisted like a Hohenzollern pretzel around her little finger. It had been that way from the day they met, and she sauntered up to him saying in High German, "Hello, hideous, is that your real nose or did you walk into a banana bush?"

Facts about how bananas grow aside, he'd been drawn to her like a snake to a hole, like a bat to a cave, like a horny young man to a temptress. Her hair had been as thick and lustrous as hot tar, black and shining and utterly captivating, her eyes two black pools from which he could never drink enough. Her lips had opened like the deepest darkest heart of an autumn rose, and he'd been consumed. Even after twelve years of marriage, Krampus could never slake the thirst that came over him when they kissed. Malignity still made him ache with desire, itching and moaning with it, hairy and hot with it, throbbing and aching like a man with a fever.

Problems only arose when they weren't kissing.

Case in point: The day after Elton's birthday she volunteered to teach a late afternoon workshop for her coven about 1,001 apps for genetically modified fruits. Krampus swore she did it to avoid hearing him practice. But she said she'd been planning to teach the course all along. Comparing apples to oranges was hard work and the other witches were Luddites, just like him, so somebody had to create the proper spreadsheets. Thinking she was talking about laundry, he quickly changed the subject. No point in picking up one more chore when he was overloaded as it was.

"Get an Apple," one of the minor trolls who reported to him once advised, "and it'll be a lot easier." Krampus took his head off, literally, having gleaned from listening to Malignity that one fruit should never be touted over the other. But after the decapitation he began to wonder if he mightn't have been a bit hasty. There were more and more bad apples to log, but no oranges.

Which reminded him, he still had to make dinner.

Elton would eat anything Krampus could dredge up from the dungeon freezer. Elk hearts, moose liver, buzzard breasts, he'd gobble up anything that could be nuked and slathered in enough catsup to make it look like prey. Sweet little Marguerite, only six, was also content to nibble on whatever was set before her as long as she couldn't see it. Unfortunately their oldest, twelve-year-old Stella, was rapidly outgrowing that infantile culinary obsession. She'd developed a curious yen for sushi, although give her a plate of home-scraped whale blubber and see how fast she'd run from the table shouting,

"Dad, stop trying to make me fat."

To the outside world he was Krampus, all-powerful, all-knowing, his black heart better than radar, sonar or any other tracking system to detect wickedness in children. But to his own kids he was just Dad. Actually he detested the name Dad, so American, so unlike the beautiful Bavarian titles that had once rolled off the tongue in paeans of awed homage, lieber vader, beloved father, respectfully loving terms like that.

"Dad." He said it aloud, stuck out his own tongue, which was a yard long, red as a coxcomb, and stinking of pickled herring, then shook himself. At least his offspring didn't behave like the brats in his ledger. Those imps called their parents so many shocking things that he couldn't even write them down in full but simply used first and last letters with a dash in between.

Another electronic wail screeched down the spiral stone staircase like a fallen angel on its way to the fiery pit. "Elton, put that damn thing away and do your homework!"

"Wah-wah-wah," the guitar taunted.

Krampus drew himself up to his full height, nine feet, eight inches from cloven hoof to the hairy pelt of his scalp. Counting his horns, which added another eight inches, he stood 124 inches or 314.96 centimeters, the measurement he preferred for its Teutonic accuracy. "Wait until your mother gets home. Then we'll hear squealing, young man."

Yours, he added silently, not mine, I hope.

Krampus lifted the lid of the giant freezer to grope through the icy vapor for a container of gutted game, by which he didn't mean a box of Parcheesi or Candyland missing some pieces. The tastiest game to his mind was truly awful offal, killed fresh and aged to disintegrating tenderness, but at this time of year, frozen would have to do. Clutching a plastic receptacle labeled bear kidneys, he clomped back up to the kitchen.

Marguerite was sitting at the table with a box full of gnawed crayons and a coloring book. The page she was working on showed a holiday scene of Santa Claus merrily flying through the sky in a sleigh drawn by a spiraling slew of reindeer. "Dad?" She looked up at him with eyes as black as coals. "Why don't they make coloring books about you?"

"Because I'm not a big, fat phony ho-ho-ho kind of guy." Krampus yanked open the microwave, shoved in the iced-over box, and set it on high. "Not like that bozo."

"He has toys in his sack." Marguerite sighed. "His little girl must have a lot of toys. Very nice toys."

"Get that stuff off the table." Krampus rummaged around in the overhead cabinet for some sort of spice to kill the taste of bear kidneys. Cinnamon? Cardamom? Essence of Mom? Whoa, where'd that come from? He took the jar down and unscrewed the lid.

"Yikes." Face pale, Marguerite slammed the coloring book shut and began to sweep the broken crayons any which way back in the box. "Mummy's home."

"No, no, that's just her fragrance." Feeling slightly dizzy just from sensing her nearby, he screwed back the lid. "Mummy's little joke."

"Phew."

Krampus heard rattling. He turned to see Marguerite dumping all the crayons back out on the table. "I said to put those away."

Marguerite shrugged. "Yeah. I know." She selected a pink crayon and began to color in Santa's suit.

"Marguerite." Krampus frowned. "Put those crayons away. Now."

"You forgot the secret word," she said in a sing-song voice.

"Please."

"Nope, that's not it." She picked up a blue crayon and began to color in his beard.

"Marguerite, enough."

"Nope."

Krampus marched over to the table and held out one hairy

massive hand. "Give that book to me right now."

"Dad." Somehow she managed to give it five extra syllables, all of them expressed in a high whine. "I want to color."

"And I want you to give me that book and then set the table."

"I don't want to."

In a flash, the air was filled with confetti.

"Dad?" Stella materialized out of nowhere. For a split second he thought she'd suddenly started growing fur on her feet, then realized she'd only stuffed cotton balls between her toes so that her silver toenail polish would dry faster. "What's for supper?"

"He tore up my book!" Eyes blazing, tears streaming, cheeks bright red, Marguerite grabbed a handful of crayons and threw them at Krampus. "He's jealous because I was coloring Santa Claus—"she stopped to gulp—"very nicely."

"Nicely? Hah!" Krampus threw back his head and laughed a dangerously ogre-like laugh. "His suit was pink. Pink! And the beard—well, let me tell you, little missy, your precious Santa wouldn't be thrilled to say the least to be confused with Bluebeard."

"Who's Bluebeard?" Marguerite wailed.

"Look." Stella pointed to the microwave. "Something's trying to get out."

"Ach! Mein Frosche!" Krampus wrenched open the microwave door, but it was too late. He pointed to the pile of steaming frogs, then at his daughters. "See what you've done?"

"Us?" Stella cried. "Me and Marguerite didn't do a freaking thing, did we, Marguerite?"

"No!" Marguerite banged her head on the table. "Mean old Dad did it. He cooked the poor little froggies."

"Is that what we're having for supper, Dad?" Elton asked from the kitchen doorway, his hair standing up in a ridge of brown prickles. " I thought you were only supposed to eat the legs."

"Of course that's not supper, dummkopf." Krampus longed to beat all three of them with a willow switch until they begged for mercy. "They were hibernating in the freezer. Until spring."

"Then why'd you nuke them?" Elton asked.

Cords stood out on his forehead. "Somebody stuck the wrong label on the box. Oh, when I find out who did it, they will be sorry, so sorry, so very, very sorry."

"Not as sorry as the frogs," Elton said.

"I wish we could put Dad in the microwave," Marguerite screamed. "I wish we could cook him until he popped!"

Krampus spun on his hooves. "Pop? You want me to pop?" Banging open the cupboard door, he ripped a big, black plastic garbage bag out of its box. "I'll show you pop."

"Dad," Elton shouted, his face red with excitement, "you're out of control."

"Control? You want to see control?" Snapping the bag in the air to open it, he shoved it down over Marguerite's head and shoulders. "You see what happens to rude, insolent, nasty, wicked children?" Yanking her off the chair, he pulled the bag down over her knees and ankles and then turned her upside down. "They get sacked." Yanking the drawstring shut, he flung open the back door and tossed the sack into the snow. "Come and get it, wolves."

To his astonishment, a great winged creature swooped down out of nowhere, snatched up the bag and flapped off toward the little village at the foot of the mountain. "No, wait, stop." Jigging in frustration and slapping his cheeks, Krampus shouted over and over for the bird to come back.

Only the wail of the rising wind replied.

It wasn't the answer he wanted.

"Dad," Elton yelled, "what about dinner?"

Stella shouted, "What should we tell Mum?"

But Krampus, panting, sweat freezing on his brow, stumbling, sliding, sometimes falling, deaf to anything but the flapping of wings high above, was already halfway down the mountainside.

"Hey, you, come here." Picking up a chunk of ice, Krampus hurled it at the swooping pterodactyl. "Stupid bird." How the prehistoric creature had ended up scavenging on a mountain in the Alps was a mystery that didn't intrigue him in the least. "Go back to being extinct, and while you're at it, drop my daughter."

With a screech, the massive bat with a snake's body and the eyes of a gremlin circled him, going round and round in the upscale hotel parking lot until Krampus thought he'd lose his lunch. "Ark-ark-ark," it croaked, the sack hanging from its beak like a baby dangling from a stork in old wives' tales.

"You coward." Krampus balled a fist and shook it at the monstrous creature. "Come down here and say that." When the creature dipped lower, he hissed, "She tastes like witch."

"Ptooey." Having spit out the plastic bag into the dumpster, the pterodactyl made one more circle and took deadly aim.

"Scheisse." Krampus wiped off the steaming bird droppings as best he could with his sleeve, paying particular attention to the fuzzy spot between his horns. "Get stuffed."

With one more squawk, the bird vanished into history.

Up, up Krampus went, scaling the big blue dumpster with the ease of a mountain goat. Perching on the edge, his terrified gaze roved over the slumping bags. Where had the creature tossed her?

"Marguerite?" He watched to see if anything squirmed beneath the black plastic sea. "It's me. Dad."

What a terrible mistake he'd made, tossing away his own daughter in a fury like some sort of redneck lowlife. No time, though, for ethnic parsing, political prejudice or the like. He had to find her before Malignity found out what he'd done, or he was toast. Literally, toast.

"Marguerite?" His yellow eyes bored into the accumulated mountains of garbage. "I have to tell you something."

He'd never apologized to anyone in his life. That wasn't the Krampus way. It wasn't the way Malignity approached life either.

Once upon a time, somewhere deep in the gene pool, the two of them had come from good stock, no doubt, kind people who'd opened the door at a timid knock on a snowy December eve and found themselves forever enslaved to the forces of darkness. But even darkness had its uses. If only he could smuggle his little girl back into the castle before Malignity got home, all would be well. When it came to the children his wife was a she-wolf.

"Marguerite? Please come out." Once more the yellow eyes swept the mounds of trash. "I don't blame you for being angry with me." Overhead, the full moon gazed down at him with a horrified face. The air was turning icier, just like the blood in his veins. "I didn't mean to frighten you." Aw, baloney, of course he did. No lying, not tonight. "I mean, I did want to frighten you. But I never thought someone would steal you. I swear it."

What was it like to have a child stuffed in a sack and carted off to meet the Devil? He'd never given it a thought. But now he knew what other parents felt.

It sucked.

"You really shouldn't have talked back to me, you know. And what you said—about Santa Claus and how he would treat his little girl—well, that hurt." Even to his own ears he sounded like one great, big, whining boob. Clearing his throat, he tried a deep bass boom. "Little girls must respect their fathers."

Was that a rustle?

"I may not be Father Christmas but I still am very fond of my little girl. Showering her with cheap toys is no way to show her how much I care."

Faintly he heard something that sounded like a long, drawn-out fart. His heart lifted. His darling little girl was mocking him, which meant she was all right. She'd survived her abduction—all right, it wasn't really an abduction because he had put her out with the trash—and the freezing cold weather, and her fright.

"Don't sass me, young lady." Where on earth had that come from?

That wasn't what he had meant to say at all. He clamped his hand over his mouth and took a deep breath. When he exhaled an icy cloud formed in front of his face. "I mean, come out, come out, wherever you are."

The words and tone were jolly. Probably that would scare her even more. They didn't do jolly in their house. That was for losers, weaklings. "No, what I mean is, get out of that bag at once."

The garbage bags lay still.

"I'm going to count to three. One…two…"

Below him, footsteps crunched. "Krampus."

The nape of his neck burned with guilt and fear. "Yes?"

"Stella and Elton tell me you were cruel to Marguerite."

He didn't dare turn. "Not cruel, exactly. Just…" He paused to think of a word, any word. "Just."

"Just what, you bully?" She was directly beneath him now.

"I mean I was just. Fair. You know, meting out justice."

"Ah. I see." A snowball smacked him hard on the back of the head. Even though his skull was very thick and his hairy scalp had grown numb from the cold, it smarted. "You meted out justice and now I'm doing the same."

"Did you put a stone in that snowball?" he asked, rubbing the spot.

"Of course."

Another hit him with such force he tumbled into the dumpster. "Marguerite?"

The plastic bag beneath him rustled. "What?"

"Oh, child." Tugging at the knotted ties, he could have wept as her little head popped up. Words of joy and sorrow flowed through him like water through a thirsty man's fingers, impossible to catch. All he could say was, "There you are. There you are."

"Dad!" She gaped over his shoulder. "Watch out! Mummy's coming!"

The blow caught him neatly between the shoulder blades. "Do

you want to lose your job?"

He thought about his job in that split second before she whacked him again with a broken broomstick. "Yes." When no further blows fell on him, he turned. "I hate my job. I want to be the one everybody loves and praises and can't wait to see."

"You?" Malignity whacked him even harder.

"Why not?"

"You want to be a goody-two-shoes? A wimp? You? The scourge of wicked children everywhere? Fat chance."

He looked from his daughter's frightened face to the moon's. "I can change."

"Over my dead body," Malignity hissed. "St. Krampus. Doesn't exactly have a ring to it, does it?"

Before he could answer, Marguerite tugged at his arm. "Dad, you're the best dad there is."

He felt his eyes filling. "I am?"

"Of course not." His little girl laughed up into his face. "You're terrible. And when I grow up, I want to be terrible, too. Just like you and Mummy."

"I'm sure you will be," he said, and shoved her back down into the sack. Standing with difficulty among the shifting bags, he tossed the sack over his shoulder. "Let's go home."

"I'll tell you right now, I'm not cooking," Malignity snarled as she vanished over the edge of the dumpster.

"Thank heaven for that," Krampus growled.

From the sack came a sly giggle. "Pizza!"

# A WINTER SCOURGE

## TAMSIN SHOWBROOK

DCI Hazel Helmsley stared at the house of her recently deceased but long estranged mother through the windscreen of her rented car. She was glad she'd let her ex have the kids for Christmas. Fighting through a crush of other Orlando-bound Brits, only to spend half their school holidays at meetings and trawling the house of a relative they'd never met, wouldn't have been likely to win her 'Mother of the Year'.

She turned the engine off, stared at the house a bit more, popped another tab of nicotine gum. Today was a chain-chewing day.

A mosquito's whine pierced her inertia and a split second later her hand was drawing away from the dashboard. In its wake, a dark smear was left, blood trailing from the thin end like an oversize tongue. She stuck hers out at the corpse.

Bastard thing.

What a mess.

In fairness, the email from Mum's solicitors had warned her about the state of the place. The other lakefront houses in this area, it had also curtly mentioned, were kept immaculate, and monitored (in accordance with a signed agreement) by the Lake Toho West Residents' Association. The elder Mrs Helmsley appeared to have forgotten this.

Like a rotten tooth in an otherwise well-brushed mouth, Mum's place hunched at the top of its drive. Creepers had wormed their way into the rotting clapboard, and one of the panels in the picture window overlooking the lake had been put out. The mesh cover over the veranda and swimming pool—according to the plans there were both—would most likely be full of gaping holes too. Hazel wouldn't have been surprised if there were snakes in the pool, or even an alligator. She didn't dare check yet. Clearing human wildlife from the streets back home in Bradford was one thing; actual wildlife here was another matter.

"Thanks a bloody bunch, Mum," she muttered.

She'd picked up the death certificate and ashes first thing, then met with the lawyers. There was no point in keeping the place—her life was complicated enough without managing a holiday home. Or managing those that managed it.

She thought about the pile of paperwork on her desk at the station and shuddered.

The other houses stretched away to the left and right of Mum's, smug under an overwhelming array of tasteful and not-so-tasteful decorations. December 22, and Santa and his reindeer were wilting under the Florida sun. Hazel got a sudden hankering for frost or even the pouring rain so often a feature of Christmases back in Yorkshire.

At least her mother hadn't picked hurricane season to die—the humidity wasn't as bad as she'd expected, especially on a bright afternoon like this and so close to open water. And it was an amazing spot. Lake Toho sparkled, in almost painful technicolor, under a yolk-yellow sun, and passing planes had cross-stitched vapor trails onto the sky's deep blue.

Inside wasn't a total write-off, thank God. Yes, it was dusty and there was a weird feeling, like the lake might wash in at any moment, but overall it wasn't in appalling shape. Hazel could see how bright it would be when the blinds were pulled up, especially with the white walls and floorboards. Mum had always had a thing for them…

She wiped away the first tears she'd cried since receiving the news and made her way round the ground floor, raising the blinds as she went. Specimen cases lay everywhere, along with lab equipment which seemed to have been abandoned mid-experiment. The walls were covered with scientific prints of flora and fauna. Mummified potted plants leered from sills and tables. Mum had been a biochemist specializing in gene splicing and had a lifelong fascination with wetland species, the insects in particular. Hence a job with a prestigious research company in Florida, after years of globetrotting and dragging Hazel with her. Until Hazel was old enough to say no. No more.

As she walked, noting things she'd like to save and what would have to go, long dark hairs collected against her sneaker soles. It struck her as odd because in the last picture she'd seen of Mum, in a nature journal, her usual ponytail had turned steel-grey.

The kitchen was the worst: dark in spite of the light outside, and the bulb in the ceiling light was broken. There was moldy half-eaten stuff everywhere; it stank of rotting vegetation; the bin was overflowing; a half-eaten pizza lay on the table…

Hang on.

Oh great: squatters. The pizza looked and smelled relatively fresh. In fact—Oh shit! It was still warm.

Hazel stood stock still, listened.

House creaking in the breeze.

Distant road noise.

Kids having fun somewhere…

No audible sign of anyone else.

"Hello?" she called at the walls. "I know there's someone here. Show yourself."

Laughing inside at the irony, she pulled her mobile out to call the police. She wondered whether whoever came out would arrive toting a gun and crab-walk round the house in the dark, à la every American police drama that made it across the pond. She'd seen people who'd been shot, been trained in how to use a gun, but like all police officers in the UK rarely carried one for her work. But guns didn't scare her; what people were capable of did scare her. Yet a certain amount of fear was healthy. As for mystery, that was what made life interesting.

No reception.

She located a paring knife in the cutlery drawer.

Once she got back to the car, she'd call the police again and they could investigate. And if they wouldn't, then she'd call a private security firm. She peered at the grimy windows, but couldn't make out anything beyond them. Whoever or whatever was here could be out the back.

She gripped the knife.

As she headed for the front door, her mobile shattered the peace, making her jump so high she nearly end up on the first floor. Reception must just be an issue in the kitchen.

It was her eldest, Rose, who chirruped, "Hey, Mum."

"Hey, sweetheart." Hazel flicked her gaze side to side, turned three-sixty. "How's things?" She tucked the phone between chin and shoulder and yanked open a door in the living room. It led down to the basement. Bad idea, by herself. She shut the door. Upstairs would be a bad idea too. Her inner detective sulked but conceded the point to inner security guard.

She got pangs as she focused on Rose's news and drew her trainer toe through the dust. Inner security guard kept nudging her to leave, but inner detective was hooked by the scene and kept scanning the living room for any other signs of occupation. It was just as Rose started talking about Karen, who was Hazel's ex-husband Mark's latest hobby, that she noticed the claw. At least, she thought it was a claw. God, had alligators gotten inside?

It was on the sofa, and massive: at least three inches long, and needle sharp when she tested the point, puncturing her fingertip. A clump of hair sat next to the claw. It was different from the long hairs that had collected under her trainer soles. This was rough and greasy and so dark it was… It was there, but it was like… like it was empty. Like it was a tiny clump-of-hair shaped hole in time and space. The more she looked at it, the colder she felt.

The claw though, like the pizza, was warm when she touched it. What the hell was this?

Shuddering, she placed it in a side pocket of her rucksack as evidence of strange goings-on for the local police. She was still half-listening to Rose telling her how fantastic Karen was and how she'd got a Mazda RX8, when she tried to pick up the hair. But her fingers refused to connect. Probably just as well.

Rose had finished her account of the day so far. Before signing off, Hazel told her she loved her and Reed—who was on his dad's iPad and therefore nowhere close to bothered about talking to her.

Outside, leaning on the car, she called the nearest police station, but mentioned nothing about the claw or the hair. Like they'd send a patrol car out based on a request from a lunatic tourist, even if that tourist did technically do the same job as them.

As she hung up, promised a patrol in the next five minutes, a throat cleared behind her.

A tiny woman was standing there, so pale and thin she resembled a sliver of moonlight. Her denim dungarees, massive straw sunhat and canvas messenger bag looked like they could fall right through her. A long plait of silver hair coiled down her back.

"Excuse me." The woman's bright words curled with a strange accent—definitely not American. "Is this your house?"

"My mum's. I think there might be squatters in there. Just called the police. And you are…?"

"Nicola." The woman smiled, extended a hand. "Nicola Santos.

I'm thinking about buying a place here."

Her palm scraped Hazel's as they shook hands.

"I apologize." Nicola showed her the skin, which was hard and cracked like a dry riverbed. Hazel felt conscious of her own, soft and pink by comparison. "I work in a very harsh environment," Nicola added. "There's no moisturizer in the world'll sort out these babies." She gave a light laugh.

Never in her life had Hazel seen anyone less likely to work in a harsh environment. And she realized as she looked harder, that Nicola was probably younger than her—the silver hair must have gone that way prematurely or be a conscious choice.

Nicola's dark eyes were unblinking. "What made you think there were squatters?"

What color were her eyes? Hazel couldn't pin it down.

She explained the situation. Nicola's polite expression never faltered as she listened, even when the bit about the claw and the hair somehow slipped out.

"Very strange," she mused. "May I see the claw?"

Hazel rummaged in her bag, produced it. Nicola turned it over and over on her palm, frowning.

"Very strange," she repeated, casting a glance at the living room window before giving the claw back. Just as she opened her mouth again, the promised police patrol car drew up. A portly uniformed figure in mirrored sunglasses got out. He gave them a courteous nod.

"Afternoon, ma'am. Understand you might have some trouble here?"

"Yes," Hazel replied, "I was just telling…"

"Nicola," Nicola filled in. "You should make a list for this officer, Hazel. Y'know? Of everything suspicious. Lists are good. I'll come back later if that's okay. I'd love to get a look round. I'm only in town for the next twenty-four hours, then I have to go back north for work."

"Okay." Hazel felt a glimmer of relief at the prospect of a potential quick sale. “This place’ll need a lot of work though.”

Nicola smiled. “I like a challenge. And I’m going to have to move soon. Where I live, it’s not the same as it used to be: fading at the edges. Y’know?”

“Kind of.”

“And I’ve always liked the idea of a warmer climate.”

Hazel nodded, then followed Nicola’s progress for a minute or two. Nicola glided past the police officer and down the drive, lopsided from the bag dragging on her shoulder. As she turned left, towards Kissimmee, she rubbed her stomach.

Blinking, Hazel straightened her dress. “Come in, officer.”

“Best if you stay here, Ma’am.” The police officer’s smile made Hazel bristle. “I know what I’m doing.”

A short while later the officer departed. He’d made, he said, a thorough inspection and found nothing untoward except some snakes in the swimming pool, for which he gave her the number of a local pest control firm.

“Probably scared off the squatters when they heard your key in the lock,” he said, shrugging. “We’ll keep an eye on the place though, don’t you worry yourself none.”

As he left, Hazel ran her thumb the length of the claw in her bag once more, felt the grooves and the warmth it still somehow held.

She opened the boot of the rental car, pulled out four flattened packing boxes and made her way inside. The living room lights worked when she flicked the switch. After setting the boxes down, she reassembled them and wondered where to begin.

Upstairs.

There wouldn’t be much of any real value; Mum’s rings, in a tiny plastic bag, had been handed over with everything else at the coroner’s office. Mum had never bothered much with material stuff and she’d have a fit if she thought Hazel was keeping everything. Dad had been the sentimental one, which had made it tough when he’d gone. She'd only been twelve. Mum had seemed so cold about it all: "Chin up, Hazel!" Until his funeral, when she'd broken down then not spoken to a soul for the rest of the day.

Shit, Mum's funeral. The arrangements once she got back to the UK. She closed her eyes a sec, then made her way up.

The shed hair was worse up here, and there was a stench. Something like sulphur and wet dog. Coming from the bathroom.

When she nudged the door open, her eyes widened. How had the officer not seen this?

The bath was full of dark hair, and several claws like the one she'd found downstairs were littered across the floor. What was more unsettling was the cold. Frost rimed the tiles and the water in the blocked sink had iced over. Each claw was surrounded by a puddle of melted ice. What the hell?

She retreated. Must be the stress of it all. Must be. The stench of wet dog clung, deep in her nostrils.

In Mum's room, she slipped the jewelry on a dresser into an envelope. Family portraits, Mum's passport and her battered copy of Darwin's *Theory of Evolution,* she placed in her bag. When she pressed her nose to the clothes hanging in the wardrobe, they didn't smell like she remembered Mum's clothes smelling. A heaviness and a dullness stole through her. She recalled the fight they'd had about Mark when she'd announced they were getting married.

"You were right," she muttered. "Chalk it up to experience."

Slowly, she closed the wardrobe door and left the room. She considered checking the bathroom again but didn't trust herself.

Downstairs, having grabbed a box, she went through to the kitchen, stared at the mess. It needed to go before she could think about packing anything.

Mum had a bowl, covered in periwinkles, she remembered from when she was little. She'd like the kids to have it some—

She could hear somebody whistling. "Physical" by Olivia Newton John. It was coming from out the back.

Shit.

She set down the box and crept as quietly as she could to the window. The day had been weird so far, but this was…

The movements of the snakes in the swimming pool were no longer languid, but frantic.

Then she saw why.

Something was getting up from the decrepit lounger at the poolside. Its twisted body, gangly limbs and huge head were all pale pink, flecked here and there with dark specks that seemed to flit from one place to another. It had to be seven feet tall at least. From its backside, a long thin tail switched to and fro as if testing the air. Two curved horns spread up and out from its forehead, past the points of its huge ears. The fingers on its gnarled outsize hands were tipped with claws like the ones Hazel had seen scattered on the sofa and in the bathroom. And even in here, she could hear the scrape of its cloven-hooved feet against the concrete.

The thing stopped at the very edge of the pool. Its eyes, enormous glowing embers set in a goblin-like face, scanned the scum-covered surface of the pool, and its mouth opened, revealing jagged yellow teeth. A glob of thick saliva over-spilled, tracing a glistening line to the water.

The snakes were wild now, darting this way and that, as if searching for escape. Then, on the far side, one broke the surface, raised its head, and began to slide onto the concrete. The next moment, there was a just smear of blood on the grey, and the snake was being swallowed, head first, by the thing still humming "Physical" through its nose. The snake's tail was coiled around the huge tongue the creature had unleashed to catch it, but slowly and surely it was pulled free and drawn down the creature's gullet.

Hazel stood, rooted to the spot, until the tip of the snake's tail disappeared. But then the thing turned, leaving no doubt that it was male, and stared, head cocked. His eyes flashed, a smile spread across his face and with one claw, he beckoned.

She still didn't move. What the fuck was that thing?

You could go out there and find out, her inner detective teased.

Shut your gob! Inner security guard retorted.

You shut yours! She spends her life taking risks and taking charge.

"Hello?" The thing said, his mouth moving in a very human way. "Daughter of Annette Helmsley? I've no interest in hurting you. Come out here. She told me you would come." His voice was a silken hiss.

Hazel remembered to breathe. The sudden hit of oxygen made her dizzy, but at least she now felt like she could move if she wanted to.

"Come out," the creature repeated. "I need to talk to you about this house. I like it here. It is warm, and I have been cold for so long. I wish to stay. Your mother told me you would let me stay. Because you are kind, and you were always a good girl. I remember."

Grasping the counter, Hazel tore herself away from the creature's gaze, focused on the windowsill. What the hell did he mean? How could he remember? She noticed then, the periwinkle bowl almost completely hidden under the trailing leaves of a spider plant.

The creature spoke again. "I knew your mother. She was a fascinating woman. I sought her out for that reason and my own heart was pained when hers became unstable. Come out and I'll tell you about the amazing work we were doing. I'll tell you why I'm here. It'll make an excellent story for your own children too. Rose and Reed like a good story, don't they? All children do."

The cold sensation inside Hazel burrowed a little deeper, made itself more comfortable. She prodded the periwinkle bowl, to make sure it was real. How could she run? Whatever that thing was, it looked like it would be fast.

Chiding herself even as she did it, she crossed to the back door and stepped out. She summoned what little composure she had left and managed to demand, "Who or what the hell are you? And what do you think you're doing in my mother's house?"

The creature threw his head back in a raucous laugh, like a donkey braying, and slapped his knees. When he brought himself under control, he clip-clopped a little closer. Hazel held her ground.

"I," he drew himself up to his full height, "am Krampus. I am pleased to make your acquaintance, Hazel, daughter of Annette Helmsley. You are of law?"

"I'm a detective chief inspector."

"I assumed as much. You smell of inquisition."

She what?

And Krampus?

She'd heard a bit of the legend. She remembered her fury when Mark had let Rose watch a film about Krampus two years ago and Rose not sleeping properly for weeks after.

Closer up, Krampus' skin resembled that of a plucked chicken and the black things took shape. They were some kind of insects. A familiar whine sounded in her ear, and she reached her hand up to swat.

Before she could, Krampus muttered some words in a tongue she didn't recognize and the whine disappeared. One of the insects settled on his cheek and he made a soft chittering noise, like a parent soothing a child, his eyes half-closing as if in contentment.

"What are those… things all over you?" Hazel shuddered in anticipation of his reply.

He smiled. "My own children. Only born recently. They feed on me, grow strong. They are good children, do as they are told. They will not harm you. Your mother helped me make them. She was very clever. Come closer. See."

"Thanks, but I think I'll just stay here."

Krampus shrugged, clopped back to the sun lounger and sat, legs spread obscenely wide.

Hazel winced. "D'you mind?"

The tip of Krampus' huge tongue protruded a little as he smiled. He ran it over his top lip. "I forget proprieties sometimes. A hazard of living by oneself." He crossed his legs. "I used to be more… discreet, but I remove my pelt every day now."

"I know, the bathroom's covered."

"Apologies. Your mother made me tidy, but since she has gone, I forget… I want to feel the sun on my skin, warm my bones, get," he twirled a finger in concentration, "the magazines tell me, vitamin D. I am old, old as humanity itself, and I need to take care of myself. Do not misunderstand: I was warm before, but only a functional warmth, enough to let my limbs move, enough to work. Work is overrated though. And so are snow and ice."

"So you've retired to Florida?"

"Retired. Yes." His eyes gleamed, though what with, Hazel couldn't fathom. "Retiring."

"Well, from what I know about you, I'm sure all the kids'll be happy." She rummaged in her bag, produced the claw. "I take it this is yours?"

A throaty gurgle she took for a chuckle escaped him. He held up his left hand. All the fingers were tipped with even longer claws. The thumb however, which he waggled, had only a pointed stump protruding from its end.

"When it is fully grown again," he said, sounding not a little proud, "it will be longer than that one. Keep that. A… souvenir."

Hazel shrugged, replaced it in her bag.

"So." She sat down on an old plastic garden chair. "How was my mum helping you with whatever all those things on you are?"

"She found me the right ones. These are gallinippers." He put one on a claw tip, held it up. "Your mother could do the right things with them. I lacked the knowledge."

Hazel squinted. It looked like a massive—

"Mosquitoes." His smile broadened. "Beautiful. They will not hurt you. I have instructed them." His tongue extended to take the insect from the claw, and he let it sit there a moment before it buzzed to his left arm. "Gallinippers can bite through clothing. Their tongues are like saws. Oh for such a tongue. I could…" His eyes glazed; the tongue retracted. It must have been two feet long at least.

Get out, Hazel! Now! her inner security guard barked.

Oh go fuck yourself, you big baby, inner detective snarled.

If Mum could deal with this, whatever he was, so could she.

"So," She cleared her throat. "They feed on you? Just you?"

"Variety is, as they say, the spice of life. They do like me best though." He pointed up at the mesh roof and Hazel had to fight an urge to vomit. The sky wasn't visible for a trembling dark gauze of mosquito bodies. "Your mother found their interactions with me interesting."

Hazel processed the information so far, calculated the possible outcomes of this encounter. What did it matter whether this thing was who he said he was? What did it matter whether he was real and not a product of her fervid stressed out imagination?

She'd pack up a few of Mum's bits and bobs, see the solicitors again tomorrow, sell the house. And then this would be someone else's problem. If it even existed.

She needed a shower and some sleep and a hug from her kids. She needed her friends and the closure Mum's funeral would bring. Maybe she could get an earlier flight home, be back for Christmas Day. Mum's fight wasn't her fight. She—

There was a loud knock on the front door. Krampus' ears twitched. He sniffed the air and scowled. "Ugh, she's back."

"Who?"

He sighed. "I am going out for a while."

"You're…"

He opened the porch cover's door and stepped into the garden. The mosquitoes descended en masse, swooping over Hazel's head and forming a huge cloud around him as he strode towards a cedar copse.

"What do you mean?" Hazel yelled after him.

Only a cackle rang from the end of the garden.

The knocking came again.

"Bloody hell!" Hazel slammed the door, then realizing she was covered in sweat, wiped her forehead and hurried through the house.

Logic dictated whoever was behind the front door was someone Krampus didn't want seeing him, so it was worth finding out their identity.

She put the door on the chain before opening it. Visible through the crack, was the woman who'd wanted to look round the house earlier. She'd taken her straw hat off and her hair shone in the early dusk. In her hands was a plain red cakebox, tied with a white ribbon. What was her name again?

The woman beamed. "Hello again. Nicola Santos. We spoke earlier? Did you solve your mystery? The claw and the hair?"

Hazel folded her arms. "What's going on?"

"May I come in, please? I've brought cake and I can help you." She proffered the box. "Krampus is an exhibitionist; always has been. I suspected he was staying here, but I had no business intruding in your house uninvited if he wasn't inside, and he's never been in when I've called previously."

After unlatching the chain and pulling the door open wider, Hazel stared at her. "Are you?"

Nicola nodded. "A version. Not the most common version, I grant you, but legends are flexible, aren't they?"

"I suppose you'd better come in."

They walked in silence through to the kitchen, but Hazel could feel an uncomfortable pressure building in her skull. Two fictional things in which she'd stopped believing on her ninth Christmas—when she'd seen her dad filling the stocking at the foot of her bed at 1am—seemed somehow to be real.

Sod this for a lark.

She wondered if she could get a late flight home tonight. Someone could be paid from a safe distance to box up Mum's stuff and she'd let the lawyers sort everything else out. She needed to get her head together.

In the kitchen, Nicola tutted at the mess. "I do apologize." She tapped the door frame.

The whole room shuddered.

Yelling, Hazel grabbed at the table, closed her eyes. When she opened them, the ceiling light, in which the bulb had previously been broken, illuminated clear, clean surfaces. She sniffed. The smell of rubbish was gone; only a trace of the Krampus' wet dog smell persisted. Mum's periwinkle bowl sat in the middle of the table.

Nicola winced, rubbed her stomach. "Much better. Worth it."

Before Hazel could ask what was worth it, Nicola took two plates from a cupboard, placed a large red velvet cupcake on each, and passed one to Hazel.

"Thanks, but I'm not really…" Hazel put the plate down next to the bowl, took the spent wad of nicotine gum from her mouth and shook it into the bin before popping another. "What's this all about? Krampus said he was here because Mum was helping him with something. And there were all these mosquitoes on him."

"Mosquitoes?"

"Big ones. Feeding on him."

Nicola's eyes narrowed. "Hmm." She took a massive bite of cupcake.

"What?" Hazel cracked the fresh gum tab between her molars.

Nicola sighed. "Naughty and nice. If I had my way, the world would be nice all the time. But that's not nature. So I reward goodness in the fresh shoots of humanity and remain hopeful."

"You're not real."

"I'm standing here talking to you."

"But you're not. I stopped believing in you when I was nine."

"You stopped believing in a version of me: a friendly rotund old man in red who bestows joy once a year. The Krampus you saw earlier is his counterpart, but he's also my counterpart. He has only one guise: twisted and bestial. We are two sides of the same coin."

"So, you're good and he's evil?"

Nicola's smile returned. Hazel thought she detected a hint of sympathy in its curve, and felt indignation stir again.

"I believe," Nicola said through another huge mouthful of cake, "in fairness. He doesn't. Unchecked, he'd love nothing more than to spread misery year-round among everyone, not just the young and naïve. I should've kept a tighter rein on him; he wants to retire, but I can't let him. Orders from above. He vanished a couple of your months ago—in a dreadful mood—and I've had to cover for him."

"He left here when he smelled you."

"I'm not surprised. No one wants their big sister spoiling their fun, do they?"

"Sister?!"

"Two sides, same coin." Nicola crumpled the cupcake case and, with expert aim, tossed it into the bin. "You must understand, our home is not what it was. We live at the top of your world, but it's dissolving. You perceive it as the ice-caps; It's something else to us, and—Do excuse me one moment." A chime had sounded from her bag. She produced a smartphone, scrolled down through what looked like a news alert, pursed her lips. "Could you drive me to Towering Typhoons Adventure Park?"

"I have no idea where that is."

"I have a map. There's been an occurrence."

"An occurrence?"

"Yes. Involving mosquitoes."

"I—No, I'm sorry. I just want to get everything sorted and get home."

"Why did you and your mother not speak?"

Hazel glared at Nicola. "None of your business." Her resolve melted under the tiny woman's gaze, however. "I made a choice. She thought it was a bad one. Irritatingly, it turns out she was right. But there was too much water under the bridge by then."

"I promise you it would be a good choice to drive me to the theme park. He's hurting people. Not seriously. Yet. But he is hurting them. And I can stop him. This is his way of crying for help."

*This* was a mystery that had turned into a domestic.

"If you're who you say you are, can't you just take your sleigh and reindeer?"

"Versions, remember?"

The sun dipped below the horizon as they reached the freeway, sitting in silence. Hazel pondered vivid memories of 'spare' presents in her stockings until her epiphany. They'd be simple things: a small puzzle, a set of pencils, a wooden necklace, but always beautifully made. A discussion had always followed the point when her parents had first seen her using them, because neither of them could ever remember buying or wrapping them. They'd shrug it off and Hazel had assumed that it was just one of those things. Her friends had also never mentioned it. They'd most likely written it off as a parental joke too.

Several ambulances flashed by the car, sirens in overdrive, all heading the same direction.

Everything glittered. You could go blind living here.

The radio made regular announcements about an emergency at Towering Typhoons—a huge cloud of mosquitoes and children causing havoc, smashing things up, attacking their parents. The word "unprecedented" kept being used.

Nicola ground her teeth. "I'd no idea things had got this bad in his head."

Outside the park was chaos. Emergency services were trapped in lines of fleeing traffic. They heard horns beeping through the dusk almost a mile from the entrance. As they drew closer, raised voices mingled with the cacophony.

"We need to walk," Nicola announced.

"We?"

"Despite duping her, Krampus clearly liked your mother and likes you as well. I'd appreciate your help."

"You're joking. I'm still not sure if this is actually happening. Besides, I told you I've got kids back in the UK. I can't just—Whoa!"

The steering wheel pulled itself free of her grasp and the car veered into the forecourt of a tinseled gas station, screeching to a neat stop in a parking bay. A sun-bleached Santa grinned and winked at her from the wall, promising a free Christmas-scented car freshener with every fill-up over twenty dollars.

"Shit!" Hazel flung her door open and stepped out into a haze of gas fumes and freeway dust. She took several deep breaths, coughed hard.

Nicola came round, wearing an apologetic smile. "We have to walk," she repeated. "Or run. Every second counts."

Towering Typhoons' rides were visible from here, their lights cutting gleaming trails through the semi-dark. The longer Hazel focused on them, the brighter they became and the more her lungs calmed. Go on, inner detective urged. The game is afoot!

"In for a penny then," Hazel muttered. "Come on. I'm catching a plane in the morning though; this is ridiculous."

They took off down the side of the road, Hazel managing to avoid the deepest of the potholes and ruts, Nicola seeming to glide over them. A few other people looked to have had the same idea. It wouldn't take many more to abandon their cars, Hazel reflected, before there was an even bigger incident on the services' hands.

The gates were closed when they got to the entrance. On the other side, people were battering on them, pleading to be let out. Nicola murmured a few words and they swung open, releasing a frantic tide, mostly adults.

Nicola and Hazel waited until the stream petered out, then slipped through the gates and hunkered down in a ticket booth.

It was no quieter, despite the roar of the crowd now being behind them; the rides and stalls were all still working. Mariah Carey was wailing that she didn't want a lot for Christmas. Official announcements competed against her for Hazel and Nicola's attention, as did myriad lights.

They might have been alone—the staff had fled with the

visitors—if it hadn't been for the gremlin-like creatures darting from stand to stand, ride to ride, grabbing and chewing and tearing and clawing, all the time emitting the same cackle Hazel had heard from Krampus. In fact, they looked a bit like—Oh.

"Yes," Nicola sighed, "that must be what the mosquitoes were for. Every one of those will be a child that's been bitten. Miniature versions of him: his own army of minions." She muttered something in a language Hazel didn't recognize. It didn't sound complimentary.

They watched as the madness continued outside then moved on elsewhere. Hazel wondered why none of the infected children had left with the crowd, but chided herself: if you had the chance to go wild in a theme park, why leave?

They crept out of the booth to the nearest touchscreen guide that hadn't been wrecked.

"If you were half-crazed with bitterness, where would you hide in here?" Nicola asked.

"I wouldn't. I'd be proud of how much chaos I'd caused. And if I was looking for attention, I'd put myself in plain sight once I'd achieved my goal. Especially if I knew someone was already—"

She yanked Nicola down behind a pretzel stand. Seconds later, a massive police squad ran past. As soon as they were safely out of the way, Nicola tugged on Hazel's sleeve and brought her back to the map.

"There." She pointed at the biggest ride: Journey To Oz. "He'll be there."

They made their way through the park, keeping to the shadows, ducking to avoid any stray mini-krampuses. After a couple of minutes, the cacophony became relative silence. The distant noise of the crowd and the freeway and the mini-krampuses filtered through as Hazel's hearing adjusted, punctuated by the walkie-talkie buzz of police voices.

The park was huge, and Journey To Oz was on the far side, on the shore of a huge lake which formed part of the ride. At the center of the lake was a tiny island, whose lighting spread across the lake in a thousand different colors and drowned the stars from the sky immediately above. Next to a paddleboat steamer docked near where Nicola and Hazel came to a halt was a notice advertising trips around the lake: "Your whirlwind tour starts here!"

"The island's a nature reserve and food court," Hazel said, tapping the board. "Interesting mix. Makes you wonder what might be in—" There was movement in the sky above the island. She gasped and nudged Nicola. "Look!"

A huge cloud, like a murmuration of starlings, was swaying to and fro, silhouetted against the light-polluted sky.

Hazel spotted something else. "Come on, we're going for a ride." She ignored the huge paddle steamer, instead running for an emergency speed boat docked alongside. Jumping in, she looked up at Nicola. "Can you get this go—"

The engine burst to life as Nicola snapped her fingers and boarded too.

"God help me, I think I'm actually enjoying this," Hazel muttered. "If any of it's really happening."

A helicopter circled overhead. The dark cloud over the island, which had disappeared, now re-emerged from the trees and swept towards the chopper at frightening speed.

"Shit," Nicola muttered, opening the boat's throttle a little wider.

The helicopter was swallowed by the cloud, its propellers sending streams of deeper darkness this way and that. They rebounded each time, were re-absorbed. Two people-shaped shadows fell from the helicopter, landing with hard splashes in the lake. The chopper veered down, crashing in the water as Nicola docked the speedboat. For a moment the 'copter's blades twitched, then its lights went out. Hazel held her breath in anticipation of an explosion, but the engine simply whimpered and died.

The two figures who had jumped were swimming for the island shore, the cloud hanging above them. When they changed direction, heading back towards the park, the cloud stopped following, maintained its course towards the center of the island.

"Come on," Nicola urged, springing from the boat.

Hazel followed and they sprinted up a hard-trodden dirt path. Litter blew back and forth in the evening breeze and twice Hazel almost came a cropper on greasy burger wrappers. As the path curved upwards, a scent of fast food and candyfloss strengthened and they burst out of the trees into the food court.

The whole set-up, like the main park, was dressed for Christmas. Too-bright, pie-eyed cartoon characters clutching candy canes bobbed up and down from the roofs of every concession and "Santa Claus Is Comin' to Town" blared from the speakers.

Hazel dragged breath back into her lungs, as Nicola performed a circuit of the court. The tiny woman seemed unaffected by their run and the stress of the situation.

A voice rang out from the cedars whose branches dripped deeper darkness over the buildings.

"I like this one, but they never got the words quite right."

A blur twisted the air into a black knot around itself as it described an arc into the center of the court. It unfurled and straightened into Krampus. The fairy lights illuminated his body, still mostly pink, but shadowing with a new growth of hair. He cast a glance around the space before settling himself spread-legged on a storm cloud-shaped bench. Then he twirled a finger, grinned, sang along.

"She knows when you are sleeping. She knows when you're awake. She knows if you've been bad…"

At that, he turned the full force of his stare on Hazel and let his tongue dangle its full length, almost to his knees. His eyes glowed red but so cold Hazel couldn't prevent herself shaking a little. Retracting his tongue, he pursed his lips and whistled.

The cloud of mosquitoes swarmed down on him, covering his nakedness with a thick fur of themselves. It was hard to decide which version was more disturbing. A couple of mini-krampuses slunk up behind him too. He patted their heads as they panted.

"Good children," he hissed.

"Brother!" Nicola strode towards him from the doorway of a place advertising pizza by the slice. "This stops here! Look at yourself!"

Krampus checked his claws. "No one asked you for your opinion, sister. Get back to your empire."

"What empire, you deluded fool? I need you. Especially now, with things the way they are. We have to make plans."

"I have made plans." He stood up, the mosquito fur on his left arm shivering as he made a grand gesture. "I plan on having some fun with my immortal coil. I've earned it. The good folk we service are seeing to it that we are squeezed out of this existence, so I have decided to become a nomad. The lifestyle suits me. You can run the family business and keep any profits. You and your lists and your bottom lines and your smiling judgments. If I'm going to do someone's dirty work, it'll be my own from now on."

Nicola shifted her bag strap and answered low and level, "I know best, Kram. That's why the Authorities—"

Krampus let out what Hazel thought at first must be a shriek of pain and threw himself on the ground. But as the dust around his thrashing legs settled, she realized he was laughing. The children were giggling too. Nicola did not look amused in the slightest.

Hauling himself up, Krampus towered over her. "The Authorities make…" The tip of his tongue re-emerged a moment, as though catching and savoring the taste of his own words. "…a fat oaf of you for these people. They let their imaginations bloat you with grease and sugar until you can barely move. Until you need dumb beasts to pull you through the skies so you can scatter your good will everywhere. And the Authorities make a beast of me. They make me into fear itself to make people better. And that's all I'm doing, making them better. Making the future better. Before I retire." He tickled one child's chin. "My children will spread chaos. Chaos is good, not bad. Chaos is honest. I am sick of threatening the young into submission."

The chop of another helicopter filled the air above and a search light bleached the scene to painful brightness. Krampus scowled as the rush of air shoved his 'fur' back and forth, exposing the skin beneath, then gestured with his middle finger. The mosquitoes swarmed the helicopter. Within seconds it was covered and began to flounder.

Nicola muttered something, a hole opened up in the cloak of insects on the helicopter and Krampus screamed at her.

"Bitch! Leave us alone! We're doing good work."

The mini-krampuses flew at Nicola and she sailed backwards through the air, landing with force on a picnic table, which collapsed. Hazel's rushed over to where Nicola lay amid fiber-glass planks and struts. The mini-krampuses were tugging at her hair, scratching her arms. Hazel yanked them off and held them, wriggling and gnashing, at arm's length. Nicola got up, dusted herself down.

"You and your tantrums, Kram," she sighed. "When are you going to realize they do nothing except cause trouble for both of us?" She tapped each mini-krampus on the head. In the blink of an eye, two small children were lying asleep on the floor at Hazel's feet. Nicola rubbed her stomach again. "This is wasting my energy. You haven't even thought about the mess you're making. And you couldn't have picked summer to do it? Or even better, January? You inconsiderate—"

Krampus' mosquitoes swooped. Hazel winced, imagining the sensation of that many biting all at once, but then was astonished to see them form a ball above Nicola's head, like the kind Hazel had seen small fish on nature documentaries form when under attack. They remained in place, spinning, swirling, unable to move out of some invisible confine as Nicola stepped from underneath them.

"You aren't as strong as me," she told her brother. "The Authorities have granted me—"

"You're only stronger because more people believe in you. How come you're the only one allowed broods and a god complex?" Krampus turned to Hazel. "Without belief, she's nothing: a barren nothing. Now you…" He looked her up and down, grinning. "You and I…" His tongue whipped out, drew a fine line across her cheek, retracted.

Hazel shuddered but maintained her steady gaze.

"No?" Krampus continued to smile. "A pity. You can still bear children. It's a shame your mother was past that. We'd make a fine experiment, you and I. My sister: she gives birth every year to the dreams and wishes of innocents. Can't stop. She never gets her own dreams though."

Nicola glowered. "I bring forth joy. I don't need—" She gasped, the whole of her shivered, and the air around her convulsed. Her glower became a grimace and the ball of mosquitoes gave a fierce twitch. Something inside Hazel snapped. Finally able to move again, she ran over to Nicola, rubbed her back.

"What's the matter?"

Nicola whispered, "My gifts are ready. I need to prepare to deliver. I should have let the Authorities deal with him."

Cocking his head on one side, Krampus let his tongue roll back out to its full length, panted a moment, before withdrawing it once more. "Soon… You need to return to the North, don't you? I can taste them squirming inside you; all those desires, all that greed."

"I'm not going back to the North without you," Nicola gasped, straightening up.

Krampus laughed. "These creatures don't want us anymore. Every year you have fewer children believing and you bring forth less and I get to do less work. And they're destroying our way through to them anyway, along with this planet." His voice softened. "Stay here. I've plans. Such beautiful plans for my retirement. Imagine a world full of my children. They will have no need of gifts to make them happy. They will be free and wild."

"They'll be your pets," Nicola snapped. "You couldn't just have gotten a hamster."

She beckoned at the ball. A single mosquito described a lazy path to rest on her finger. When she brought it closer to her face, it quivered, gauzy wings catching the glow of the fairy lights. Hazel peered too. It was no more and no less ugly than any other mosquito she'd ever seen.

But then the top of its head flipped back like the whole thing was one giant set of jaws. The opening was fringed by miniscule teeth like fiber optic needles and what would have been its proboscis unfurled. Except it wasn't a proboscis, it was miniature version of the Krampus' tongue. A single bead of saliva dripped from it and Hazel had the odd sensation it was staring at her.

"My mum helped you make this?"

Krampus gave a satisfied nod. "With a little…"

"I don't want to know."

"Oh, I can be very charming, in every sense of the word, as I think you're finding out." He waggled the tip of his tongue again, and Hazel felt a disturbing mix of repulsion and a compulsion to go to him. Krampus' eyes gleamed and Nicola's voice sounded as though from a distance.

"You can be so disgusting, Kram."

Hazel was shaken out of her trance as Krampus crowed, "I believe that's part of my job, sister."

A scuffle of footprints sounded from the trees behind Hazel and Nicola and a radio coughed, "Stay in touch."

"Police." Hazel was certain.

"Most likely. We must move fast." Nicola muttered. She delved in her bag and pulled out what looked like a shard of glass. "This takes a lot of energy and I don't know if my gifts can survive the process, or whether we'll be seen, but it has to be done." She began drawing a circle on the ground, muttering all the time.

Krampus kept staring at the far side of the court, then at the black mass above Nicola and Hazel. He looked pained and his voice became a whine.

"Let them go, sister. Please. They cannot survive if—"

The circle lines lit up and the breeze became a howling wind. Nicola searched her bag again, thrust a huge red coat at Hazel. Before Hazel had a chance to ask, the temperature dropped away around them.

Krampus howled as the mosquito ball rimed with frost and collapsed to half its size.

"Come here, brother." Nicola's voice was soft. Her face, by contrast, had sharpened, but not with anger, Hazel realized. Whatever she was doing was eating away at her. "Or I'll close the entrance once I'm back home and leave you for the humans. You know that if the entrance closes, you have no powers at all. And if you run, it'll be my duty to find you and kill you. Come here, and we can discuss this. There's no more time for games. If I'd known you were so unhappy, I'd—"

The ground inside the circle crazed. Fragments fell in on themselves to reveal only blackness beneath. Hazel began to lose the feeling in her hands and feet as the temperature plummeted again. The whole court had frosted now.

Combined with the decorations, it might have got her in the Christmas spirit had everything else not been going to shit.

As Krampus marched over, the ground inside the circle fell away completely, and an Arctic whirlwind blasted upward. Nicola grabbed Hannah's hand, pulled her forward and—

Pale blue.

Loads.

Miles of it.

Hazel winced, brought the scene into focus, scrambled to her feet. Her lungs felt like they were in a vice, her lips stuck together. She pressed her hands, which were in huge mittens, to her face until she could breathe through her mouth and nose properly, then hugged herself. The red greatcoat had covered her; its hem dusted the ground and the hood had been pulled up over her head. It stank like Krampus' fur, and scratched, but it went a long way to keeping the cold out. Beyond her own fogged breath all she could see was the blue white of snow. But there was still something odd, like someone had cast a net over the scene, and the edges of the landscape beyond were ragged. She became conscious of raised voices behind her.

When she turned, Krampus and Nicola were there. Beyond them, a darkness had opened up in the landscape, an archway of nothing that pushed against the indigo Arctic night. The cold in Hazel's bones deepened.

Nicola jabbed her brother's chest, jabbed again, gestured at the pitch black, her face full of fury. Then she fell onto the snow and lay clutching her stomach. Hazel ran to help, but found herself running on the spot. No matter how fast she went, the pair got no closer.

Then Nicola exploded.

Not in a blood and guts way, more like a supernova. Hazel stopped running, stunned, as what looked like ashes spread into the air and began to filter through the gauze. She caught one, felt it thrum in her fist. When she opened her hand, the thing hovered a moment then joined its fellows on the wind once more. They flew higher and higher until they became indistinguishable from the night sky.

A hand settled on her shoulder and she whipped around.

Nicola was standing there, but she was transparent. A wan smile spread across her face. "Thank you for your help," she croaked.

"What's wrong with you?" Hazel asked.

"Just takes it out of me, that's all. The children will still get their presents this year. They'll be smaller, because I've had to fix what my fool of a brother has done, but it's the thought that counts."

Hazel managed a nod. "Where are we?"

"What can you see?"

"Snow and ice but darkness too, like the mouth of a cave."

"Well done." Nicola's eyes had lit up. "You're at the gateway between your world and where we come from. It needs a cold place and a strong magnetic source to work, so your world's Poles are perfect. Sadly though… well, you know. I only come here once a year: I feed on belief and I reward it, so the cycle continues. It's cold on the other side too, though. Everywhere. Krampus has always preferred it this side of the gateway."

Her brother licked his chops as the Arctic wind whipped harder. "I can escape it here. My pelt may feel cold to you, but everything is relative. In our world, it defends me against the worst. But I still crave more warmth than this place can offer."

He shivered, and Hazel felt a twinge of sympathy.

If he was cold with his fur though, how did Nicola stay warm wherever it was?

"Cold," Nicola seemed to read her mind, "passes straight through me. Everything does. Apart from belief: the idea that I exist, that I have form."

Hazel's brain buzzed with the concepts. Its preference was always for tangible facts, bagged and tagged. "So what happens now?"

"I'd like to buy your mother's house. And it's not just a ruse to look around this time." Nicola's gaze was steady. "This episode has proven we need it. For my brother. Provided he uses it wisely. Any more incidents like the one we've seen today and I'll have to destroy him." Krampus huffed and his sister continued. "Think of the house purchase as my first true gift to a human adult." Smiling, Nicola stepped over to her brother. "No more 'babies' or takeover attempts. I'll be watching. The Authorities will be watching. I'll persuade them to grant you a different form. I'm sorry I didn't listen to you before."

Krampus sighed and nodded, reminding Hazel of Rose whenever she told her off for something and got only a grudging acceptance of wrongdoing. "I will find a hobby."

"Wood-turning's good," Nicola enthused. "Children love—" Her brother glared. "Or something else. And you've got to stay in training anyway. I'll need you in a couple of days and same time next year."

"You know the Authorities?" Hazel faltered as Nicola frowned. "What are they?"

"Dictators," Krampus muttered, drawing a hoof through the snow. "We should stand up to them."

Tutting, Nicola replied, "They make things, the tiny things your people keep trying to unravel, then hold them together. They play at being gods."

"*Play*," Krampus snarled.

Before Hazel could ask any more questions, she found herself standing on the porch of Mum's house. The coat and mittens had gone, though their smell persisted. Night had also gone, replaced by the heat of the Florida sun. What time was it? What day was it? She checked her watch: 2 pm, the 23rd. Even her bones felt swollen with fatigue and they itched inside. Nicotine. She scrabbled in a pocket, popped a gum tab and put it in her mouth. The chewing improved her focus.

Her rental car still sat in the drive. In its back seat were the packing boxes, taped up.

When she tried her key in the front door lock, it refused to turn. Having given up thinking of anything as weird, she rang the bell.

"One moment," a gravelly voice called. A few seconds later, the door opened. A gangly man stood there, dressed in stonewash jeans and a black t-shirt. His face was sun-pinked, the hair on his head coarse and dark and greying at the edges. At the sight of Hazel, his lines on his cheeks deepened with a smile.

"I thought so," he chuckled. "I knew that was inquisition I could smell. It's taken you so long to return. Do you like my new form? I can go to the market now, or even take up golf, during my semi-retirement. And my sister says I can revert to my old form when needed. Like tomorrow." His eyes gleamed in anticipation, the tiniest trace of red visible in the pupils. "Before she returned to the North, my sister arranged the business details for this house. You should check your bank account after Christmas. She also helped me to pack your mother's things; I knew what was important to her." He blinked. "One thing though." He reached for something hidden from view by the door.

Hazel felt a lump rise in her throat as he passed her Mum's periwinkle bowl. It contained a tiny fir tree with a blue bow around its trunk.

"An early Merry Christmas to you. Do stop by if you're in the neighborhood. I'll cook. Bring your children. But tell them they must be good. Or else. And you may tell them, as they still believe, that I have seen the lists for this year and they are on my sister's. Just."

Hazel heard laughter, realized it was hers and clapped a hand to her mouth.

Krampus grinned. "You laugh like your mother. If… No. A safe flight home, Hazel Helmsley. And now, if you will excuse me, I have rays to catch? Yes, catch."

He held his hand out and Hazel shook it, felt the cold still coursing through him, the incongruous warmth of his nails. Then the door closed.

She faltered her way to the car, set the bowl in the passenger seat and picked up the airline ticket someone had placed there. It was for 10pm today; she'd be back in Bradford in time to see Rose and Reed for Christmas.

Windows down, she drove the car onto the main road and followed the shore of Lake Toho. The radio was telling her that an incident involving the Towering Typhoons theme park had been resolved, but the damage to the park itself would take weeks to fix. She turned it off.

Sunlight waltzed on the water. The air was full of the laughter and chatter of happy families. And a light breeze waved an inflatable Santa's arms.

# BAD PARENTS

## E. M. Eastick

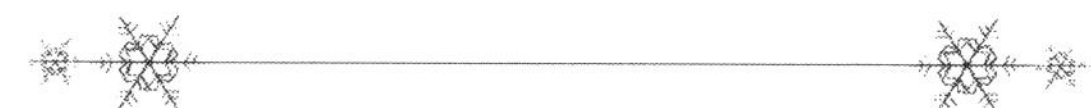

Saint Nick dropped the sack from his shoulder, and it landed with a thud beside the glowing hearth. The beast in the armchair woke to the noise and snarled at the disturbance to his sleep.

"I need you, buddy." Saint Nick slumped into a chair made of roughly bound sticks, and it crackled under his weight. He rested his elbows on his knees, leaning toward the beast, and then sat back when the stench of rotten meat assaulted him.

The beast grunted as he flicked a long tongue over a protuberant eyeball red with sleep.

"Look at this." Saint Nick nodded a bushy gray beard at the lifeless sack. "Finding a well-behaved kid in this village is like trying to find a sock in a snowstorm. It was bad last year, but this year—"

He sighed. "I need you back, Kram."

The wood in the fireplace shifted and sent a spark of embers onto the dirt floor.

"How many times do I need to tell you? I'm retired, Nick." With a hairy finger, the beast scratched the base of one of his horns.

"But these kids are brutal. I overheard the parents saying Timmy put a snake in his nanny's shoe, Steven threw eggs at the schoolmaster, and Margaret attacked Harry's trainset with an axe, while Harry was playing with it."

"Not my fault. Not my problem." The Krampus dug a gob of snot from a flaring nostril and wiped it on his tongue.

"I know, I know, those parents should be ashamed of themselves for letting it get to this." Saint Nick ran a big hand over his moustache. "But seriously, Kram, you're the only one who can fix it."

With surprising agility, the Krampus shot to his hooves, his tail whipping around his knees. "I told you, Nick, I'm done with killing kids." He speared a crooked finger in the direction of the village.

"Those parents need to be held accountable. I'm sick to death of cleaning up their messes." The saliva on the Krampus's fangs gleamed in the firelight.

"Okay, okay, take it easy, man." Slowly, Saint Nick rose to his feet and heaved the sack over his shoulder. "You're right, of course. Like you said last year, bad parenting leads to bad children, but instead of bitching about it—" Holding his breath, he stepped toward the Krampus until their noses were almost touching. "Why don't you do something about it?"

"What are you talking about?"

Unable to hold his breath any longer, Saint Nick turned for the door. "If you're not going to kidnap the brats, why don't you help the parents change them? It'd make my job a hell of a lot easier."

"Sounds like the cold's finally gotten to you, old man." The Krampus stamped a hoof and settled back into his armchair, his tail flicking farewell to the jolly giver of gifts.

As Saint Nick squeezed himself and his sack through the cabin door, he called over his shoulder. "I'll tell the elves to spread the word."

"What word?" roared the Krampus, but the door slammed the question back into his face.

❄

The reel buzzed as the Krampus cast the line out across the calm green surface of the creek. He never caught anything. He suspected the fish had all died long ago, when the upstream mine, now abandoned, used to spew contaminated wastewater from its operations into the waterways.

Still, he enjoyed lounging on the bank and listening to the blackbirds squabble. It reminded him that he never had to deal with another child screaming into his ear, begging to be released from the chains, and pleading for his or her life. Ah yes, retirement agreed with him, all right.

On the opposite bank, a pair of fawns edged their way to the water's edge and dropped their heads to drink. The Krampus watched them and unexpectedly felt the tug of loneliness, a longing to share his life with someone who understood him. The village folk may have danced through the lanes pretending to be him, to scare their children into good behavior (which obviously didn't work), but they never took the time to understand him.

The Krampus clucked his tongue to get the fawns' attentions, and then tried a smile when they looked up at him. At the sight of the Krampus's hairy limbs, sharp teeth, and curled horns, the deer turned and sprinted into the woods, their gangly legs tripping over themselves in their panic to get away. The Krampus sighed and packed up his fishing gear.

As he carried his rod and tackle box back to the cabin, agitated voices coming from inside made him stop. Thieves wouldn't make such noise, he figured. He didn't have anything to steal, anyway. Who else would have a use for old bundles of birch and rusty chains?

Dropping his fishing gear, the Krampus strode into his house through the front door and stood with his hands on his goaty hips. The room was full of men and women from the village. They appeared to be arguing with each other and fell silent under the Krampus's scowl.

"Please," said a woman dressed in the heavy brown wool of winter.

"Come and take our children. They're out of control." As if to support the claim, loud howls followed by a shrill scream rang from the direction of the village.

A man with a thick black beard and who wore a heavy pelt coat wrapped an arm around the woman. "That's not why we're here, love," he said quietly. "We agreed."

A second man of around the same age, but clean shaven, stepped forward. "You agreed, Wesley. The rest of us just want the Krampus to do his job."

The crowd began arguing again until the Krampus couldn't take it any longer. Raising his arms, he roared, "Quiet!"

The villagers fell silent and looked at him.

"I'm retired," said the Krampus. "So you can all get out!"

"But we need you," pleaded the first woman as she shrugged off Wesley's arm. "The children are destroying the village."

"And whose fault is that, eh?" said the Krampus. In turn, he stared in the eyes of every person in the room and felt the shiver of satisfaction when they cowered from his gaze. "You're all bad, bad parents. That's why the children are running amok."

He cocked his head at a niggling feeling inside him. "How did you lot find me, anyway? Only one person knew about my retirement home."

The man called Wesley stepped forward. "Saint Nick told us where you were on the condition that we let you help us." The wooly man turned to the other villagers. "We promised him we'd try."

"It'd be easier if the Krampus just hauled the children off to Hell and be done with it," said a woman's voice from the back.

"Easier, yes," argued Wesley. "But we gave the old guy our words. Doesn't that mean anything?"

The Krampus stood with his weight on one hoof and his arms crossed. He didn't give a damn about anyone giving their word. He just wanted them all to leave.

"Wesley's right," said a man with a soft voice. He flicked blond hair out of his eyes and stepped forward until he stood directly in front of the Krampus. "We promised jolly old Saint Nick, so here we are."

After a round of mumbles, the more argumentative villagers seemed to resign themselves to the merit of keeping promises and turned their eyes to the Krampus, too. "Here we are," they echoed.

The Krampus kept his arms crossed. "What the hell are you lot talking about?"

The blond-haired man gently placed a hand on the Krampus's shoulder and then just as gently pulled it away when the Krampus snarled at him. He swallowed before he spoke. "We want you to help us become better parents."

"You what?"

"Saint Nick said you'd teach us about good parenting practices."

"He what?"

"We need help, Mr. Krampus," said the man. The crowd mumbled concurrence.

"All right, all right," growled the Krampus. "If I help you, will you all get lost—forever?"

The villagers nodded and uttered their agreement.

Without another word, the Krampus built the fire while the villagers shuffled around behind him, arranging themselves into a tight circle. The Krampus turned to sad, but expectant faces watching him, waiting for him to start.

"Okay," he said pointing to Wesley. "Let's start with you."

Wesley sat on the stick chair and wringed his hands. With his head low, he exhaled loudly. "I never thought it would be this hard," he said before raising his eyes and taking a breath. "My name is Wesley, and I'm a bad parent."

The Krampus nodded. "That's a good first step, Wesley. Well done." He tried to ignore the woman at the back whispering to her neighbor: "He really is a bad parent, you know. Never pays those kids any attention." The Krampus was grateful to whoever shushed the woman before she could say any more.

"And what about you?" The Krampus nodded to the blond man.

The man appeared to be shaking. When he spoke, his voice quavered. "My name is Barry, and I'm a bad parent."

"Not as bad as Wesley," whispered the mysterious voice, which was followed by a stern "Sshh."

After the whole circle of villagers had admitted their bad parenting, some folks sweating profusely and others bursting into tears, the Krampus yawned and wanted nothing more than to crawl into the bed that six villagers had taken as a seat.

"All right, well done, everybody," he said without feeling. "Your homework for tonight is to listen to your children. Got that?"

A room of blank faces looked at him. Twenty pairs of eyes blinked at him. "You mean, listen to them whine and scream and swear?" asked Wesley's wife, who the Krampus now knew was named Roberta.

"No," said the Krampus, disappointed. "Ask them how their day was, or who their friends are, or what their favorite subject at school is."

The eyes blinked again.

"And then listen to what they have to say," continued the Krampus.

When the villagers began mumbling to one another, the Krampus stood and walked to the door. Swinging it wide open, he called, "Right, now off you go, everybody. Go and listen to your children."

Still mumbling its confusion, a lackluster crowd dribbled outside and into the woods, now cloaked with the darkness and coldness of night. The Krampus slammed the door, but heard Wesley's voice float back to him. "Thank you, Mr. Krampus. We'll see you tomorrow."

The Krampus stoked the fire, flopped onto his bed, and listened to the distant uproar of children breaking things as they tore through the village.

The next morning, the Krampus stood beside his raised flower beds containing the bulbs he'd planted in the fall, and regarded the dust-covering of snow that had fallen during the night. Because of the cold, and because of their bad form in general, the Krampus guessed the village parents wouldn't bother with any more bad parenting meetings.

"Hello," sang a voice from the front of his cabin. "Are you here, Mr. Krampus?"

The Krampus considered hoofing it through the woods and hiding out by the creek, but when a second voice called out, "We're here for our meeting, Mr. Krampus," the Krampus rolled his eyes and joined the crowd gathered by his front door.

He didn't expect more parents to turn up at his home. The familiar faces from the day before ushered the newcomers through the narrow doorway and chattered excitedly about their Yuletide preparations.

"Perhaps this year the children will sit down to eat without throwing the food across the table," said one woman as she lowered herself onto the rock the Krampus used for his hot pots and pans at meal times.

"Perhaps they'll even have a bath for the occasion," said the woman beside her. The two giggled at their fantasies.

When the village folk were settled inside the Krampus's cabin with little room to spare, the Krampus cleared his throat. "All right, today we're going to talk about how our bad parenting affects day-to-day life." He nodded his pointy chin toward the blond-haired man called Barry.

"Well," said Barry with a slight shake in his voice. "Sometimes I—" His eyes glistened with the threat of tears. "Sometimes I let my son, Mason, stay up past midnight."

The Krampus raised a hand to the chorus of gasps. "We're not here to judge," he said. "Go on, Barry."

"I've noticed when Mason stays up late, he's grumpy the whole of the next day. Sometimes he screams all the way to the market." The confession was too much for the man. He released a torrent of sobs, which attracted a spatter of sympathetic words from the others.

The Krampus sighed as he checked his long fingernails. He picked out grime from under a thumbnail and then scratched his butt. Inspecting the thumbnail again, he nodded with approval at the new level of grime. "Okay, okay," he said to quieten down the group. "You." He pointed to a thin stern-looking woman sitting behind a stout man.

The woman straightened her back and squared her shoulders. "With all due respect, Mr. Krampus," she said. "I don't see how any of this is helping. With only eleven days left till Yuletide, I hardly think this kind of self-deprecation is going to help us control those awful children. Why can't you just take them away like you use to?"

The Krampus crossed his arms. "You must be confusing me with the Pied Piper, ma'am." He curled his top lip back and ran his tongue over his fangs. "And the Pied Piper I most definitely am not."

"Fine, fine," said the woman as she glanced around the tiny room. "But I see you still have your birch bundles and your chains over there in the corner. And I bet you still have your thorny baskets around here somewhere."

The baskets were under the lean-to round the back, the Krampus knew, but he wasn't about to admit it.

"Why don't you just take the brats?" asked the woman.

The Krampus stood and stamped a hoof.

"Because I'm retired," he shouted. "And parents need to take responsibility for their children. Now, all of you, get out and leave me alone."

"She didn't mean it," pleaded Wesley. "We need your help."

The Krampus turned to the man with the black beard and found himself calming. He was actually beginning to like the dad who wanted to be a better parent. "Did you listen?" he asked.

Wesley wobbled his head vaguely. "Well, I tried. But Margaret has become pretty attached to that axe of hers. I asked how her day was, and she took a swipe at my leg."

"But at least you tried," said the Krampus.

"Yes, I tried," said Wesley. "I really did."

"We all did," said Barry amid nodding heads.

"It's a waste of time," said the thin woman. The Krampus guessed she must have been the one who had whispered insults during the last meeting.

"While we're here, the kids are breaking things, and stealing things, and killing things." She lifted her skirts and strode through the door. "I don't want anything more to do with this nonsense."

With angry eyes, she turned back to the Krampus.

"And I suggest you come out of retirement immediately, or I'll summon—the priests."

The other villagers gasped. The Krampus groaned.

The woman stormed off into the woods.

Roberta touched the Krampus on a grizzly elbow. "Don't worry about Mary," she said softly. "She's just letting off steam. Her husband died of food poisoning—something in a fish he caught in the river—last month, and her four-year-old, Hilda, buried her hamster last night."

"Aw, that's sad," said Barry. "I didn't know Fuzzy died."

"He didn't," said Roberta. "Not for a while, anyway."

Shaking his head, wondering how Mary's ex-husband had managed to catch a fish and he hadn't, the Krampus settled back into his armchair.

"Should we continue, then?"

The villagers settled back into a circle. In the ensuing silence, the sounds of splintering wood and shattering glass reached them from the village. The Krampus wondered if Mary was right. Maybe the bad parent meetings were a waste a time.

❄

On the eve of Yuletide, the parents from the village dribbled into the Krampus's cabin and settled themselves into their usual meeting places. Nobody spoke and nobody smiled. Red and tired eyes looked like they hadn't closed in weeks, and even dressed in heavy winter garments, it was clear many of the villagers had lost weight since the meetings had started.

After stoking the fire, for the chill of evening had descended on them quickly, the Krampus scratched his hairy chin as he regarded each person. "I never said being a good parent was easy."

Exhausted faces looked back at him. Barry ran a hand down his haggard face. "It's *not* easy," he drawled. "It's *hard.*"

"But I have faith in all of you," said the Krampus, not feeling any faith at all and suspecting the flatness in his voice told them as much.

"We've tried," said Wesley. "We really have."

"You can't give up now," said the Krampus. This time, he did mean it. If the parents gave up and the children continued to misbehave badly, Saint Nick would insist that the Krampus come out of retirement.

"What else can we do?" asked Roberta. "We've tried listening to them, encouraging them, supporting them, hugging them—we've even tried bribing them."

"The only thing we haven't tried is…" Barry choked on the words he dreaded to hear.

"Beating them," Roberta said shakily.

"Come on now," roared the Krampus. "Violence is not the answer."

A village of doubtful eyes turned on him.

"Okay, maybe sometimes it is," said the Krampus. "But these are children you're talking about. *Your* children."

Wesley crumpled to the dirt floor and sobbed.

"Horrible children."

In between Wesley's sobs came the distinct, but faint crackle of burning timber. "What's that?" asked a woman closest to the door.

The Krampus strode outside with the villagers, the edges of the doorway crumbling a little with the rush of bodies. They stopped and stared at the flames leaping above the tree canopy in the distance.

"It's the children," said Roberta. "They're out of control."

Pleading eyes turned to the Krampus. "Help us," said Wesley through a beard glistening with tears and snot. "Save us."

The Krampus looked at his fishing rod and tackle box in the shadows of the cabin wall. He looked at the raised beds he hoped would flourish with tulips and irises in the spring. And then he looked at the miserable, bad parents from the village and felt a stab of guilt deep in his gut.

Perhaps the widow, Mary, understood children better than all of them—he wondered if she liked fishing. With a sigh, the Krampus turned back to the cabin door. "I'll get my chains," he said. The rattle of steel and rustle of birch were lost in the cheers of bad, but very happy, parents.

# MEMO FROM SANTA

## Jude Tulli

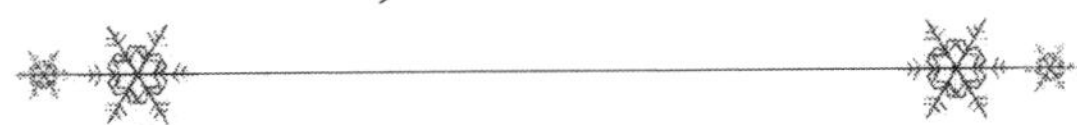

From: The Laptop of Santa Claus
To: All Children
Cc: All Parents of Current Children; Krampus, Billy G.
Re: New Wish List Submission Guidelines and Reorganizational Announcements

Dear Children,

As you know, there are more of you each year, and your jolly old Santa must continually improve his delivery processes in order to accommodate a growing number of growing girls and boys, many of whom make increasingly expensive, extensive and, quite frankly, exhaustive requests.

It is my pleasure to announce the enlistment of a new independent contractor to help Santa meet all of his Christmas Eve commitments in a timely and accurate fashion. Billy G. Krampus, Ph.D. in Child Psychology and Behavioral Corrections, will now be handling all of your wish list submissions. He's asked me to ask you to follow his new guidelines so we can better serve you.

Dr. Krampus graduated Magma cone Lava from Under World University (4U, as it's affectionately known, having two regular "U"s plus one double). All the changes outlined below have passed a rigorous beta-testing protocol with a volunteer polar bear community here at the North Pole, and have been certified FYOG-compliant ("For Your Own Good").

Dr. Krampus' requirements follow.

Did I hit all the bullet points we talked about? Where's the off button? That take will have to be good enough; Prancer needs her vitamins or she gets tired early and then wakes everyone up in the middle of the night. Oh, THIS button. See, technology is my frie—

—S. Claus
*Dictated but not read.*

Children,

Beginning this year, you are to kindly fill out the following self-review and address it to:

Dr. Krampus
Equator

Be sure to affix a first-class stamp; the mail doesn't deliver itself, now!

----- print and cut here ---------(Aiming to figure out how to add scissor icons by next year)-----------------

## CHILD'S SELF-REVIEW FORM

I, ______________________________, do hereby swear by my soul* that I believe my Goodness Rating to be a ____ out of 5, where 1 = Truly Horrifying, 2 = Somewhat Disturbing, 3 = Neither Terrible nor Wonderful, 4 = Mostly Good Most of the Time, and 5 = People Tell Me They See a Halo Above My Head.

______________________________ ____________

Signature date

______________________________ ____________

Signature of Parent or Legal Guardian date

*I hereby acknowledge that falsification of my self-evaluation constitutes grounds for immediate soul-harvest of myself and/or my child.

----- print and cut here -----------------------(Next year, promise. Where have I heard that before?)---------

Just give it your best guesstimate and don't lose any sleep over the wording of the document; legal formalities give even Dr. K. a headache.

We need to receive these no later than November 7, so if you're not finished with yours by Halloween, kindly refrain from extorting candy from neighbors until you've completed the form and dropped it in the nearest mailbox with your non-refundable $10 self-evaluation review fee.

If you must send your form up to a week late please include your $10 fee plus an irrevocable $100 can't-follow-simple-directions and probably-don't-color-inside-the-lines-either fee ($110 total). Beyond a week late, your rating will sustain a one point penalty and your parents will be assessed a $500 lack-of-participatory-spirit fee. "Lost in the mail" is not a valid excuse even if it's true.

Now, once we have received your self-evaluation or declared it AWOL, we'll respond with your Formal Yuletide Unalterable Assessment no later than November 30. AS THE THIRD ADJECTIVE DICTATES, THERE IS NO APPEALS PROCESS FOR FYUAs. I know what you teenagers are thinking, and it's pure coincidence that the same acronym could stand for something contrary to the spirit of the season.

You must be a 3.5 or higher if you are to receive desirable presents. We realize that in previous years the cutoff was 3.0, and we apologize, but Santa's new helper (yours truly) eats more than 10 elves and can't afford to work for the sheer joy of a sleigh-ride a year (though it IS quite fun, and Rudolph is even more endearing than I imagined him when I was a kid. It's just that it takes a long time to pay off the school that put the "Dr." in Dr. K. You'll know how that is soon enough.)

This is not personal. It's simple cost containment, kids. With the world population growing as it is, and our budget shrinking, we're forced to be creative in our ever-changing methods, lest Christmas be cancelled entirely. Not to mention that, from the looks of him, Santa was ready to retire half a century ago. Between you and me, he can't afford to quit because he keeps kicking his own personal funds into the Christmas kitty. He's just too much of a giver for his own good.

If you are a 3.49 or below, DO NOT SEND US A WISH LIST. Sending a wish list without a wish list-entitled rating will result in *two* punishments from the list below. Those children who make amends with those they have irritated this year might (it has not yet been decided) escape punishment. It should be noted that in all of these cases NO PRESENTS OF VALUE WILL BE RECEIVED THIS YEAR. As there is a coal shortage, it has not yet been decided whether we will proceed with plan B for this year's Symbolic Message of Concretized Disappointment in Naughty Children (SMoCDiNC; trademark pending). You'll be notified by e-mail once a decision's been made.

## POSSIBLE PUNISHMENTS FOR CHILDREN SCORING BETWEEN 0.0 AND 3.49

**3.0 - 3.49**: Dr. K. will personally spill the milk you leave for Santa and deposit copious cookie crumbs on the table, chairs and floor. He then, at his sole discretion, might call Child Protective Services to alert them of the pigsty conditions your parents maintain for you. Hoof-prints on linoleum will not come out with bleach; try vinegar and water or a Krampushine® brand steam cleaner, available in stores now.

**2.0 - 2.99**: Dr. K. will send minions to spray your tree with scents specially formulated to entice your companion animals to knock it over no matter how many times you set it right. If you have no tree, this will include one fully-trimmed evergreen to be billed to your parents at three times the fair market value. If you have no companion animals, this will include the complimentary installation of a pet door and the relocation of no fewer than three wild raccoons/possum/kangaroos* to your neighborhood/yard/living room.

* This list is not exhaustive; actual species employed is contingent upon local ordinances and availability.

**1.0 - 1.99**: Dr. K. will send minions of minions to jam all your electronic gaming devices from December 24 at 12:01 a.m. until the morning of your first day back to school. Said devices will remain "fritzy" anytime you turn them on prior to completion of homework assignments/chores/calling your grandparents just to tell them you love them.

**0.0 - 0.99**: Dr. K.'s special minions of minions of minions will sublet (rent free) your closet and/or the living space beneath your bed and monitor your performance until next year's review.

Naturally, they will remain invisible to parents, siblings and friends. No one else will notice how loudly they breathe at night, either. Pleasant dreams.

You might be wondering why the higher the rating, the more personal the attention. It is Dr. Krampus' experience that a personal punishment is often the encouragement a child on the brink of success needs to improve the following year's performance. Conversely, an impersonal punishment ensures the worst-behaved children receive the message that they acted so badly they are not worth my time unless they clean up their acts and roll over a new snowball.

If your rating exceeds the cutoff mark, you may send us a wish list. No one will get a 5, so if your FYUA says you're a 3.5 to a 4.99, this means you.

## WISH LIST SUBMISSION GUIDELINES:

Divide your rating by 5. Round up. This is the number of items you may request on your wish list. This year's maximum retail value per gift is $7.99 INCLUDING TAX, EVEN FOR INTERNET ORDERS. We are passing the savings from volume delivery on to you. Believe me, we are strictly non-profit and by that I mean these new guidelines are a desperate attempt to break even for a change. Have you seen the price of reindeer alfalfa flakes?

Please do not request items on behalf of anyone else. Only list what YOU want for Christmas, and prepare yourself for the grim reality that you might receive something entirely different.

Remember, presents are commodities. We are lucky to have them, and the proper response is *gratitude.*

Please do personalize your letter. Dr. Krampus is no different from your teachers and parents in enjoying a word of praise here and there, sincere or otherwise.

SLANDER OR LIBEL OF OTHER CHILDREN WILL DECREASE YOUR RATING BY ONE POINT.

TALKING UP NAUGHTY CHILDREN FOR WHOM YOU FEEL SORRY WILL ALSO DECREASE YOUR RATING. TWO POINTS.

Don't be too formal, but don't be too conversational, either. We are not judges or clergy, nor are we your friends or family. We are here to do a job, and do it right.

You can log on to my wish list letter critique forum if you wish to see sample letters and my reactions to them. Here's an example of one gone wildly astray:

*Dear Santa,* (WRONG! ADDRESS ALL WISH LISTS TO ME NOW, DR. KRAMPUS.)

*I saw you in the department store the other day and I gave you a hug.* (Personalizing up the wrong tree—Santa will not be reading wish lists this year; just me and my zombie army of interns.) *I love you, Santa.*

(I am now predisposed to curse your present. Write to Santa during the off-season. No one remembers him then, and he's got plenty of free time to correspond.)

*I hope you can forgive my sister for not eating all her veggies all the time.* (Talking up naughty child penalty assessed.) *She wants a Weebox Station this year!* (Only tell me what YOU want. She will tell me what she wants if she is entitled to do so.)

*This year I would like a bike with training wheels, because I tried my sister's bike and I fell off too much.* (Bicycles exceed the price ceiling. You're getting a temporary tattoo kit of Dr. K. imagery, so next year you'll remember whom you're writing to.) *And a new car for my parents since our old one died and Mommy has to take my sister's bike to work.* (There is so much wrong with this I shouldn't even have to explain.)

*Please give Rudolph a kiss on his glowy red nose for me,* (He has a cold right now, so ew!)

[Name withheld for fear readers might ostracize child for writing such a horrible letter.]

Instead, try to write something more like this:

*Dr. K!*

*Your totally da bomb and I love your approach to child psycho, dawg! When I grow up I wanna look and act and be just like you!* (It sounds over the top and is a bit grammary, but I'm catching the drift. I'm on board with this kid from the opening line.)

*Imma be surprised this year, cuz I trust you, dawg! You my main man, and you know what I want better then I do.* (I might make a slight exception to the gift value policy for this one. The numbers have yet to be crunched, but a jet ski might not be out of the question.)

*Saw you outsida da Wol-Shoppe the other day. Gave you my ice cream, 'member?* (I DO remember! Who doesn't love ice cream?)

*Stay cool!*

[Name withheld for fear readers might beg author to ghostwrite their letters. If you're nervous, I can hook you up with a staff ghostwriter for $9.99 pre-paid to the equator address. All proceeds will be invested in presents for this year. A matching amount may be reallocated to the punishment fund.]

****

PLEASE RETAIN THIS MESSAGE AND RE-READ IT SEVERAL TIMES BEFORE ATTEMPTING TO FOLLOW THE DIRECTIONS.

I know change can be hard, and learning a new procedure can be a challenge. You should see the Santa Sleigh-rider's manual. A thousand pages and NO INDEX!

I'm confident, however, that with everyone's cooperation we can make this one the BEST CHRISTMAS EVER!

One for all and all 4U,

Dr. Billy G. Krampus
Independent Contractor
Santa's Workshop, Inc.
(Teleworking Live from the Equator)

# ABOUT THE AUTHORS

**Steven Grimm** writes fiction based on classic fairy tales, including "Faithful Henry" from the *Frozen Fairy Tales* anthology. He also writes Cauldron Comics' *Silver and Gold*, a webcomic about a transgender Cinderella who fights to save LGBTIQ+ lives in a world where Fairyland is a daily nightmare. Find Steven's work at his *Saved by Fairy Tales* blog: SavedByFairyTales.com.

**Lissa Marie Redmond** is a retired police detective turned writer. She lives and writes in Buffalo, New York with her husband and two daughters.

**Beth Mann** is a fiction writer living in South West England, where she divides her time between reading, writing, and drinking tea. In 2014 she completed an MA in Creative Writing at Bath Spa University, and also co-edited that year's student anthology, *Beginnings*. She takes her inspiration from myths and legends of all shapes and sizes; her short story "The Last Werwolf in Germany" is forthcoming in Falmouth University's supernatural-themed journal *Revenant*.

**Anya J. Davis** is from Devon, in the South West of England. She has had short stories published in World Weaver Press's *Speculative Story Bites* anthology, Massacre Magazine and more, and another was long-listed for the 2016 Exeter Writers Short Story competition. You can find her on Twitter: @traumahound23.

**E.J. Hagadorn** is the author of numerous works of fiction and poetry. When not writing he is often seen taking road trips, lurking in graveyards, or sleeping at his desk. His work can be found at www.ejhagadorn.com

**S.E. Foley** has always had a thing for writing, but never seemed to find time to do it. After her spouse left her and she survived cancer, she has changed her view on what is important. She makes time to write between two jobs and raising her son.

**Brad P. Christy** is the author of the short stories: *Miseryland*, *Angel Dust*, *'Twas the Fifth of December*, and *Cape Hadel*. He is a member of the Writers' League of Texas, and holds a Bachelor of Arts degree in Creative Writing and English. Brad lived in Germany for three years where he immersed himself in their culture and folklore, and now resides in the Pacific Northwest with his wife.

After thirty years at sea, **Ross Baxter** now concentrates on writing sci-fi and horror fiction. In December 2014 he won the *Horror Novel Review.Com* best creation short fiction prize. Married to a Norwegian and with two Anglo-Viking kids, Ross now lives in Derby, England.

**Nancy Brewka-Clark** sold her first short fiction to *The Boston Globe Magazine* in 1983. Since then her work has been published or produced in multiple genres from murder mysteries to sonnets to one-minute plays. Please visit nancybrewkaclark.com for more information.

**Tamsin Showbrook** lives in Manchester, UK, and when she's not doing her day jobs or having fun with her kids, she writes at great length (novels) and hardly any length (flash fiction, short stories, poetry). She's been published by WWP previously, in Rhonda Parrish's *Sirens* anthology, and some of her other work has been published under her real name. You can contact Tamsin at: tamsin.showbrook@gmail.com.

Australian born **E. M. Eastick** is a retired environmental manager, avid traveler, and writer of no-fixed form or genre. Her creative efforts can be found in *Mad Scientist Journal*, *Ember*, and a number of anthologies. Currently living in Colorado, E. M. can be found lurking as a co-writer at www.arielstone.com.

**Jude Tulli** lives in the Sonoran Desert (which can get much hotter than the equator) with his beloved wife Trish and a small pride of housecats. You can check out his novelette *Faegotten* today on a Kindle near you.

# ABOUT THE ANTHOLOGIST

**Kate Wolford** is a writer, editor, and blogger living in the Midwest. Fairy tales are her specialty. Previous books include *Beyond the Glass Slipper: Ten Neglected Fairy Tales to Fall in Love With*, *Krampusnacht: Twelve Nights of Krampus*, and *Frozen Fairy Tales*, all published by World Weaver Press. She maintains a 'zine, *Enchanted Conversation: A Fairy Tale Magazine*, at FairyTaleMagazine.com.

Thank you for reading!
We hope you'll leave an honest review at Amazon, Goodreads, or wherever you discuss books online.

Leaving a review means a lot for the author and editors who worked so hard to create this book.

Please sign up for our newsletter for news about upcoming titles, submission opportunities, special discounts, & more.

WorldWeaverPress.com/newsletter-signup

## ALSO EDITED BY KATE WOLFORD

**Krampusnacht: Twelve Nights of Krampus**
A Christmas Krampus anthology
Edited by Kate Wolford

For bad children, a lump of coal from Santa is positively light punishment when Krampus is ready and waiting to beat them with a stick, wrap them in chains, and drag them down to hell—all with St. Nick's encouragement and approval.

*Krampusnacht* holds within its pages twelve tales of Krampus triumphant, usurped, befriended, and much more. From evil children (and adults) who get their due, to those who pull one over on the ancient "Christmas Devil." From historic Europe, to the North Pole, to present day American suburbia, these all new stories embark on a revitalization of the Krampus tradition.

Whether you choose to read *Krampusnacht* over twelve dark and scary nights or devour it in one *nacht* of joy and terror, these stories are sure to add chills and magic to any winter's reading.

Featuring original stories by Elizabeth Twist, Elise Forier Edie, Jill Corddry, Colleen H. Robbins, Caren Gussoff, Lissa Sloan, Patrick Evans, Guy Burtenshaw, Jeff Provine, Mark Mills, Cheresse Burke, and Scott Farrell.

"A kaleidoscope of Krampus tales featuring enjoyable twists and turns. Imaginative and entertaining."
— Monte Beauchamp, *Krampus: The Devil of Christmas*

"From funny to pure terror. The writers also tell us their inspiration for each story which helps put us in the right frame of mind. I really enjoyed all these tales, and it was a great introduction to Krampus for me. I like that he is about justice, not just doing harm for the sake of evil. What makes it even better is that he has Santa's blessing. **This is a must-read for the upcoming holiday season.**"
— *Bitten By Books*

# ALSO EDITED BY KATE WOLFORD

**FROZEN FAIRY TALES**

an anthology of winter fairy tale retellings

Edited by Kate Wolford

**Winter is *not* coming. Winter is here.** As unique and beautifully formed as a snowflake, each of these fifteen stories spins a brand new tale or offers a fresh take on an old favorite like Jack Frost, The Snow Queen, or The Frog King. From a drafty castle to a blustery Japanese village, from a snow-packed road to the cozy hearth of a farmhouse, from an empty coffee house in Buffalo, New York, to a cold night outside a university library, these stories fully explore the perils and possibilities of the snow, wind, ice, and bone-chilling cold that traditional fairy tale characters seldom encounter.

In the bleak midwinter, heed the irresistible call of fairy tales. Just open these pages, snuggle down, and wait for an icy blast of fantasy to carry you away. With all new stories of love, adventure, sorrow, and triumph by Tina Anton, Amanda Bergloff, Gavin Bradley, L.A. Christensen, Steven Grimm, Christina Ruth Johnson, Rowan Lindstrom, Alison McBain, Aimee Ogden, J. Patrick Pazdziora, Lissa Marie Redmond, Anna Salonen, Lissa Sloan, Charity Tahmaseb, and David Turnbull to help you dream through the cold days and nights of this most dreaded season.

"*Frozen Fairy Tales* is a solid anthology."
—*Fairy Tale Fandom*

"[*Frozen Fairy Tales*] would make an excellent Christmas present—it can be enjoyed for the next few months and doesn't have to be put away with the holiday decorations!"
—*Tales of Faerie*

# ALSO EDITED BY KATE WOLFORD

**BEYOND THE GLASS SLIPPER**
Ten Neglected Fairy Tales to Fall In Love With
Edited by Kate Wolford

***Some fairy tales everyone knows—these aren't those tales.*** These are tales of kings who get deposed and pigs who get married. These are ten tales, much neglected. Editor of *Enchanted Conversation: A Fairy Tale Magazine*, Kate Wolford, introduces and annotates each tale in a manner that won't leave novices of fairy tale studies lost in the woods to grandmother's house, yet with a depth of research and a delight in posing intriguing puzzles that will cause folklorists and savvy readers to find this collection a delicious new delicacy.

*Beyond the Glass Slipper* is about more than just reading fairy tales—it's about connecting to them. It's about thinking of the fairy tale as a precursor to *Saturday Night Live* as much as it is to any princess-movie franchise: the tales within these pages abound with outrageous spectacle and absurdist vignettes, ripe with humor that pokes fun at ourselves and our society.

Never stuffy or pedantic, Kate Wolford proves she's the college professor you always wish you had: smart, nurturing, and plugged into pop culture. Wolford invites us into a discussion of how these tales fit into our modern cinematic lives and connect the larger body of fairy tales, then asks—no, *insists*—that we create our own theories and connections. A thinking man's first step into an ocean of little known folklore.

"I have lost count of the books I've read presenting a collection of fairy tales but I can guarantee I've rarely enjoyed reading any collection like I did *Beyond the Glass Slipper*."
— *Fairy Tale News*

## MORE FAIRY TALE TITLES FROM WORLD WEAVER PRESS

### OPAL

Fae of Fire and Stone, Book One

Kristina Wojtaszek

"A fairy tale within a fairy tale within a fairy tale—the narratives fit together like interlocking pieces of a puzzle, beautifully told."
—Zachary Petit, Editor *Writer's Digest*

***White as snow, stained with blood, her talons black as ebony...*** In this retwisting of the classic Snow White tale, the daughter of an owl is forced into human shape by a wizard who's come to guide her from her wintry tundra home down to the colorful world of men and Fae, and the father she's never known. She struggles with her human shape and grieves for her dead mother—a mother whose past she must unravel if men and Fae are to live peacefully together.

"Twists and turns and surprises that kept me up well into the night. Fantasy and fairy tale lovers will eat this up and be left wanting more!" —Kate Wolford, *Enchanted Conversation: A Fairy Tale Magazine*

"Lyrical, beautiful, and haunting...OPAL is truly a hidden gem. Wojtaszek [is] a talented new author and one well worth watching."
—YA Fantastic Book Review

"Fans of fairy tale retellings and stories involving Faeries will fall in love with Opal." —Chapter by Chapter

### CHAR

Fae of Fire and Stone, Book Two

*An isolated fae must travel a century into the past to rewrite the book that will save her people.*

Kristina Wojtaszek

## MORE FAIRY TALE TITLES FROM WORLD WEAVER PRESS

### THE FALLING OF THE MOON

*Moonfall Mayhem, Book One*

A. E. Decker

In the gloomy mountains of Shadowvale, Ascot Abberdorf is expected to marry a lugubrious Count and settle down to a quiet life terrorizing the villagers. Instead, armed with a book of fairy tales, her faithful bat-winged cat, and whatever silverware she can pinch, Ascot heads east, to the mysterious Daylands, where her book promises she can find True Love and Happily Ever After, if she only follows her heart.

Determined to win the hand of Prince Parvanel, Ascot storms the Kingdom of Albright. With the book's guidance, she's confident she'll overcome any obstacles the imperious Queen Bettina Anna throws in her way, be they witches, evil stepmothers, or Big Bad Wolves.

Unfortunately, the book doesn't cover reluctant princes, wolves who read Dostoyevsky instead of blowing down houses, or a guild of Godmothers whose motivations may not be as pure as three drops of blood on a sweep of snow. Most annoying of all is the captain of the guard who swears he'll see the moon fall before she weds Prince Parvanel.

There are stories… and then there are *stories*, and if her parade of shifty shenanigans continues, Ascot might have to rewrite her own tale lest she end most Unhappily Ever After!

"A unique and clever fantasy, *The Falling of the Moon* is a thoroughly entertaining read from first page to last. Very highly recommended and certain to be an enduring favorite."
—Midwest Book Review

"A great read for anyone looking for something cheerful to read. Five shiny stars." —Kat Mandu, *One Book Two*

# MORE FAIRY TALE TITLES FROM WORLD WEAVER PRESS

## FAE

Anthology of Fairies

Rhonda Parrish's Magical Menageries, Volume One

Meet Robin Goodfellow as you've never seen him before, watch damsels in distress rescue themselves, get swept away with the selkies and enjoy tales of hobs, green men, pixies and phookas. One thing is for certain, these are not your grandmother's fairy tales.

With an introduction by Sara Cleto and Brittany Warman, and all new stories from Sidney Blaylock Jr., Amanda Block, Kari Castor, Beth Cato, Liz Colter, Rhonda Eikamp, Lor Graham, Alexis A. Hunter, L.S. Johnson, Jon Arthur Kitson, Adria Laycraft, Lauren Liebowitz, Christine Morgan, Shannon Phillips, Sara Puls, Laura VanArendonk Baugh, and Kristina Wojtaszek.

## CORVIDAE

Rhonda Parrish's Magical Menageries, Volume Two

Featuring works by Jane Yolen, Mike Allen, C.S.E. Cooney, M.L.D. Curelas, Tim Deal, Megan Engelhardt, Megan Fennell, Adria Laycraft, Kat Otis, Michael S. Pack, Sara Puls, Michael M. Rader, Mark Rapacz, Angela Slatter, Laura VanArendonk Baugh, and Leslie Van Zwol.

## SCARECROW

Rhonda Parrish's Magical Menageries, Volume Three

Featuring all new work by Jane Yolen, Andrew Bud Adams, Laura Blackwood, Amanda Block, Scott Burtness, Amanda C. Davis, Megan Fennell, Kim Goldberg, Katherine Marzinsky, Craig Pay, Sara Puls, Holly Schofield, Virginia Carraway Stark, Laura VanArendonk Baugh, and Kristina Wojtaszek.

## MORE FAIRY TALE TITLES FROM WORLD WEAVER PRESS

### WOLVES AND WITCHES

a fairy tale collection by

Amanda C. Davis and Megan Engelhardt

***Witches have stories too.*** So do mermaids, millers' daughters, princes (charming or otherwise), even big bad wolves. They may be a bit darker—fewer enchanted ball gowns, more iron shoes. Happily-ever-after? Depends on who you ask. In *Wolves and Witches,* sisters Amanda C. Davis and Megan Engelhardt weave sixteen stories and poems out of familiar fairy tales, letting them show their teeth.

"Sisters Amanda C. Davis and Megan Engelhardt are the female Brothers Grimm."
—K. Allen Wood, Shock Totem

"Dark and delicious revenge-filled tales! I Highly Recommend this fun and small collection of short stories."
—Fangs, Wands & Fairy Dust.

### SPECULATIVE STORY BITES

Edited by Sarena Ulibarri

Fifteen bite-sized stories, offering a sampler platter of fantasy, science fiction, and paranormal horror. Within these pages, you'll find flower fairies, alien brothels, were-bears, and sentient houses. Step inside a museum where all the displays are haunted, follow a siren into the underworld as she searches for Persephone, and discover the doors that lie, literally, behind the heart.

Featuring stories by Shannon Phillips, Adam Gaylord, Rebecca Roland, Dianne Williams, M.T. Reiten, Larry Hodges, Anya J. Davis, Jamie Lackey, Megan Neumann, Kristina Wojtaszek, Gregory Scheckler, Sandi Leibowitz, Nora Mulligan, Tom Howard, and A.E. Decker.

# NEW AND FORTHCOMING FROM WORLD WEAVER PRESS

**Bite Somebody**

Paranormal Romance

*Immortality is just living longer with more embarrassment.*

Sara Dobie Bauer

**Beyond the Glass Slipper**

Ten Neglected Fairy Tales to Fall In Love With

*Some fairy tales everyone knows—these aren't those tales.*

Edited by Kate Wolford

**Campaign 2100: Game of Scorpions**

Political Satire Science Fiction

*A third party, and an alien, take on a corrupt world government.*

Larry Hodges

**Shards of History**

Fantasy

*Only she knows the truth that can save her people.*

Rebecca Roland

**Fractured Days**

Shards of History, Book Two

*Malia returns home the hero of a war she can't remember.*

Rebecca Roland

**The Falling of the Moon**

Moonfall Mayhem, Book One

*If Ascot wants a happy ending, she'll have to write it herself.*

A.E. Decker

**The Meddlers of Moonshine**

Moonfall Mayhem, Book Two

A.E. Decker

## NEW AND FORTHCOMING FROM WORLD WEAVER PRESS

**Opal**

Fae of Fire and Stone, Book One

*The daughter of an owl is forced into human shape by a wizard who's come to guide her down to the colorful world of men and Fae.*

Kristina Wojtaszek

**Char**

Fae of Fire and Stone, Book Two

*An isolated fae must travel a century into the past to rewrite the book that will save her people.*

Kristina Wojtaszek

**The Haunted Housewives of Allister, Alabama**

Cleo Tidwell Paranormal Mystery, Book One

*Who knew one gaudy Velvet Elvis could lead to such a heap of haunted trouble?*

Susan Abel Sullivan

**The Weredog Whisperer**

Cleo Tidwell Paranormal Mystery, Book Two

*The Tidwells are supposed to be on spring break on the Florida Gulf Coast, not up to their eyeballs in paranormal hijinks… again.*

Susan Abel Sullivan

**Heir to the Lamp**

Genie Chronicles, Book One (YA)

*A family secret, a mysterious lamp, a dangerous Order with the mad desire to possess both.*

Michelle Lowery Combs

## NEW AND FORTHCOMING FROM WORLD WEAVER PRESS

**Solomon's Bell**

Genie Chronicles, Book Two (YA)

*Ginn thinks she has problems at home until she magically lands herself in 16th Century Prague.*

Michelle Lowery Combs

**Murder in the Generative Kitchen**

Science Fiction

*Does your smart kitchen know you better than you know yourself?*

Meg Pontecorvo

**Omega Rising**

Wolf King, Book One

*Cass Nolan has been forced to avoid the burn of human touch for her whole life, until Nathan shows up at her ranch.*

Anna Kyle

**Skye Falling**

Wolf King, Book Two

*Skye, a Fae-shapeshifter halfing, could die if she doesn't find out how to wake her dormant wolf.*

Anna Kyle

**Legally Undead**

Vampirachy, Book One

*A reluctant vampire hunter, stalking New York City as only a scorned bride can.*

Margo Bond Collins

**For more on these and other titles**

visit WorldWeaverPress.com

* * *

World Weaver Press
Publishing fantasy, paranormal, and science fiction.
We believe in great storytelling.
WorldWeaverPress.com

Printed in Great Britain
by Amazon